D1570803

Benediction

BENEDICTION
A Book of Stories

Neal Chandler

University of Utah Press
Salt Lake City
1989

Volume Three, Publications in Mormon Studies
Linda King Newell, editor

Publications in Mormon Studies was established to encourage creation and submission of work on Mormon-related topics that would be of interest to scholars and the general public. The initiation of the series represents an acknowledgment by the Press and the editor of the region's rich historical and literary heritage and of the quality of work being done in various areas of Mormon studies today.
ISSN 0893-4916

The following stories first appeared in *Dialogue: A Journal of Mormon Thought*—
"Benediction," volume 18, no. 1, Spring 1985
"Roger Across the Looking Glass," volume 17, no. 1, Spring 1984
"The Only Divinely Authorized Plan for Financial Success in This Life or the Next," volume 18, no. 3, Fall 1985
Permission to reprint granted by *Dialogue*.

Library of Congress Cataloging-in-Publication Data

Chandler, Neal, 1942–
Benediction, a book of stories / by Neal Chandler.
p. cm. — (Publications in Mormon studies, ISSN 0893-4916 ; v. 3)
ISBN 0-87480-329-2
1. Mormons—Fiction. I. Title. II. Series.
PS3553.H27124B46 1989
813'.54—dc19 89-4780
CIP

For Beck, who gives me the space
and forgives me the time

Ordained Order of Contents

The Call

When Emmett was sixteen, the bishop called him into his office for an unscheduled interview, a sort of spiritual wellness spot check, prompted, the boy suspected, by his Explorer leader and by his own mother who felt that he was not fellowshipping well with the youth. This was true. Though of goodly parents, Emmett was awkward and irregular of stature and did not fit smoothly into any of the natural alliances of adolescence. He liked team sports even less than various team captains liked having finally to choose him. His few athletic successes were dictated entirely by the relative usefulness of pure, inert mass or height in the constellations of activity around him. Only once had there been an exception to this. And, as English teachers used to say when English teachers still taught English, the exception proved the rule. It came during the first fully suited-up gym class of a new basketball season. Emmett was loafing and shooting with the others, awaiting the—for him inevitably demoralizing—choosing down of teams. Suddenly, out of nowhere, he sank a twenty-two-footer. "Swishhh." And then another. And another. And yet another. Flawlessly he split the strings as if he were Bingo Bobby Smith and did this daily for an easy living. He couldn't miss. He couldn't believe it. Neither could Gordy Hubbard. Gordy was a jock, one of those five-foot-four-inch-cubed crown princes of P.E., born with a varsity gym shoe in his mouth. "What you been doing, piss-ant, eating Wheaties?" Gordy had first pick, and he picked Emmett. Emmett! Number one, in the very first round. And he called him "the Killer Piss-ant," and Emmett played on Gordy's nearly invincible team nearly an entire season. He played. But the truth is he never hit another outside shot, not one, not in ten weeks, and, what's more, he had serious trouble making even standing, two-handed layups. By the end of the first week, Gordy had stopped calling him "the Killer Piss-ant." He forbade

Emmett to shoot. Then he forbade him to dribble. By the end of the second week, Hubbard turned ugly and resorted to insult. "That's it, Lard-ass, don't move! Just stand there!"

There were girls, of course. Girls in Algebra. Girls in sweaters. Girls in magazines and on penny-arcade cards under the mattress. But utter biochemical preoccupation with things female expressed itself in Emmett as utter social paralysis. He fell painfully in love with a girl as ethereal and slight as the paper ladies on his box spring seemed corporeal and earthy. Away from her, he couldn't even remember her face, but he fought to remember. Fought to be faithful. To wait and to endure in forbearance. He watched her wistfully in the halls at school, placing himself strategically to catch her eye and say "Hi" and then rush on importantly to nowhere in particular. He called her only rarely, always hemming and muffing the lines he'd practiced a hundred times in his head, but her absolute politeness in refusal was certain and redemptive.

"Gee, I can't that night." A week's reprieve from existential dread. "I'm sorry." License to dream. "But thanks for asking." She was an angel.

Emmett didn't have a car. He had no desire to own one, not at the price of supporting it, nor did he work on cars. And, most crippling of all, he discovered—after a failed flirtation—that he didn't even like Rock 'n' Roll. He didn't listen, didn't keep track of songs or singers, didn't dance, didn't care. He was hopeless and found his friends where, obviously, he had to—on the fringes of normalcy: guys who, like himself, hadn't worked out well; guys who still wore earmuffs and their Levis cuffed; guys who didn't go to church, or who did, but asked premeditated questions; guys who conducted Brahms and Shostakovich in the back seat of the family Studebaker; guys who read "Pogo"; guys who wrote poetry. Sooner or later guys like that will get you called in for an unscheduled interview.

The bishop smiled his fatherly smile across the desk. He had his coat off, and he pulled at one suspender in a sage gesture Emmett had seen on television. "Well, young man, I understand you've been hanging out with the 'brains.' " He said "brains" in quotation marks.

Emmett shrugged, caught off guard. But if rumor had it that he was hanging with the "brains," well, he was willing to live with that particular ignominy. No one in the Explorers' troop had much to fear from his grade-point average. Emmett knew that, but it made him all the more ready to believe that, in fact, their hearts and circumscribed horizons crouched in orbit far below his own more exalted sphere. "I guess," he said.

"Well, that's fine. Fine." The word in the bishop's mouth didn't sound fine at all. "But I'd like you to remember that you can't answer every question in life with human reason. The logic of men is all right in its place, but the really important answers are spiritual. Do you understand what I'm saying, Emmett?"

It was M.I.A. night, and Emmett was wearing forbidden Levis. He leaned back now on outstretched elbows and, with a new and heady sense of identity, slouched down and forward into the seat, hooking one leg up and over the arm of the upholstered chair. The arm, however, was higher than he'd calculated, and, instead of looking casually insurgent, his looming knee seemed silly. He wanted to pull it back again, but he couldn't, not right away. Not without retreating ignominiously and altogether from the maverick posture he'd just assumed.

The awkward truth was that, while the bishop felt constrained to reason with Emmett over the limits of reason, the "brains," about whom he worried, consulted with the young man principally on the mysteries of sports and auto mechanics and women. Emmett's ticket to both forums seemed to be lack of genuine qualification for either. He had become a sidekick—but a sidekick only—to stars, an artless Gabby or Poncho to the real Roy Rogers and Cisco Kids of the mind.

"What do you want to do after school and after your mission? What would you like to be?" The bishop leaned back on his elbows too and crossed his legs. He was trying, the boy supposed, to be a regular guy, a pal, and to set the suspect at ease, but the question, like all serious questions not of his own devising, took Emmett by surprise.

"I don't know about a mission."

The bishop frowned. "Of course you'll go on a mission."

"But when I get out of school, I'm going to be a writer." Emmett made this weighty decision at the very moment of its announcement. He knew no more then about being a writer than about being a chemical engineer, which had been his decision and would have been his answer had the bishop asked him a year earlier. In fact, he still especially liked the sound of "chemical engineering." The symmetrically technical syllables. And the lab coats, of course. And architectural arrays of glass tubing converging in conical beakers. But he hadn't actually ever taken chemistry. The periodic table dominated the chemistry classroom. You could see it from the hall, insinuating some darkly promiscuous liaison with math. And a still small voice had ever bade Emmett to keep himself pure and unspotted from math.

Writing was his first dalliance after chemical engineering. A kind of blind date. Creative Writing was third period opposite Chemistry. It was also a-mathematical, and Emmett was on the rebound. Writers, after all, lived in San Francisco or Europe, and Europe was probably better even than lab coats. And so, despite a poverty of syllables, he told the bishop he wanted to be a writer. The bishop in turn frowned even harder and pulled at his suspender for wisdom. Emmett sat under his glum eye with a knee looming absurdly between them and feeling as sure of himself as if the whole world were watching him pick his nose.

"A writer. Well . . . I think that's a fine idea." The words were pronounced with carefully metered enthusiasm. "I think the Church could use a good writer. Did you know," an editorial shift in tone made Emmett look up, expecting yet another tug at the bishop's suspenders, but the counselor had missed his own cue, "that except for the scriptures, only two books in this dispensation have qualified as required reading for the Church? Apostle Talmage wrote both of them in the temple." He closed one eye and let that sink in for a moment. "It's not easy to be a real writer, young man. It's a noble ambition, and I admire that. But what I meant was, how are you going to make a living?"

The bishop's response was, of course, as appallingly naive and eyebrow-tightening to Emmett as his own had been to the bishop. No one wrote church books in San Francisco. Apostles never even went to San Francisco, did they? Why would they? And did anyone anywhere ever really write church books? Weren't they just inflicted whole and indigestible from heaven? The specter of earnest scriptural commentaries and pious edification cast a shadow over Emmett's just-fertilized writing career even darker than the periodic table had cast over his lab coat. Only in this case it was even worse. If he'd told the bishop he wanted to be a chemical engineer, there would have been no further questions about making a living. What he had, in fact, told him not only ignited this concern, it spread the blaze to others. The only way now to calm him and to temper his report to Emmett's mother was to back down. But you cannot back down with your leg hooked ridiculously over the arm of a chair. When you're caught picking your nose, you can't just shrug and put the stuff back where you got it.

"I'm going to write stories," he announced. "Science fiction."

The great stillness that followed was filled with serious talk, and in order finally to escape, Emmett had to promise the bishop he would think it all over, and pray about it, and then come back to talk again. The bishop was a good man, and a wise one, and the question he forced on Emmett then has not left him in peace much since. It preoccupies his wife, his creditors, even Emmett (though always in that order) still today. Yet for all his prescience, what the bishop imparted in that meeting was not wisdom. It was calling. The attentive look in the eye of authority, the way the bishop's eyebrows had drawn suspiciously together, the long, serious, appraising silence that fell in upon Emmett's answers like a lurking sentry. A heedless innocent had been detained for questioning on a byway to Damascus, and when the interrogation was over, when the boy reached home again and looked into the bedroom mirror and thought about it, he knew that, for the first time in his life, he was really on to something.

Space Abductors

Marvin Chisolm put the key in the ignition and started the engine.

"Dad, can we get three movies?"

"Sure, son." In the mirror he watched the garage door descend behind them as he waited for the traffic to clear.

"But I don't want a Disney one. I hate *A Hundred and One Dalmatians*."

"Sure, son." It was cold, and he was tired and resented having to go out again. The Volvo's heater—he put his hand up to the vent—almost justified the price of the car.

"I don't want *King Kong*, either. I like it okay, but I don't want to get it this time."

The sky was that deep, gunmetal blue that comes on a clear night just before darkness, and the long, leafless trees seemed starved and sullen behind the street lamps. He felt older. The feeling surprised him, but he couldn't dismiss it, and he watched his veined hands on the steering wheel.

"I want to get *Space Abductors* again and a new one. Maybe *Jaws*."

"Huh?"

"The third movie, Dad, I wanna get . . . "

"No, son, we're only getting two movies."

"But you said . . . "

"I said we're getting two movies. One for you and the girls, and one for your mother and I." He thought for a troubled moment. "Me. I think it's your mother and me." He didn't really know anymore. He'd forgotten.

"But it's my turn to choose. The girls chose last time."

"Fine, son, it's your turn to choose."

For his thirty-fifth birthday his racquetball buddies had given him a framed color photograph of the bald spot growing slowly but steadily out of sight and mind on the back of his head. The children had whooped with delight, and he had laughed too and then forgotten about it. But you don't get old at birthday parties. You age after dinner in front of the television, or re-reading the financial news in an upgraded seat on the evening flight, or in bed with the children asleep and listening in the next room. He watched his hands.

"Then I choose *Space Abductors*. It's a great movie, Dad. It's my favorite."

"Mmm-hmmmm."

"It's about this alien starship that lands on this house out in the desert only the people don't know it's a starship 'cause they're asleep and when they wake up and look out the window it looks like winter—but not under a starship—just winter with snow and icicles and everything and they go outside to see what happened because they're supposed to be in the desert and they find this ice cave that you can tell by the music they shouldn't go in there but they do anyway and this door shuts behind them and this old guy tries to stop it but it slams down on his arm like a giant razor blade and cuts it off and he's on the inside but his arm is outside in the snow and there's all this blood and you can still see the fingers moving and everything. Dad, can your fingers really keep on moving when your arm's cut off? Dad?"

"Yes, son."

The sky transmuted to an even deeper, almost unbearably melancholy indigo and then, quite suddenly, to black.

"And this voice comes out and says they're kidnapped because they're not really just people living in the desert. This guy—it's a young one and he still has his arms and everything—he's really a test pilot and the lady is a scientist working for the government on a secret space project and the aliens have been watching them out in space for a long time and they're going to take them back to their galaxy and suck the information out of their brains."

Marvin checked the rear-view mirror and accelerated through a yellow light.

"And then the part comes where they show the name of the movie. It's called 'Space Abductors,' Dad. And then they show a whole bunch of other names and then they take the lady scientist and the man to the commander of the starship who looks just like a regular human but you find out later he's really a monster lizard, kind of, but he can turn himself into a human or a robot or anything he feels like but he's really a lizard and when they're through sucking information out of people's brains they hang 'em up on hooks in these big refrigerator things and the old guy's already in there except for his arm isn't on but he's still alive—they keep them alive in there and they suck their blood out real slow in these long tube things and that's what the monsters live on in space but the man and woman don't know about it yet but it's pretty neat."

When they got to the video store, he sent the boy to find his movie, and went himself to the "T" section of the display for the one his wife had ordered. She'd written the title down for him, but he didn't need to look. She was like the kids. She watched the same movies over and over. He'd brought this one home before. All the same, he couldn't find it, and finally he gave up and asked the girl at the counter. She smiled indulgently.

"It's like the library," she explained. "The 'the' doesn't count."

He remembered he'd made the same mistake before. *The Way We Were* was posted under W for "Way." When he reached for the little tag, he found a half-dozen or more of them on the hook.

Meanwhile, his son was waiting for him at the desk with his own tag, and he took it and read the title.

"Are you sure you want this movie?"

"Sure, Dad. It's great. I've seen it lots of times."

"What's it rated?"

"I think it's PG." The boy looked worried. "But I hate G movies, Dad; even the girls hate G movies, except Jennifer."

"And your mother let you watch it?"

"Sure!"

"You're absolutely certain?"

"Da-aad!" He squeaked with exasperation.

They stood and waited their turn at the counter in silence. The man ahead of them was short and fat with oily brown ringlets falling in bulbous spirals over his dirty gas-station shirt. The tags spread out on the counter in front of him had no names, only numbers. That meant the films were X-rated. The man's mouth was X-rated, too.

"Dad."

Marvin felt a tug at his jacket, but the summons was only whispered, and he was listening to the conversation in front of them.

"Dad!" The whisper became adamant.

"Yes, son."

"He used the F-word. I heard him."

Straightening up again quickly, Marvin slid a discreet hand over his son's mouth. However, he also smiled his empathy past the fat man's shoulder at the clerk, who rolled her eyes and smiled beholdenly back. It was, in fact, a wonderful smile. She was a very pretty girl, fresh and blond with buttermilk skin and a last hurrah of adolescent freckles. And she wore a soft, peach-colored sweater with an open neck and obviously . . . he stepped a little to the side to see more clearly . . . obviously no bra at all underneath. The sweater was roomy but insubstantial, and it clung with liquid fidelity to the swelling orbs below, which seemed for all the world as taut and prim and perfect as a sculpture. Yet, when she moved, even ever so slightly, the bright, membranous covering rolled and pitched as sweetly and wantonly as a water bed. Marvin knew he was staring, but the girl was busy with the X-rated gas-station person, and there was no one else at the counter.

When it was his turn, he asked her how long she'd been working at the video store and if she were from around there, whether she liked her work and whether she thought she would go back to school again. Did she have a boy friend? A pretty girl like her surely ought to have a boy friend. He also tried hard to look only at her eyes, but when she leaned over to get the plastic bag for his videos, the front of her sweater collapsed irresponsibly downward and he found himself staring point-blank into the very center of the universe. It was breathtaking. Literally. He stood there transfixed and anaerobic, unable to move or to breathe at all until it was too late. Until she had already looked up again and discovered the unmistakable trajectory of his undisguisable absorption.

While she finished up the order, putting his videos and the charge slip into the bag, the girl smiled to herself the same world-weary smile she had earlier smiled at Marvin over the greasy shoulder of the X-rated gas-station person.

When he left the store, he was angry. He yelled at his son and made him readjust his seat belt. If the boy couldn't ride safely, he wouldn't ride at all. But after a while the anger subsided, and Marvin found himself staring absently ahead into the darkness. He ached somewhere . . . somewhere he couldn't identify, and far away in the distance a voice seemed to be speaking to him.

"The grenade blows the whole door off the air lock, Dad, and they find out it's really the ice cave so they escape out of the ship but they don't know the aliens are still tracking them on radar and the lizard monster is already inside their house when they get there but they don't know it and when the lady goes into the bedroom alone the music is really scary and the monster knocks her down on the bed and rips her blouse off . . . "

"What, son?" Marvin slowed the car. And then he stopped it. "It did what?"

"It's okay, Dad!"

"I thought you said this movie was PG."

"It's okay. We close our eyes. Really. Mom makes us and the girls close their eyes for that whole part anyway because they're scared but I think it's great except the blouse stuff. I don't care about that except it makes her boy friend real mad and gives him this great idea how to hook up the water pipes to the death ray generator in the starship and then he hides in the shower and makes noise so the monster will come after him and it nearly gets him with this claw that shoots out green acid but he ducks and it barely misses him and he turns on the water which doesn't electrocute him because he's wearing sneakers and anyway he's standing in the bathtub which is insulated."

Marvin looked incredulous.

"You know, Dad, insulated. It's fiberglass."

"Oh."

"But the monster is barefoot in a whole bunch of water on the floor so it gets zapped like anything and you can see its eyes melt right in its head and there's this great sizzling noise and the girls scream the whole time which is pretty stupid because it's the monster that's getting electrocuted and the woman's all safe and everything and then after that there's a whole bunch of really disgusting kissing stuff in the bedroom."

"With her blouse still ripped off?" Marvin was paying close attention now.

"But, Dad, don't worry. I hate the kissing stuff. I always turn it off way before they start that garbage. Really!"

"I don't know, son. I think I'd better look at this movie before I let you watch it."

"Da-aaad," the boy sounded like a truck over-winding first gear, "I've seen it four times already."

When he opened the door from the garage to the kitchen, his son darted under his arm with the plastic bag from the video store and broke for the family room.

"Rob! ROB!"

The boy stopped in the hall, but didn't turn around.

"I told you I'd have to look at it first."

"But Da-aad!"

"Is that you, Marvin?"

His wife was calling from upstairs. He didn't answer.

"Where have you been?"

"You sent me to get your videos."

"Well, how long can it take?" He didn't answer.

"I promised the children they could watch their movie before bed, and Jennifer's already asleep."

"We went straight there and came straight back."

"Well, make them get started, or they'll be up all night."

The fugitive standing motionless in the hallway broke again for the family room.

"Rob!" Marvin walked into the hallway behind him and looked up the stairs, but his wife was in the bedroom. "I don't know about this movie."

"Well, what did you get for them?" The edge in her voice narrowed.

"I don't know. He says he's seen it four times already, but it sure isn't Disney."

"Robbie doesn't like Disney, dear. We promised the children if they did their jobs and finished their practicing, they could have a movie, and you promised me you'd cover this awful hole up here and move the dresser back against the wall."

"The plumber said we had to keep it open for a while to check for leaks."

"That was twelve days ago, dear." She paused maliciously. "Did you check?"

He didn't answer.

Rob was at the door of the family room now, looking back at him.

"I'll tell you what, son, you go ahead and watch it, but when it gets to the part you told me about . . . "

"The blouse part?"

"Yeh, the blouse part. You pause the machine and come and get me. I think I'd better have a look at this movie. And I think you'd better prepare yourself, young man, for the possibility that I won't let you watch it again. We're not just anybody here. We have standards in this house, and rules."

"But what about when the monster gets electrocuted, Dad? It's the best part."

"Your electrocution is fine, son, but there are certain things in this world a boy was just not meant to see."

Marvin shook his head, and then he scratched it, and when he heard movie music coming from the family room, he went on upstairs to check for leaks in the plumbing in the hole in the wall behind the dresser.

The Only Divinely Authorized Plan for Financial Success in This Life or the Next

"Thelm, the man is standing in his own way. If only he would get the vision of this thing, see the potential, the tremendous opportunities. If he'd just drop those skeptical blinders long enough to see what's really going on in this world . . . " Carmen Maria Stavely, whose exotic given names trailed a deliberately homespun life like forgotten party streamers, raised both imploring hands from the breadboard on her kitchen table. There were traces of dough, like vestigial webs, between her fingers, and a haze of mottled beige flour softened her angular white forearms and conservative, pin-striped hair as though she had been airbrushed into her genteelly dilapidating kitchen by Andrew Wyeth. Her voice, however, and her adamant gunmetal eyes remained as impermeable and abrupt as broken slate.

At the far end of the table, her friend Thelma silently mixed and measured ingredients with that vaguely desperate preoccupation of the inept. It was some seconds before she realized that Carmen had ceased to knead the dough on the table in front of her and was poised over the breadboard as if it were a pulpit.

"Nineteen months, Thelm. Wednesday, it will be one year and seven months to the day that Walter lost his job. And he didn't just lose it, either. He threw it over, threw it right in their faces like a dirty rag, because—" her eyes retreated a little, "because it's a matter of principle. And nobody understands any better than I do, Thelm, or than you do for that matter, that you have simply got to live by your principles. Walter turned round and walked away from that place, and he's never looked back. And there'll be no criticizing or second-guessing from me or from the children. We know what went on down there. We're proud of him." Thelma, who very much liked Walter, nodded earnest agreement, but was reluctant to smile or speak up. And her caution was her good fortune, for Carmen reversed field without warning. "I'll tell you this. No matter what people say, you can't eat pride. You can't pay the bills with it. It won't keep up the mortgage; and when you get down to it, it won't even help you hold your head up. Just you go down there to the savings and loan, or the gas company, or even the hardware store, and tell them that you're not going to pay again this month because 'You see, sir, it's all a matter of principle, sir,' and then you watch and tell me how high your head is when you come out again. I've been apologizing to those go-fers of Mammon for nineteen months, so don't anyone tell me about pride. I can't afford it. I've got six children, and I can't afford it."

This was not like Carmen. Though she kept precise accounts of the world's evils, when she spoke of family, she was normally as partisan and as carefully sweet as the Avon lady. She had not spoken like this with friends before, certainly never with any of the ladies from church. But Thelma, who was new, was also different. She was not a talker. Instead, from long habit and by genetic predisposition, she was a woman talked about.

Since her early teens she had been indentured to a body whose breathtaking and bountiful femaleness was itself a destiny, so that for decades she had exerted little more than damage control over her own life. But now, at last and inevitably, her earthly vessel had begun to run awkwardly aground. And though she made use of this shipwreck to free herself and to change the course of her life, she was nonetheless like the last surviving priestess of some razed and discredited temple who continues from blind habit—and the inability to do otherwise—to practice her ancient custodial art upon the ruin. She wore her dyed hair in the electric hues and styles that once made Rhonda Fleming's fortune. And her floral print dresses were as dumbfoundingly undomestic as her open-toed pumps and violet nail gloss. Sitting in church, she was a vision of transcendental cheek, an aging child of Babylon come in cheerful obliviousness to winter on Mount Zion.

And so the congregation talked. But despite their talking, she came. And if the truth were known, she came with a will, for though spectacularly out of context and as foreign as garden compost to the carefully aseptic practices of piety, Thelma Hunsaker Rydell had come among them to take not her place, but refuge.

Perched now in Carmen Stavely's kitchen, she was like a giant flowering lotus in a pantry herb garden. She dominated the room with flaunted color and inutility all the while she struggled with the bowls and cups and measuring spoons on the table before her. Carmen, however, seemed not to notice. The truth is that, though she loved to brandish the Lord's terrible swift sword, she was not finally capable of pointing it at real, flesh-and-blood persons. In her own way she was as incongruously innocent as her guest. The two had, in fact, become fast friends—more than friends, for each filled an acute need in the other. Thelma was the willing acolyte, a submissive and even anxious pupil in search of keys and passwords to a better and more peaceable kingdom. Carmen, on the other hand, was an incorrigible but seriously disheartened teacher who very much needed a disciple possessed of eyes to see and ears to hear.

They read in the scriptures together, and Carmen explained at length, jealously shepherding her charge through the jungles of interpretation. She led Thelma gently but unswervingly by the pure light of orthodoxy as only Carmen understood it. And while she led her, she introduced her as well to certain other blessings: the consolation of natural herbs, the joys of honey, pure and unrefined, the regenerative power of legumes and of raw milk, and the open revelation of whole, home-ground wheat. And, truthfully, all that she gave and all that she did for her new friend was repaid her an hundredfold in gratification. For, unlike Walter, who merely tolerated his wife's sacrificial devotions to a higher order of nutrition, and unlike her children, who, she knew, cheated, Thelma embraced vegetarianism as sincerely and enthusiastically as if all along she had only been waiting to be asked. In the logic of her emotions, in fact, the surrender of flesh seemed a natural consequence, an ordained penance, and a modest price to pay for release from the past.

Together, the two women shared abstinence and enlightenment in growing communion. In the course of just a few months, Carmen opened Thelma's understanding to the first and last principles of history and politics, of medicine and cosmetics, of nutrition and housekeeping and home economics. And on this particular day, because it was very much on her mind, and because only eighteen hours earlier a terribly important—and equally inconclusive—meeting had taken place in her own living room, Carmen rehearsed her pupil for the umpteenth time in the virtues of a certain superlative cleaning agent. It was—on principle—the only such product Carmen allowed in her home. The Stavelys washed everything with it from their teeth to their rusting Ford station wagon, and Carmen hoarded an entire two years' supply in a basement cupboard no bigger than a bread box. Like other enlightened users, she rendered moral tribute to its pure and unfrilled utility by calling it simply "the product." And, as with so many things, her unwavering product loyalty was rooted in true religion.

"It's concentrated, Thelm. That's the whole thing. It's absolutely concentrated. Do you realize what the women of this country are paying out every single day for useless fillers? A cup of this and a cup of that. Do you have any idea how that adds up? But no matter, they just keep pouring it right down their drains, right down the tubes, right down into the pockets of the corporations, the multi-nationals. And while those gangsters get richer and richer, what do we get? Well, I'll just tell you. We get filler! Forty, fifty, sixty percent . . . it's infuriating, absolutely infuriating!"

She pinned the glutinous mass under her small fists unrelentingly to the floured mat on the board. Then, releasing all at once, she looked up with resignation. "It's our own fault, you know. Walter showed me an article in *Newsweek*. We don't subscribe, of course. Those magazine people are all owned, body and soul, by the multinationals, and I won't let him. But he buys it at the drugstore anyway, and I guess I don't mind as long as the money doesn't come out of household, and he doesn't leave it lying around for the children. Sometimes, I think they even print the truth in there—when it serves their purpose. I think this was the truth, Thelm, because this company did a test, a marketing one, and offered genuine, pure concentrate to the public. Imagine! And do you know that 73.2 percent of the women tested—seventy-three point two!"—Carmen was addicted to dramatic repetition—"paid no attention whatsoever to the directions on the box. Bright red letters, big as you please, and women went right on pouring a cup of this and a cup of that until their machines choked up like stuffed zucchini. And the cost, well, it went absolutely through the ceiling, and the first thing you know they're all clamoring to the corporation to 'please' let them have their fillers back."

Pain settled over Carmen's high alabaster brow like the mark of Cain. "Can't you just see it? Can't you just visualize the chairman and the smart aleck vice president of sales slapping each other on the back and gloating all over the boardroom? If that story doesn't just have the clarion ring of truth to it! You should have seen Walter. Couldn't have been any more pleased if he'd thought it up himself. Oh, he didn't say anything, but the silence nearly cost him a hernia. Dear Lord, is it any wonder that many are called, but few are chosen? When it comes to women, Thelm, sometimes, I confess, I think the fewer the better. Sometimes I'm not very charitable." Deftly she reversed the heaving victim on her board and this time fairly slammed it down into the bed of flour, which woofed out on either side and then slowly dissipated in magnified particles through the angular afternoon sunlight.

"I guess," offered Thelma, now experienced enough to know a response was expected, "I guess they just didn't understand the importance." And then in a tone of concession. "I suppose it's not very surprising, is it?" She was half apologizing, wondering if she herself were not guilty of having poured an unrecognized fortune in genuine concentrate through the glutted bowels of some hapless machine. More than one had succumbed to her prodigal stewardship.

Thelma was now separating dough into loaves and setting them aside to rise again. "How many are we making, Carmen, dear?" She changed the subject with a decisive cheerfulness, hoping to divert attention from her own probable complicity in this sorry affair. And she watched with relief as her mentor's quick mind tracked rapidly and systematically out of its distraction to lodge the question neatly into context. "Thirty-six. They want thirty-six this time. We're a great hit. Especially the honey-cinnamon. Brother Glover is printing up new labels right now. Every single ingredient listed in big old-fashioned letters right across the top, and 'Mrs. Stavely's Natural Breads' in fine print at the bottom. That was my idea. We can pick them up in the morning on our way to the shop."

Carmen completed her final series on the breadboard stylishly with a double underhook and an improvised guillotine of artful wickedness. "There! And they are paying us right up front this time. Just like downtown." She relished this acquired bit of business-speak, though her anxious mind was foraging far ahead of the pleasure. "But it's not enough, Thelm. It's never enough, and it's gone before I ever see it. Walter has simply got to see the light." The sun percolated from her mood again. "He's fifty-four years old, and they're not hiring account executives at the old folks' home. What is the man thinking of? Last night in that living room out there, right in front of witnesses who'll swear to every word I'm telling you, Kevin Houston offered my husband a distributorship—a dis*trib*utorship, Thelma." She paused to underscore the inconceivable. "And Walter behaves as if he were deaf . . . or crazy . . . or senile! Did he say, 'Yes, sir, this is the chance we've been praying for'? Oh no! He didn't even say no! He just embarrassed me and seven perfectly unsuspecting people to death, that's all. I could have choked him. I could still choke him."

Thelma tried to reflect appropriate distress. She knew Kevin Houston. He taught Bible classes every Sunday to overflow crowds of hushed and wet-eyed admirers. More importantly still, he was known to be the young wizard behind the organization that sold and distributed "the product." He was a much-heralded, much-admired, phenomenal success. And he was not secretive or niggardly with his magic, either. There were meetings, seminars with flip charts and flow charts and ardent testimonials, and Carmen Stavely went more willingly, almost, than to church, for she returned truly encouraged and uplifted. But her unemployed husband would not go with her; and so, Thelma guessed, she had resolutely brought Mohammed to the mountain, though apparently with disappointing, even disastrous results.

Thelma hurt for her friend. Yet her sympathy taxed her scruples because, if the truth were known, she did not entirely like Kevin Houston. At first she had credited the unwelcome shadow of aversion to his wife, a tall, dental redhead, who smiled and popped her gum with the steely self-assurance of a knuckle-ball pitcher. But it wasn't his wife; it was Brother Houston himself, though the reason was hard for Thelma to put her finger on. Perhaps it was the involuntary way he courted women, his pure adolescent sincerity, the vulnerable eagerness to please; or perhaps it was the ready masculine command over every needful and unneedful thing. He was a charming show-off, not unlike certain other remarkable men she had known, and not known, and, unfortunately, married. In his presence, she felt uncomfortably at home. And if she followed and listened to him as enthusiastically as anyone, it was never without a troublesome pang of self-betrayal. But these misgivings were still vague and beyond Thelma's capacity for articulation, so that when she came, as she felt she must, to Walter's defense, she had little choice but to travel on borrowed light.

"The Potters say they're not going to get involved with Brother Houston because his business is what you call a pyramid scheme. Maybe that's what Walter is thinking, dear. Maybe you shouldn't be getting involved in a pyramid scheme either." Thelma knew she was in over her head, but the open scorn that blossomed in Carmen's face told her she had trodden on something ripe and dreadful.

"Sylvia Potter is as dim as dusk, and so is her husband. Of course it's a pyramid, Thelma. What else would it be? Now, you just get out a dollar bill and take a good look at it."

Thelma, though readily contrite, did not have a dollar, and Carmen rummaged angrily through her cupboards until she found one, then spread it out dramatically under the nose of the blushing lotus lady at her kitchen table.

"Now, what do you see?"

Thelma stared blankly down at the bill.

"Oh, for heaven's sake, not there!" Frantic with irritation, Carmen reached down, flipped the bill over, and pointed. "Here!"

Thelma was astounded. "Why, it's a pyramid."

"Of course it's a pyramid. And what does it say right there?"

The words were Latin, but Thelma obediently mispronounced each in turn as it was pointed to, and then, when she had finished, Carmen translated the lot just as if Latin were as familiar to her as the *Reader's Digest*: " 'God's new-order-of-the-world-now-established-among-men.' " Carmen completed a second instructional pass round the pyramid with her finger. "It's God's own plan, Thelm, put here in a free country with a free market and free enterprise. That's what a pyramid is, it's capitalism—Christian capitalism—and it's there because the founding fathers of this country, men like . . . "

She flipped the dollar bill over once more and poked with her finger until Thelma read, "George Washington."

"Exactly! Honorable men like George Washington, whom God raised up for that very purpose, put it in the Constitution and on the back of that dollar bill so that every eye might see and every tongue confess the truth of what I'm telling you right now. Of course it's a pyramid! Anyone with any education and any proper history and common sense knows it has to be a pyramid, because that is what this country is all about. When you've got a pyramid, you've got the only divinely authorized plan for financial success in this life or the next."

Carmen drew herself up at the table and was very solemn. "There are laws, Sister Rydell, decreed before the very foundations of this world, and if a man wants any blessing at all in heaven or on earth, then he'll only get it through obedience to the law on which that blessing depends. And when Kevin Houston offers you a distributorship in your own living room, it's not just some business he's talking about. It's a corporation in the very image of the eternal. It's an executive position in the new order of the world. And that's an investment that thieves don't steal nor moths, nor rust, nor anybody else corrupt. That pyramid scheme you're talking about is an answer to prayer, pure and simple. Last night Kevin Houston offered my poor drowning husband a steamship, an entire, luxury steamship. And it's so big and so marvelous and so absolutely beyond imagining that Walter can't even see it. He's as blind to it as a dug-up mole to sunlight, and if I don't find some way to open his eyes, then he and I and the lot of us are going to go down right here in plain sight of rescue."

Thelma was by now well aware of just whom she had inadvertently provoked. She recognized the vocabulary and the high, dramatic, Sabbath-School tone. "What," she asked defensively, "did Walter say when Brother Houston made his offer?" And her tactic worked, for Carmen ignored the question entirely, though her uncharacteristic silence made it obvious that it oppressed her. She was already stacking bowls and pans and filling the sink with water, but sooner or later the thorn would have to be excised from her narrow chest. After a moment or more of struggle, she opted for sooner.

"Do you know what he said?" She turned with both anger and incredulity in her voice. "Do you? He said, 'Young man, your fly is open.' " Thelma choked and struggled for control over the involuntary muscles in her diaphragm.

Carmen, meanwhile, raged. "That's it! The whole thing! The exact words! An hour, an entire hour spent explaining the program, step by step, right out of scripture so any child could understand. And all Walter Stavely sees is an open zipper. It's disgusting. In front of all those people. I've never been so embarrassed in my life. And poor Brother Houston didn't even have time to turn around and zip himself up before Walter hightailed it into the kitchen like some scamp child who knows he's in for the dickens. If I were his mother instead of his wife, I'd strangle him." She went back to her dishes. "And what am I going to tell Kevin Houston? The man's a Samaritan . . . There's no other word, a Samaritan. 'An offer's an offer,' he said, just as if nothing in the world had happened. But whatever am I going to say to him when he calls this evening?"

"Can't you take the distributorship yourself?" Thelma abandoned Walter to his fate. But Carmen kept to her dishes and replied as automatically as if the words were memorized.

"Walter Stavely is the head of this family. It's his responsibility. It's his decision, and he has got to make it. If you cut off the head of the family, Thelm, you kill the body, too. Some solutions are just no solution at all."

"Well, have you asked him?" Thelma persisted.

"Yes, of course I have. This morning. Out there in the garden. He was tying up those tomato plants again, though it's so late in the season, I don't know why he bothers. I asked him straight out, 'What do I tell him, Walter? I've got to give the man an answer.' "

"Well?"

"Well, he looked up grinning like a bad joke and said, 'My dear, the man's a flasher, and I never go into business with flashers.' " Thelma choked again, but Carmen hadn't finished. "Now, flashers aren't necessarily bad people. Walter wants that understood. In fact, they have a certain basic honesty—very up front, so to speak. Isn't that clever, Thelm?" Thelma was paralyzed, unable to raise her eyes from the table. "Don't you think that's very clever of Walter? Sat out there all morning thinking up his clever answer. And when he'd given it, he looked at me with his old man's eyes and said, 'I'm sorry, Carmen. I suppose he's a nice enough fellow, and, yes, he knows a thing or two about the world, but I promise you that young man will show you things you never wanted to see.' And then he went back to tying up those damned tomatoes just as if he'd really said something . . . and just as if those poor exhausted plants would go right on bearing all winter long, and the mortgage wouldn't fall due, and the roof didn't leak, and the transmission in the station wagon wasn't going, and Kathryn and Walter, Junior, didn't need help with their tuition, and the final insurance notices weren't out there unopened, because I can't face them, and the water bill, and the taxes . . . " And her voice trailed off into a litany without shore or boundary.

A long time passed. The afternoon dissolved into autumn gloom, and Thelma realized with a start that her teacher, her sure-minded, millennial sponsor, was sobbing quietly into the dishwater. She sat for a while in self-conscious silence, unsure of what to do, but in the end her instincts were stronger than her brief acquaintance with discretion. She went to Carmen Stavely, folded this narrow, bristling bird of a woman into the schooled softness of her great, fading, vagabond bosom, and held her like an older sister or like the mother she'd never been, while her friend cried helplessly, and God on his inscrutable pyramid sent raw winter rain down upon the very spot where Walter Stavely had so carefully tied up the tomatoes.

The Onlooker

In the early Fall of the final year of his mission, he drove an ancient Volkswagen van from Bremen to a small city on the Friesian coast. When he reached the marshes and the narrow dikes along the Ems, it was nearly dark, and low storm clouds, moving in from the North Sea, crouched overhead like the shaggy, black underbelly of some incredible animal. Trying to avoid the storm, he turned off the main road near the village of Hesel and took a little known or used shortcut through the Ihringsfehn moors. It was not a good decision. The cobbled road was in terrible repair and had neither lights nor markers. Soon it began to rain, and with a suddenness common only in the Friesian flatlands, the rain became a flood, rolling over the van in long, inverted breakers. He slowed to a crawl. Sometimes he had to stop altogether.

With him were his companion and six missionaries. They had spent a long morning in conference meetings in Bremen, and now he was driving this small band of conference faithful back to their city on the coast. The mood was bright despite the road and the weather. There is a subtle exhilaration that animates us when we share a serious commitment, a sense of separate intimacy and of election that invests even common conversations with a heady intensity. Reconvinced and reaffirmed, they sang the hymns and the inevitable folk songs; they told stories on each other, occasionally even on themselves; and they laughed and laughed. The German sister who sat directly behind him, older and more glib and self-assured than the others, reigned over the traveling celebration. She directed the singing and told story after inexhaustible story. Now, as the rain began to pound the van, she was telling them of a once sheltered school acquaintance who mysteriously and with terrible matter-of-factness had become a Hamburg prostitute and then, one morning, murdered a sleeping army officer with the scissors she had taken along from her grandmother's sewing basket at home.

They listened to her review of the newspaper accounts with ritual horror and barely restrainable, tabloid enthusiasm. He, of course, would have liked to tell some thriller of his own—had he known one—or at least to take stage center with certain memorized passages from a former companion's "Dear John" letter, but the storm and the bad road demanded his attention. At best he clung to the periphery of the conversation, laughing and offering editorials where he could. Still, he didn't really mind, and in fact, in the back of his mind, he knew he preferred presiding to performing. At once nervous and exhilarated, he felt himself a sort of minor Moses or Abraham, guiding his tiny covenant household through a dark and stormy wilderness in a foreign land. They were in the elements. They were not of them.

It was getting very late, but with deep ditches on either side of the road and a canal somewhere up ahead, he didn't dare drive at more than ten or fifteen kilometers an hour, and this was, in fact, his good fortune, for all at once a figure broke out of the darkness just a few yards in front of the van.

As startled as ever he had been in his life, he leaped on the brake, throwing his passengers sharply forward against seats and dashboard. Just ahead in the unsteady illumination of the headlights stood a man with his outstretched arm pointing directly at the center of the windshield. Quickly, the fellow dropped his arm and, hunching sideways into the wind and rain, shuffled toward them. He was dressed as a farm hand, though he looked somehow military in a heavy jacket and a grey wool cap with a bill. As he reached the side of the van, he turned and leaned forward against the window.

Throats behind the driver gasped. Half of the man's face fell away into a hideous crater where the jawbone seemed to be missing and soft, unshaven flesh sank into a deep, pitted scar. Dark water poured from his cap and down over the mangled knot of empty skin and beard.

He said nothing. He made no sign, nor move. He merely looked from face to startled, white face through the rain-streaked window, mustering each of them in turn with a look of grim and accustomed anger. The storm wind outside had begun to rock the van with surprising little twists and jerks, but inside the air had turned to stone.

No one spoke. No one moved. Thoughts had ceased with their breathing while second after glacial second stretched itself and broke off aimlessly into the darkness. Then, after an eternity, but arriving with the measured abruptness of an anticipated explosion, someone shoved the frozen driver sharply forward against the steering wheel.

"For God's sake, get us out of here!" demanded the voice from behind him, and in the same instant his companion whirled to lock the doors on the passenger side of the van.

"Let's go!" The command came this time in deliberate, instructional English.

Unsure of himself, not knowing what to do, he looked from one insistent expression to the other and then back again to the grim eyes at the window. Attention in the van, meanwhile, had shifted from the figure outside to him. There was both annoyance and urgency in their faces, and soon he found himself pushing uncertainly at the accelerator and releasing the clutch. The van lurched clumsily, then lurched again, and almost at once the man at the window disappeared into the storm behind them.

Awkward silence did not dissipate quickly or easily, but an hour later a light, if far more cautious, mood had re-established itself among the travelers. They joked, a little weakly perhaps, about the ghost of Ihringsfehn. They sang again, and before the trip was over he had even found opportunity to recite those predictably successful passages from a classic "Dear John." The trip ended with laughter, with farewells and earnest German handshakes that were more than just obligatory. They were, it seemed, safely out of Egypt, beyond the fatal Red Sea, and they shared at least a small sense of mutual congratulation.

Yet they were not as they had been, and there was a new wariness in that parting as if the prophet, though truly he never lost the way (for he had gone very carefully) nonetheless had suddenly, inexplicably lost his footing and fallen heavily in the raw wilderness with all his unsuspecting household. For all their good-natured laughing and dusting off, they were startled and soiled and suddenly insecure. No one who was there that evening ever spoke to him again of the encounter. For all its high drama, it refused to become a testimony or a story or even a tradeable reminiscence. It crouched stubbornly apart from the streams of compliant experience, refusing to be named or counted. And so he pushed it to the edge of memory to encounter it only rarely thereafter, and unexpectedly, like a grim, incomprehensible stranger in a storm, and to return its angry stare, and then hurry on ahead again, leaving it as before behind him—and somewhere out ahead—in the dark.

Benediction

Ardmoore told Carmen Stavely, who'd been away in Idaho visiting family, that what happened that Sunday morning was absolutely confidential. The bishop had instructed all who'd been present to keep the matter strictly to themselves; and he, Ardmoore, did not think (though as usual his optimism was naive) that more than a very few people outside the ward were acquainted with the details. As for himself, he had not been present, had not, therefore, been warned or instructed by the bishop, and was reporting only what he could not help learning from the entirely unsolicited accounts of others. If what he told her was not in all respects consistent, Ardmoore would have been the first to confess confusion both at the contradictions and at the ardor with which each teller insisted upon the complete accuracy of his or her own version. Fortunately, there was general agreement on the sequence of events. The incident had occurred on the fourth of five Sundays in May and thus marked the fourth appearance of Brother Kevin Houston as the new Gospel Doctrine teacher.

The partitions in the multi-purpose room had been pushed back all the way and propped with metal folding chairs because, unfortunately (or providentially—here the opinions were as sharply as they were unevenly divided), Sister Reeva June Parish who teaches Gospel Principles had been home again with mono, and all her neophyte faithful and her missionary-surrounded investigators had come on over to hear Kevin.

The truth, as Ardmoore well knew, was that most of those people would have been there even if Reeva June, bursting with good health and sound principles, had put in her scheduled appearance. Reeva was sweet, but Kevin Houston put on a truly spectacular show; and in four weeks, word-of-mouth had already made Gospel Doctrine a standing room sellout. With the exception of

Ardmoore, who tended the flame in the clerk's office, and of the other bishopric members, whose reliable absence was a matter of form and tradition, almost everyone thinkable had been in that class, including, as is now well known, Damon Boulder himself, who had not set foot in the class—nor in the church, for that matter—the entire four weeks since his own formal and unbidden release as Gospel Doctrine instructor.

Now, Damon must have come early because he'd sat in the next to last row near the door. For the most part, people said, he was quiet and uncharacteristically reticent to speak or to take part unless called upon. But perhaps, as some now insist, he was only playing possum, biding his time, waiting. On this hotly contested question of premeditation, however, Ardmoore was, himself, unwilling to express an opinion, and it is perhaps important, before we go any further, to point out that Ardmoore had always really rather liked Damon Boulder; that he had, in fact, defended Damon at the very ward council meeting in which Bennett Sarvus, practically as his first official act as newly installed Sunday School president, had recommended Damon's release.

Leaning back and pulling lint from the cuff of his blazer, Bennett had mentioned almost offhandedly that Boulder had now been teaching the adult class for over a year. Surely it was time to release him with many thanks and to offer him some new challenge in the ward. There followed several nodding, lip-pushing "well, why not" seconds from among those present, but practically no one was taken in by this careful show of nonchalance. Bennett and his seconds had just declared war.

Utterly predictable pockets of guerilla resistance quickly formed up and returned fire. In particular, the militant and military-looking Marvin Chisolm led the counterattack. Marvin was the ward liberal, an unabashed Democrat rendered respectable by his brahman Utah roots and successful consulting business. He wore his expensive, Ivy League education openly with his mustache, his penny loafers, and his herringbone jackets. In church, his schooled reverence for the rigors of academe took the general form of irreverence for the popular accommodations of faith. In a tone of purest acid he declared himself (1) entirely satisfied with the present teacher, and (2) categorically opposed to any change that might, in Marvin's own terms, "further abet the already rampant and reprehensible

'Koolaidization' of Mormon theology." Even Ardmoore said, in a conciliatory tone, that it seemed to him a shame in a New Testament year to let go the only teacher in the stake who read Greek and who had some formal training in ancient scripture.

By this time, however, Bennett Sarvus had come to full attention atop the powder-blue sofa on which he was sitting, and he began to speak with a hushed gravity quite beyond his twenty-five and a half years. Precisely this, he explained, was the problem. Brother Boulder had, it was true, a great deal of worldly learning—which was, no doubt, commendable in its place—but at the same time he openly spurned the authorized lesson plan, and, in fact, when President Sarvus had gone personally to inquire after the manual, Damon, who couldn't even remember its title, had had no idea at all of its whereabouts, except to say that perhaps it might be "somewhere in the car." As everyone well knew, that meant somewhere awash in the ragged sea of books and papers spilling around the back of Damon's wheezing, barnacled, 1963 Plymouth station wagon, a brontosaurial conveyance bizarrely adorned with seraph's wings that Carmen Stavely's own husband Walter and the boys in his Scout troop gleefully referred to as "the Fourth Nephite." It was also common knowledge that Damon's lessons were, in fact, taken largely from whatever obscure, uncorrelated, probably even foreign and idolatrous book he happened to be poring over at the time. More than a few people, especially established, full-blooded Saints who were not afraid to speak out behind his back, complained that he talked over the heads of new members. He loved Latin words and questionable or extreme ideas, and though, yes, Damon Boulder had a great deal of worldly knowledge, Bennett, whose own field was information management, felt compelled to point out that raw, unmanaged, uncorrelated knowledge was not unlike raw weather, or raw language, or, for that matter, raw sewage. It posed a serious environmental hazard, in this case to the fragile spiritual ecology of the ward. Hadn't the scholars and intellectuals among the Jews managed with all their learning to befog the very light of Christ? Bennett, for his part, was not anxious to follow their example in the Sunday School for which he was now personally responsible.

He finished on a note of such sincere and impassioned concern that the room fell into a kind of rhetorical arrest. Even Boulder's angry supporters sat as if molded in aspic; and Ardmoore, embarrassed at his earlier comment and obvious shallowness, stared through the carpet at his feet. The bishop, however, shuffled restlessly and then coughed for attention.

"Look, Bennett," he said, "I've been through all this before." And indeed, over the years and at the behest of many, he had tried to shift the reluctant Damon Boulder from teaching into nearly every other thinkable kind of position. As a temporary Scout leader Damon had, with the saturnalian hubris of innocence, taken the entire troop skinnydipping in the pond at the stake farm. In the clerk's office he had actually, knowingly subverted certain statistical reports with figures taken, as he later freely admitted, from a table of random numbers. When questioned, he explained guilelessly, but without repentance, that though doubtless inaccurate, his impossible numbers were certainly as useful and as significant as those called for in the reports. As ward In-Service leader he'd cancelled four consecutive monthly meetings, only to occupy the entire hour and a half of the fifth reading long exhortatory passages from the *Journal of Discourses* with a bright, theatrical enthusiasm comprehensible solely to himself. He refused categorically to deal with the ward finances, insisting loudly that God and common sense forbade him to do so, and when called once, long ago, in a moment of sublimely naive inspiration to serve on the ward building committee, he had, while toiling faithfully and knowledgeably for a better than standard plan building, also written a light-hearted, fun-poking letter of complaint and suggestion to the Church Building Committee in Salt Lake City. Unfortunately, in that higher, thinner, "intermountain" air, every vestige of fun and good nature must have evaporated utterly from the document, for, on its account, Damon's then brand-new bishop suddenly found himself skewered and roasting painfully over the fire-red carpet in the office of a very angry stake president. It was a lesson he hadn't forgotten.

"I could call Damon to the bishopric." He paused, absently fishing broken animal crackers from the watch pocket in his vest while looks of horror sprouted around him like crabgrass in timelapse. "But if I did, he'd accept reluctantly and then celebrate by growing a full beard and what hair he has left to his shoulders." He looked up with a gesture of conclusion. "If the stake would let me do it, I'd retire and ordain him to teach mysteries to the high priests' quorum; but since they seem determined he's going to be the oldest active elder in the church, I'm going keep him right where he is. He likes it; and as long as he's not teaching some open heresy or other, I like it too. A little hard-core education isn't going to hurt anyone. We're just not used to it. If you think someone is seriously troubled," he added as an afterthought, "well, we have other classes, don't we?"

But the problem was that there were, in fact, no other classes. Reeva June Parish was, for reasons beyond her control, becoming seriously unreliable; and Family Relations was once again without a teacher, the last one having disappeared quite suddenly and, in fact, mercifully after the revelation of her imminent divorce. No one new had been called, and the bishopric's own wait-and-see footdragging was to blame. So it was not surprising or even unwarranted when, not many days later, a delegation of appropriately credentialed Saints went privately to the bishop's home.

In an old bathrobe, he led them to the cluttered family room where he sat, almost primly for a man of his comfortable dimensions, staring resignedly at the crackled leather of his slippers while Sunday School President Sarvus, after apologizing for the hour, polled his militant companions and then closed with another, even more impassioned appeal for retrenchment in Gospel Doctrine. When Bennett had finished, the bishop, without raising his eyes from his slippers, took a deep breath and let it go. Then, placing his hands on his knees, he thanked all present for their concern, stood, and left the room. According to Ardmoore, he must have gone straight off to bed without so much as a nodding farewell to his guests. The house beyond the family room remained dark and eerily silent; and when, after much too long a time, the bishop had not returned, the abandoned and incredulous party of kingdom patriots found its own groping way out of doors, there to caucus one more time in troubled whispers on the moonlit drive before disbanding stealthily into the night. The partisans were puzzled and pessimistically insecure about what their night ride had accomplished. Yet the very next Sunday the bishop himself—ignoring channels—called Damon Boulder in and told him he would soon be released from his teaching job in prospect of a weightier assignment. Ardmoore, who'd been in the outer office, swore to Carmen that Damon Boulder laughed out loud. And this is not improbable, for Damon too had heard it all before. It may have seemed to him at first like a private joke between old friends until, of course, the handwriting would not fade from the wall. Then he just sat in glum silence while the bishop performed his rehearsed enthusiasms across the desk.

There is no doubt Damon took it badly. He stayed away four full weeks, reappearing, as everyone now knows, on *that* fateful Sunday. The news of his return could not have spread any more quickly if it had been posted on a billboard in the parking lot; and round Rachael Holbein, one of the midnight riders, made a point of stopping Kevin Houston in the hallway, taking his sleeve, and whispering with all the theatrical subtlety of a silent-movie conspirator that Boulder was back. And, indeed, since Boulder was not known as a particularly forgiving or deferential man, Kevin might well have been apprehensive; except, of course, that he wasn't.

Kevin Houston had that particular kind of self-assurance which in a secular and sophisticated world is taken as evidence of old money. In Kevin, however, whose prosperity was, in fact, nearly as green as the banknotes in his wallet, it signaled instead a kind of fore-ordination to the high, blood bureaucracy of Zion. He spoke in the accumulated ecclesiastical jargon of four generations; and his voice, as the cynical Marvin Chisolm delighted in saying, had the "perfect grain and color of simulated walnut formica." Moreover, when he took the stage in Sunday School, he left no doubt at all in any mind, not even Marvin Chisolm's, as to who among those players present commanded top billing.

"So you gotta follow the brethren?" The sentence sliced through the room at a whining pitch and decibel level that stunned the still-conversing class members into silence. Having thus seized attention, Houston, who had not even reached the front of the class, whirled on his heel and backed the rest of the way up the center aisle. "Is that right, Brother Zimmer?" A young man in a short-sleeved white shirt and blue tie came to attention. "Ya gotta follow the brethren?" Again Kevin whined the sentence out in a minor third so nasal and obnoxious that a newborn infant would have recognized it as a taunt.

"Well, I suppose." Zimmer, though reliable, was startled and embarrassed at an answer which, while clearly correct, somehow sounded ludicrous in the face of his interrogator's tone. Once having spoken, however, he immediately regretted his vacillation and, as quickly, repented. "I mean, yes! Of course!"

Kevin kept silent for a moment, surveying the expectant class, then looked back to Elder Zimmer, now with a sardonic cast to his familiar smile. "Why?" he demanded. "You're an educated man, David." Zimmer shrugged. "Now, don't be modest, a well-educated man, and you regularly study the scriptures? Does he read the scriptures, Ariel?"

David Zimmer's wife nodded vigorous confirmation. "He certainly does," she said.

"Well, I thought so. Now tell me this, Ariel. Is he a responsible man? Does he exercise good judgment in his work, for his family, in his church assignments?" Again Ariel's affirmation was aggressive. "Then why on earth should David Zimmer, a man of education, preparation, and sound judgment, feel compelled to follow anybody's 'brethren'? Why don't those church leaders out there," he made a dismissive gesture in a vaguely westerly direction, "just leave him alone to follow his own gospel-inspired, common sense course to salvation?"

As Houston turned from Ariel to the rest of his audience, the predictable hands already fluttered aloft. There was round Rachael Holbein; there were the Cutters, Sylvia Potter, Arlon Crisp, who was elders' quorum president, and, finally, there were two of the six missionaries, all telegraphing urgent signals at the ceiling. But Kevin had something else in mind.

"Brother Chisolm, what do you think?" Marvin Chisolm had sat in class for four weeks now nursing a loud silence and an expression of weak nausea. It was time to call his bluff.

"I don't know, Kevin." Chisolm raised his eyebrows and lowered his voice so that the people behind him strained forward to hear. "I'm not even sure I know what 'following the brethren' means. Perhaps you could explain."

"It's obedience!" Rachael Holbein had read the lesson and could no longer wait to be recognized. She dashed in headlong. "It means obeying the commandments and always doing whatever you're asked." She sat back resolutely and folded her hands on the manual in her lap.

"When I do what I am asked," Marvin looked at Kevin and not at Rachael as he spoke, "I am being polite or considerate or accommodating. I am obedient, on the other hand, when I do what I am told. Perhaps that is what is meant. Perhaps urging us to follow the brethren is simply a euphemistic way of warning us to do what we are . . . "

"Now, Marvin," Houston cut him off decisively at the offending verb, yet his tone remained as smooth and sweet as whipped topping, "do you suppose it is a simple thing to direct the affairs of a world-wide church of several million Saints?"

"Of course not." Marvin didn't see the point.

"We all know, Brother Chisolm, that you have had a good deal of administrative experience yourself. So let me ask you what sort of system, what method you personally would suggest to the brethren for governing the important spiritual and, yes, even temporal affairs of an organization of millions spread all over the world?"

Marvin, who had felt a little cornered by the relentless warmth of Houston's questioning, smiled an air-conditioned smile. "I'd teach them correct principles and then let them govern themselves."

"Well now, I think that's a marvelous answer. In fact, I think it's just exactly what the Lord would have each and every one of us do . . . ultimately. But in the meantime, Brother Chisolm, tell me. How do you teach people those correct principles? I mean, how do you *really* teach them? And how do you get people—and believe me I'm including myself here—how do you get them to really govern themselves?"

When Marvin didn't answer immediately, Kevin bored in like a trial lawyer on a scent. "If we just talk to everybody, tell them about it, will that do it? If we just preach at 'em a little on Sundays, will they learn those principles, and will they live by them?" A snicker went through the class. "No one seems to want to say 'yes.' Well, why not, then? What, when you get right down to it, is the only truly effective way to teach the gospel?" He turned to the blackboard and took a piece of chalk. "I think we all know that to teach effectively, we've got to teach by . . . "

"By the spirit!" Rachael Holbein, the Cutters, and the missionaries all bleated out in unison.

"Well, of course. Certainly, you've got to teach by the spirit, now, don't you?" And Kevin wrote SPIRIT in block letters on the board. "That's an excellent answer, and we're going to get right back to it, too. But before you can teach by the spirit, you've got to teach by something else first." He wrote again: EXAMPLE. "You've got to teach by example. Isn't that right, Brother Cutter?"

"Sure is," Cutter grinned. "Actions speak a whole lot louder than words."

"They certainly do, and if you've got to be an example in order to lead the people of God, then maybe it's about time we took a good hard look at just what kind of examples our leaders are." Kevin paused and paced slowly across the front of the room in apparent self-absorption, bouncing a piece of bright yellow chalk in the palm of his hand. When he reached the windows banked shoulder high across the mint-green cinderblock wall on the far side, he stared out into the sunlit spring morning for a moment and then whirled, as if with sudden inspiration.

"Now take Peter," he announced, "the very first chief executive officer of the church, the George Washington of Christianity, so to speak. Now just what kind of a man was this Peter? Was he an all-American? Ask yourselves! Was he a genuine, all-conference, all-church champion, or was he just some guy off the street looking for a job? I mean," he raised his open palm to a vertical plane in direct line with his nose, "what do we really know about Peter?"

The class was a little stunned; and when no one showed any sign of responding, Kevin called on the elders' quorum president. "Arlon?"

Arlon Crisp, who was in the habit of speaking before he thought, always divided his sentences into two distinct parts, a universal or boiler-plate introduction and a more specific, though equally formulaic, conclusion joined by varying periods of awkwardly searching silence.

"Well, one thing we can say for certain," he began, and then foraged his crowded mind several seconds long for whatever it was that could be so certainly said, "is . . . is that . . . that he was chosen of the Lord." He smiled. But Kevin was not buying.

"Oh no, Arlon, that's too easy. What we have to figure out here today is why the Lord chose Peter in the first place. What did this man have that someone else didn't? Was it prestige? Was it education? What did the guy do for a living?"

"He was a fisherman, wasn't he?" A very pretty young girl, a convert of only a week or two, spoke with soft hesitancy from the third row.

"A what?" Kevin put his hand to his ear.

"A fisherman," the missionary on her right confirmed boldly.

"FISHERMAN?" Kevin's obvious incredulity made both respondents wince as if some terrible and terribly obvious mistake had been made. "You mean he didn't have a Ph.D. in religion? He wasn't an expert on theology? Are you trying to tell me that the man chosen by the Lord to preside over the church didn't have a doctor's degree, or a master's degree, or even a piddly little old bachelor's degree? Why, next you'll be trying to tell me he wasn't even an intellectual, that he was some sort of simple, honest working man. Well, well. Well, well. Well, well." He spoke his "wells" in melodic pairs and crossed back to the other side of the room.

"Tell me," he re-addressed the third row in slow, dramatic dismay, "was he just any old fisherman? Do we know anything else about Peter?"

By this point, most of the audience were beaming, though a few, predictably, smoldered. No one, however, was foolhardy enough to take up Kevin's newest invitation to dance. His sure orthodoxy was too subtle, too deceptive, too unorthodox. And though they loved (or loathed) the tune, no one had any further illusions about being able to mind the step. Kevin would have to answer his own question.

"Well, brothers and sisters, we know this much. We know he owned his own boat. Owned it outright. And he hired other men to work for him. This man they called 'the big fisherman' wasn't looking for any handout when the Lord and the church came along. He supported himself, supported his wife, his children—we don't know for sure how many he had, but you can bet your life he had more than two. Why, he even supported his mother-in-law. Now, that should tell you something." Kevin paused for the accumulating appreciation to catch up with him.

"Now," he continued, "I'm going to tell you another thing, something not many people have figured out yet. Old Peter was a pretty darn good business man. When the Lord called him in to head up the church organization, he was already worth a considerable amount of money. He had a savings program. Made sound investments. He was a man who'd magnified his 'talents' (and some of you had better look up the real meaning of that old Jewish word in your Bible dictionaries).

"Now," he continued, "do you want me to tell you how I know about this, how I'm absolutely certain of it? Well then," he accepted the rapt silence as assent, "I will. If you'll take your Bibles and look up First Corinthians 9, verse 5, you'll find out that when Peter was called to go out and preside in the mission field, he took his good wife right along with him. Now, in my father's family, as some of you know, we've had considerable experience in this area, and let me admonish all those priesthood bearers here today. Brethren, believe you me, you do not take your wife into the mission field unless you've first put more than enough money aside to support her in the manner to which she is bound and determined to remain accustomed. And that is the gospel truth."

When the laughter finally paled, Kevin became serious again. "In those rough, ancient times when thieves and shiftless beggars, when high-paid parasite priests and crooked Roman tax-collectors were the norm, in those dark times, not unlike our own times today, here was a man who carried his own weight, who took care of his family, who got ahead in business, a man with the stature and with the financial means and know-how to truly serve his church. Now that's something we know how to appreciate even today.

"That man was as solid and reliable as a rock. And, in fact, my brothers and sisters, did you know that 'rock' is the very meaning of the name Peter, a name, by the way, which was not given him by any earthly power? Why, his parents thought his name was Simon." Kevin shook his head in good-natured recognition of human folly. "The Lord himself gave Peter his proper name when he called him to the work. Now, don't you just suppose that the Lord knew exactly what kind of man he was hiring? Don't you just suppose that when he gave old Simon Bar-Jona, that successful, self-reliant, maritime business man from Galilee, the name 'Peter,' he was sending you and me a message, telling us that here was the kind of a man the Lord is looking for, an ensign to the nations, an example to each and every one of us." A wry wrinkle gathered itself on one side of Kevin's forehead. "Or do you suppose he gave him that name just because he had nothing better to do on a Saturday afternoon?"

Kevin waited patiently until the familiar, if now more hesitant, hands began to collect in quantum spurts and flutters, and then once again looked beyond them to the back of the room.

"Dr. Boulder, what is your opinion?"

The class froze. Kevin was having it all his own way. Chisolm was long since vanquished, and Damon Boulder's uncharacteristic silence seemed to confirm once and for all the calling and election of the new order in Gospel Doctrine. So why this? Why taunt the dragon?

Boulder himself seemed surprised. He sat a while thinking before he answered. "The giving of a name in itself is not really very remarkable, Kevin. It was a common practice for Jewish rabbis to give titles to their disciples, usually some word that pointed to promise in a situation or placed an obligation on the bearer. Christ, of course, did this more than once, and there are various examples in the Old Testament."

He paused and looked around. "As to this particular title, well, I really don't think it was a product of financial analysis, Kevin, nor of character analysis for that matter. In fact, it has always seemed to me more like wishful thinking. I, at least, would be hard put to think of a title less descriptive of the man's actual behavior."

"What do you mean by that?" Sunday School President Sarvus was standing in the back of the room where he had been watchfully presiding since shortly after the beginning of the lesson. The clarion annoyance in his voice sent a shiver through the more timid in the room, and attention closed in around the discussion like a crowd around the scene of an accident.

"Well," Boulder continued unperturbed, "he didn't show himself to be much of a rock, now did he? The man was almost fatally impulsive. When, for instance, Jesus called to him on the Sea of Gennesaret, he was all hot to get out and walk on the water, but two or three steps and his self-assurance collapsed. He nearly drowned. More importantly, he was the first and the loudest of the disciples to confess his loyalty to Christ, but we know he was also the first to deny him . . . and the most insistent. He had a temper. He was violent. Threatened people. Even cut off some poor fellow's ear. How often did he have to be slowed down, cooled off, rebuked? Oh, he mellowed as he got older, but he wasn't cured. Even after he'd been called to lead the church, he couldn't stay out of trouble. In fact, he got into so much trouble with the law in Jerusalem, he had to be released from that highly visible, presidential position and sent out into the boondocks to preside over a mission (an expedient, by the way, which is not unknown to the church in our own day). But in the mission field, I think, Peter finally hit his stride. He was a great teacher, you know, a baptizer, and because doctrinal purity was far from chief among his passions, inside the church he became a capable politician. Perhaps the best she's ever had."

"Politician?" Kevin Houston, who had been listening intently, arched his eyebrows into pointed interrogatories.

"Certainly. Somebody had to mediate between those pureblood Jewish hardliners up in Jerusalem and Paul and his liberal rabble in Rome. No easy task, you can be sure, and no one to set him apart for it, but he carried it off like a ward politician with consummate pragmatism."

"With what?" Rachael Holbein had been lost for ten minutes. None of this was in the manual.

"Pragmatism, Rachael, consummate political pragmatism. Paul complains in Galatians that his old friend and fellow missionary Peter knows all too well which side his bread is buttered on. Oh, he's an ally of sorts; but when the occasion and the realities of power require, he is not in the least above dissembling and backing down to those starched bureaucrats in Jerusalem, even when doing so violates his own inner convictions. And that, for good or for ill, is political pragmatism."

"I don't understand." Bennett Sarvus broke in again, but this time directed his metallic gaze and his question to Kevin Houston. "Is Brother Boulder insinuating that the Apostle Peter was some sort of cheap political hack?" His measured enunciation and crystal tone made it clear that he was very upset.

"Oh no," Boulder quickly responded before Kevin might intercede, "he was a very fine politician, a very successful one. He did more, perhaps, than any other to keep an early and sorely divided church together, to prevent schism. And I don't think political successes like that come cheaply, either. They are almost always bought at great personal cost. In a way that's Paul's point, isn't it? That too often we pay out again in personal integrity whatever it is we win for the integrity of the community? In any case, I was only wondering out loud—and at Brother Houston's invitation, of course—if perhaps, in retrospect, 'Simon Politikos' (Simon the Politician) might not have been a more accurate title, and, consequently, higher praise."

Boulder leaned back in his seat with his face carefully blank and with an air of dreadful satisfaction. And indeed, the marvelous spell holding the class enthralled before Kevin had so rashly conjured this spirit was gone. The crowd was visibly restless, palpably unsure and disoriented. Yet Kevin stood among the ruins of his Sunday School lesson as calm as a summer's morning. "You know," he said so quietly and with such intense reflectiveness that the class immediately forgot its agitated milling and whispering to listen, "You know, I think Brother Boulder is right."

Even Damon Boulder glanced up.

"I think he's reminding us that though Peter was a good man, a great man, a chosen man, he was not, in fact, a perfect man. Like you and like me, he was human. Isn't that right, Brother Boulder?"

Surprised at being invited back into the discussion, Damon nodded. "Peter shows us pretty clearly everything that the call to leadership involves in human privilege and weakness."

Pursing his lips, Kevin nodded. "Yup, there is certainly something to what you say. But you are wrong on one point, Damon—the point about the name—because the Lord knew exactly what he was doing when he gave that imperfect fisherman the name Peter. You know," his voice took on a sudden air of confidentiality, "when I was preparing this lesson, I ran into a real puzzle. I looked up that name Peter in a fancy dictionary I have at home. It's an old Greek dictionary. Now, the New Testament was written in Greek. Isn't that right, Damon?" Damon nodded. "And in Greek the English name Peter is spelled P-e-t-r-o-s."

Kevin wrote it on the board, turned, and winked at his audience. "You see, there's a bit of the scholar in some of the rest of us as well. And do you know, when I looked up P-e-t-r-o-s in that dictionary, it didn't mean *rock* at all. The real Greek word for *rock* is P-e-t-r-a." He spelled it out on the board and wrote the translation directly underneath. "So just what do you suppose P-e-t-r-o-s means?" He pointed to the still empty space under the first word on the board; and when everyone, including Boulder, remained silent, Kevin turned and wrote out the answer. "It means 'stone,' an ordinary stone.

"Now," he whirled and faced his audience with a bolt of new energy, "that might not seem like a very big difference to some of you, but think about it. What is a rock? I mean, there's the Rock of Gibraltar and the Rock of Ages; there's the man who built his house upon a rock, and then, of course, there's the rock of revelation upon which the Lord has built this magnificent church. Surely a rock is something pretty big, pretty darn substantial. But if that's a rock, what then is a stone?"

For a moment or more he scanned the ceiling while he dug in his trouser pocket, then pulled a smooth round chip of shale out into the sunlight and held it up between his thumb and forefinger for all to see. "Now, there is a stone, and a stone, my brothers and sisters, is also a rock. It's a little rock, a rock you can put in your pocket or skip across a lake. And so I asked myself, why did the Lord want to go and call that big, strapping, six-foot fisherman and business tycoon 'Mr. Simon Little-Rock'? It puzzled me all morning long. And then . . . then suddenly, like revelation, it came to me that it was nothing so very remarkable at all, that you and that I, that all of us do the very same thing almost daily."

Kevin advanced to a still open expanse of the bright green blackboard. "Now, take a name, almost any name like Bill, or Tom, or Jim, or even 'Rock.' " He listed the names in a column. "What do we call Bill or Jim or Tom before he's grown up, before he reaches the full stature of a man? Why, we call him Billy or Jimmy or Tommy." He added the diminutive ending to each name as he spoke it. "And we mean 'little Bill' or 'little Jim' or 'little Tom.' He's our 'little man,' we say, just as those old Greeks could have told us that 'Petros' meant 'little Rock.' So, you see, surely Peter was a rock. He was all rock, nothing but rock! Yet a rock, let's admit it, with a great deal of growing to do before he reached the full, magnificent stature of a perfected, celestial rock. Now, doesn't that just make sense? I'll just tell you it does. I'll tell you, the Lord knows just what he's doing, and just exactly what he's saying. Doesn't he?"

Flames of affirming attention that had dimmed and sputtered now burned brightly again all over the room.

"And do you know, brothers and sisters, I pondered that name." He turned to the board and filled in the final "y"; then, placing the chalk on its side, he drew a broad, yellow circle around the name. " 'Rocky' . . . there's something special about that name, isn't there, something out of the ordinary? We don't just give that name to children. In fact, we associate it with tough guys, with fighters, and with a special kind of indomitable spirit.

"Remember, back at the outset of class I said that we would get back to the spirit. Well, I'm going to keep my promise because recently I was taught something truly wonderful about spirit, something that has a tremendous bearing on the lesson the Lord wants us to learn here today. Recently, I had the privilege of attending, with my good wife, the final in a series of three remarkable films, all of which, amazingly enough, bear that same name given nearly twenty centuries ago to an enterprising Galilean fisherman with tremendous celestial potential."

While Kevin underlined the crucial name once more on the board, Marvin Chisolm, his nausea and piqued impotence at full mast, twisted around nearly 180 degrees in place to fix Damon Boulder with fierce, "for heaven's sake, do something!" eyes. Damon, however, waved Marvin off with a gesture of hand-washing indifference.

"I'm sure," Kevin continued, "some of you saw those movies as well, but let me tell you about them. Let me tell you about a young man without education or wealth or worldly sophistication, without social position or powerful friends or political influence. Let me tell you how that young man, starting from the absolute bottom-most rung of a corrupt and indifferent sports world, with only his vision, his pure heart . . . with hard work and an indomitable spirit to sustain him through setback and suffering, through temptation, trial, and travail—when those nearest and dearest forsook him, when none believed in him or in his vision or in the transcending power of his spiritual resolve . . . let me tell you how that young man became a world champion . . . and how he endured to remain a champion, overcoming the fierce enticements of worldly success, overcoming even the brutal, crushing physical onslaught of a veritable angel of hell. Yes, let me tell you about a real man with real spirit."

And Kevin Houston told them. He told them the parable of "Rocky," the difficult core of an ancient story made plain and simple in the bright, allegorical shell of a new one. He showed them the Hebrew fisherman as secret, inspiring foreshadow of the tenacious Italian Stallion, the triumphant Philadelphian in vivid similitude of the intrepid Galilean. And when he had finished his story, when he was done, somehow . . . somehow it was as if Rocky himself were right there among them, bruised, pummeled, punished, exhausted, and, yes, victorious, as magically, improbably, and inevitably victorious as virtue and goodness and truth.

Then, after a moment, Kevin Houston stepped forward into the idolizing hush and, like Dan Rather at the last day, drew the sum.

"So you see, brothers and sisters," his full, round baritone contracted to a flesh- and soul-penetrating whisper, "you see, Damon Boulder is right. The Lord cannot supply perfection in those all-too-mortal men he calls to show us the way. But he loves us, and because he loves us, he gives us, instead, the very best men there are."

Kevin paused and seemed to look every man, woman, and child directly and simultaneously in the eye. "He gives us champions, *world* champions of the spirit, heroes from his very own Righteousness Hall of Fame, to captain the team, to pace us on that straight and narrow course, to set the inspiring, endure-to-the-end example that God's loyal fans all over the world will follow to success, salvation, and celestial glory." He paused again with a fatherly and summarizing smile. "Peter may not have walked upon the water as the Lord did; but among mortals those two or three halting steps still make him the all-time, number-one, water-walking champion of the world. And that, Brother David Zimmer, my dear brothers and sisters, O ye nations of an unregenerate world, that is why we must all gladly, gratefully, humbly follow the brethren."

The ensuing silence was as tight and translucent as Jello, one of those sweet, shimmering moments that are a passionate teacher's only genuine wage. And Kevin Galinghouse Houston let it roll and glide and glitter voluptuously during the few brief seconds that remained before the final bell. When the bell rang, however, it found him alert and ready.

"Brother Boulder," there was honeyed olive branch in his radio voice, "would you please say a closing prayer for us?" The tactic was bold. Like a rabbit surprised in the brush, Damon Boulder seemed to shudder in his seat. Kevin, meanwhile, fixed him with gentle, "would you please" eyes. The day was won. It lacked only the formalities of concession. "Damon," he entreated, "we'd like your benediction."

Boulder made no move, though he stared back in what some have described as stunned disbelief. The many in the class who understood what was going on began to fidget. Yet Kevin only smiled with the long-suffering beneficence of a Buddha and waited.

After an agonizing silence, Boulder finally arose and made his way to the front of the room. When he arrived, he seemed to have found his resolve and, to the relief of everyone, turned decisively and faced the class. With ritual solemnity, he tilted his round face earthward and held it in commanding obeisance until all present fell into a cough-stifling, child-threatening silence. Kevin closed his eyes.

What happened next can be recounted. It cannot be conveyed.

"Give me an R." The words were spoken clearly enough, but even so remained wholly unintelligible to a class poised comfortably over a familiar prayer wheel. "Give me an R." This time Boulder said it louder, and several listeners glanced up as a check against their obviously errant hearing. After the third time, half the class was looking at him from under its still inclined eyebrows. "Give . . . me . . . an . . . R!" he intoned slowly, this time with pedagogical emphasis. Boulder was staring resolutely back at his timid onlookers with one fist raised to the height of his shoulder in punctuating encouragement.

At some point during the fourth incantation a light flickered, though oh so ephemerally, in the communal confusion. It flickered just enough to catch the attention of Marvin Chisolm, and then, for Marvin alone, it flashed again brilliantly. His head came up. His eyes cleared, and he came very near to raising his hand. "R," he stammered with experimental insecurity; and when Boulder cocked his head in recognition, he took courage and repeated himself with conviction, "R!"

Damon Boulder smiled. "Give me an O," he inveighed, raising his other fist, and Marvin Chisolm responded in tempo.

"O!"

"Give me a C!"

"C!" came the answer, and this time a second voice chimed in. It was the pretty young girl in the third row, so wide-eyed and freshly baptized that her name was still known only to the missionaries who hovered around her in dense-pack.

"C!" she sang out in a fresh, green soprano that took even Damon Boulder's breath, while the missionary on her right, the carefully combed and Old-Spiced boy who had baptized her, recoiled helplessly. His much younger companion on the left, however, joined with equally helpless enthusiasm in the response to Brother Boulder's subsequent calls for a "K" and then for a "Y."

"Y!" they all sang out, a chorus of three voices now, or, as some insist, four (though no one will name the fourth accomplice, and none has come forward to confess). But whether three or four, Boulder pushed them relentlessly on into the finale, raising his alternating fists in rhythmic emphasis, if also with the self-conscious awkwardness of a tubby and sedentary older man.

"Give me an "R . . . O . . . C-K-Y!"

The room reverberated with the answer, and Damon Boulder stooped as low as he dared to rise up again with his revelers and with the trombone glide of the triphthong to a dramatic, tiptoe climax.

"YYYEEEEAAAAAA ROCKEEEEEEEEY!"

When it was all over, a matter of seconds, the entire cheering section was on its feet, though at the first poisonous look from his companion, the young missionary dropped back into his seat like a cinder block. Marvin Chisolm, meanwhile, trotted to the front of the room and grabbed Damon Boulder's hand.

"Now, that's spirit, Damon. That is definitely championship spirit!" He squeezed hard and then turned quickly to Kevin, who was off a little to the side in the strange, semi-crouched position he had assumed at the first words of Damon's benediction and had not abandoned. He looked strangely contracted. Marvin reached down a little and pumped his hand as well. "I think you've really taught us something here today, Kevin. Yes sir, and that is not an every-Sunday occurrence." He pumped again and strode out of the room. The young lady, meanwhile, had disentangled herself from her gaggle of anxious missionaries and was pursuing Damon Boulder, who had already escaped down the hall. No one else had moved. No one.

It was quiet again, but the quiet was no help. The strange silence seemed to demand filling; and Kevin, though Marvin Chisolm seemed to have pumped him upright again, could find no words. He struggled, but the hundred formulae churning up from his mental archives filed back as mutely as they had come, and it was a long overdue release when Rachael Holbein broke for the door and scuttled sideways down the hall toward the bishop's office.

The rest of the story, the official aftermath, is, of course, sealed up in the records, and the bishop has expressly forbidden everyone, including Ardmoore, to talk about it. But there was one other thing, not a matter of record, which he confided to Carmen Stavely.

When he had entered the bishop's office just moments after the distraught Rachael Holbein had left it, he had found the bishop swaying precariously on his loudly squeaking, vinyl swivel chair, great round tears streaming down his flushed and helpless face. To the alarmed clerk he seemed out of control, as if he were suffering some terrible seizure, some convulsive and almost wanton attack of hysteria.

"Oh my!" gasped Carmen Stavely involuntarily. And when that same afternoon she recounted the entire affair to her closest and most trusted friend, and then later, of course, to her family over dinner—in fact, at every subsequent retelling—she inaugurated her story with a heartfelt expression of concern for the bishop. "The poor man," she sighed with a grave, sympathetic shake of her head, "the poor, dear man." And then she paused for her listeners to look up expectantly.

Roger Across the Looking Glass

The process is as invariable and explicable as the engineered logic of a machine. Yet for all its biological transparence, to Roger Talmage, educated, institutionally devout, and forty-two, the quite ordinary adjustment of his eyes from day to night vision has become a kind of erotic magic, at once marvelous and necessary. Always he is astonished at how surely and how well, only seconds after Ellen has switched off the lamp, the darkness begins again to yield up her body; and not just her body, but a renewed, ideal body somehow abstracted and transformed from the manifestly forty-one-year-old woman who had reached for the lamp switch. He waits for this. Connives for it. Manufactures and orchestrates it. And his excitement grows and localizes as the veils slip steadily away, not to music—never to music—but to an ever more insistent rhythm, which, beginning in himself, soon patterns the ritual struggle with the woman.

A breeze lifts the window shade and touches his back. He has already begun to sweat lightly, and the sudden chill abruptly summons him to his own body, to the comfortable strength of his supporting arms, the firmness of his chest. Roger Talmage has, in the past year, reclaimed his body from flaccid middle-age. He has made it hard again with brightly colored, vinyl-coated weights and countless early morning hours of running. At this moment a redeemed sense of self-possession makes every deep, thrusting movement, though deliberate wildly beyond mere intention, nonetheless unfrenzied, untroubled, and without the old anxieties of pleasure. Not unlike an Indian fakir who holds pain coolly at bay, Roger Talmage takes command of the pleasure in his body, accepting from his senses precisely and only that which he has first meted out with his will.

Through long years and until recently, sexual encounters with Ellen had been, to Roger, a burden of disappointment borne first painfully, then reluctantly, then hardly at all. As straightforwardly as he desired his wife, his desire often failed him just when it was most to be taken for granted, and he, as a consequence, was most vulnerable. Her frequent tears and his own apologies and conjured explanations left him perplexed and humiliatingly insecure over a physical attraction which had once seemed obvious and elemental.

It is true Ellen did not complain. She did not keep accounts, and, in fact, seemed all too anxious, sometimes tearfully, sometimes in bowed resignation, to accept his apparent disattraction as inevitable. When he could not dissuade her, he began in time to resent his wife's martyrdom as much as he might have resented a whore's derision. He certainly had no desire to administer her shame with his own; and so he began to avoid her body, coming to her only when his urgency and anger made a kind of success inevitable. At home he retreated into a patriarchal reserve posted carefully on one side with the children who seemed happy for the attention and on the other with steadily growing obligations at church and in the community. But as his active sensual life abated, a nagging preoccupation with sex grew. At odd moments of the work day he found himself as beset by breasts and thighs as if he were seventeen years old again; and when he had begun to masturbate, guilt and frustration quickly fed into lean and bitter, though always unspoken, reproach of the woman.

One day, his morning's ritual concern over a swollen waistline suddenly dropped into fathomless disgust at the sluggish intractability of his whole physical life. Standing before the mirror, he held the rolls of soft, opalescent flesh between thumbs and forefingers, where, like his recalcitrant manhood, it lay, not defiantly, but in flat, vegetable indifference to his person, his pride, his will. By the time he began to dress, he could hardly bear to touch himself, and when he had tied his shoes, he arose with genuine anger and not a little melodrama to leave the house and run eight wheezing, sweating blocks in his business suit before returning home to change his clothes and his life. In the following weeks and months he labored with the pious tenacity of an ascetic to bring his body to a controlled, mechanical leanness, and for the first time in almost nineteen years, took charge of his marriage bed.

None of this consciously enters Roger's mind as he coasts at the edge of his own excitement waiting for his wife's orgasm. Her breath begins to shorten. The muscles in her arms and shoulders tighten, and he opens his eyes to watch with a fascination that is only partly sensual. As his wife's excitement intensifies, his own, in fact, subsides until he becomes as much spectator as partner. Her face, obscured by the darkness, is less "Ellen" than woman. Mouth slightly open, eyes tightly shut, she seems outside herself, beyond her rhythmically contracting body, receding out into the blue darkness away from him, away from them.

Increasing his pace with the studied preoccupation of a technician, he directs her glide further, further out until the anticipated shudder erupts, shaking her body with the six-seven-eight seconds (he counts them) of silent, rocking violence that leave her gasping and disheveled on the pillow beneath him.

There is no cry, no word, no sound but breathing. His own need has acutely reasserted itself. He is very hard, and there is violence in his own movements now. Already, though, there is a satisfaction even greater than the pleasure his body is intent upon. If Roger Talmage were a less scrupulous man, he might recognize it as the exhilaration of revenge.

Uncommon winter sunlessness darkened the corridor tiles to the color of waxed cordovan, and Talmage, excused from class for a varsity debate meet, hurried through the halls past rows of grey metal lockers. Voices from a rehearsal in the auditorium registered vaguely and, passing one of the short, lighted entrance ramps, he glanced up. Then he stopped. On the ramp above him sat a girl. Her back toward him, she was leaning forward with an ear pressed to the crack between the yellow birch doors. Straight brown hair fell loosely to the middle of her back over a print dress which, pulled tight against one knee, revealed the long pale thigh of the other, extended leg. He stared involuntarily at the white flesh against the dark tiles.

She must be cutting class to listen to the rehearsal. It was something by O'Neill, something intense and serious which he had already judged pretentious for a high-school cast. He judged himself beyond such adolescent affectation, and it embarrassed him deeply. From the angle at which he watched her, he could not see her eyes, but he was immediately certain that they were tightly shut, her expression rapt and transported. Roger scowled and shook his head, but when suddenly she pulled away from the doors, he panicked, as desperate at being discovered as if he had been peering clandestinely through her bedroom window. But she only looked at him blankly, then leaned slowly forward against the doors again, leaving him almost grateful with relief.

In the ensuing weeks he encountered her everywhere. It seemed almost as if he had fallen into some invisible track running tightly and inevitably along the fact and data of her existence. She was, he learned without having inquired, a year younger than he, strange for all her prettiness, a "type" more than a girl, without discernable affiliations and often without shoes. She did not seem to have or to cultivate friends, though he saw her occasionally with other "types." He was surprised to discover she was Mormon. Certainly, he had never seen her in seminary where he knew virtually everyone. And she wrote poetry. A girl who had sat next to her all year in English and spoken with her exactly once told him. She turned in poems instead of class assignments and read Hemingway or D. H. Lawrence during exercises on pronoun agreement.

Roger was transfixed with distaste, and when the English magazine printed some of her poems, he puzzled through them for a very long time in private, ready to turn the page at the least intrusion. He did not like what he read. The language was perhaps clever and cynical, but the poems seemed overheated, full of naive indignation. Haunted by the fear of being or of being thought immature, Roger had sometime since disassociated himself from his own adolescence, and he found the pretension of neatly rhymed social outrage almost unbearable. In the end he felt as embarrassed as he had at their first encounter in the corridor. He closed the little magazine firmly, as if to cover her shame once and for all and to put her resolutely behind him, but in fact he returned several times to reread the poems.

Almost involuntarily he had begun to look for her in the halls between classes. He said nothing, but he stared and knew that she—equally mute—had begun to acknowledge these encounters. The childishness of the game disturbed him. She was neither so attractive nor so strange as to explain his compulsion. And yet this embarrassed fixation on a girl he neither knew nor consciously wanted to know, in the end, proved stronger and more persistent than his attraction to any of the pretty and thoroughly reasonable girls he dated and kissed and coaxed in his father's Pontiac. Long after graduation, other girls forgotten, he still carried her strange memory like a small knot of scar tissue which one rediscovers from time to time in surprised moments of self-examination.

On Wednesday, 7 April 1959, Ellen Mitford Church and Roger Allen Talmage exchanged wedding vows in the Salt Lake temple. The bride, daughter of Dr. Edward Church and a woman remarkable to those in attendance chiefly by her absence at the temple ceremony, was a graduate of the University of Utah where she had majored in English and helped edit the campus literary quarterly. In an ordinary white gown and an attitude of resolved optimism, Ellen was, even for a bride, more than ordinarily beautiful.

The groom, whose smiling parents presided over the event, not officially, of course, but as a matter of habit, was then completing his junior year in business and American government. A returned missionary and honors student, he served in student government and belonged to the appropriate pre-professional and honors societies. At the insistence of his bride, he also wore white, though seasonally premature (as his mother could not help pointing out) and not nearly so well. He felt self-conscious about his winter pallor against the pale gabardine, and as the long evening wore on, his normal groom's anxieties seemed to grow out of reasonable proportion.

When he had begun to worry that perspiration might be showing through his collar, he reacted with a magisterial brusqueness normally very foreign to his nature. He began to conduct the ceremonial introductions with an almost military impatience, prodding startled guests who up until that point had made only very leisurely progress across the back court and around the key-hole to the spot just out-of-bounds where the reception line waited under a portable canopy of roses and candles. Roger had attended dozens of wedding receptions in this and other almost identical halls, but at some point during the evening the oppressive falseness of a barely camouflaged gymnasium took hold of his usually reticent imagination. It occurred to him that the entire reception was like nothing so much as the obligatory public handshaking of prizefighters before a bout. Standing next to him, literally at the edge of an arena, Ellen seemed as pliantly uncomplicated and lovely as a man could wish. But she was not uncomplicated. She remained somehow an enigma, and had he ever accused her of being obscure or difficult, she herself would have nodded in vague acknowledgment. Roger smiled mechanically and hurried the curious spectators along to his parents down the line, all the while waiting half playfully and half in earnest for the sign that would send his bride and himself each to their respective corners to await the starting bells of the struggle of their lives.

It was, in fact, this very thought or, rather, the accompanying picture of his slender bride trotting grimly away across the court in her soft white gown and twelve-ounce fighting gloves that rescued Roger. He laughed out loud, though carefully, and as his pulse quieted over this ambushed bit of paranoia, he managed to regain some of the familiar calm and social grace people expected of him.

Once again in control, he had only to look at his bride as she was, standing beside him, to dispel overwrought fears of an Ellen who had existed primarily in his adolescent imagination. The impression he had carried away from high school had become a fixation, a kind of graven image, so rigid and ritual that, returning from his mission, it had literally been weeks into the first quarter of school before he had realized with astonishment that the long-limbed girl he regularly watched across the lecture hall was, in fact, his bizarre high-school poetess. She sat across from him in class now with the erect propriety of someone waiting to speak in church. Her hair carefully cut, she wore narrow skirts and nylons and heels that did marvelous things for her legs. And when he asked her out, she obliged with a smile and a voice which, though more brittle than he would have liked, sounded reasonable and unpretentious.

The change had seemed incredible, almost perfect, as if she had undergone some marvelous conversion in anticipation of his return. During their courtship he began to see a hidden, higher purpose in the attraction that had so puzzled and disturbed him in high school.

Only once during their engagement had there been any unpleasantness. It came over a small thing, a poem she showed him in a moment of risked intimacy. She thought—or said she thought—it was funny, a certain way of looking at marriage. She had titled it "Stewardship," a word that seemed to address him directly and made him wary. He read it slowly, rereading the short lines in intense discomfort.

There are tulips marching princesses at night.
In gangs of one (or sometimes more)
Our ladies struggle, chokechained, through the park
And clutch their hemlines grimly
To the one remaining breast
And drag their tender shins
Across the lawn,
While tulips, pressing straight
Toward the dawn,
Harass the balking columns
In a jealous fury, lest
They lose their sweating charges to the dark.
With thrashing leaves and flower roars,
They prod their dour damsels toward the light.

When he had finished, her back was to him, and she was busy with something at the desk. Her silence was transparent anticipation, but he had little to offer. He didn't find the poem funny. In fact, what little of it he could make sense of offended him, though he didn't say so. Instead, he probed awkwardly for the point she was trying to make, but his questions only seemed to dismay her. She tried to explain that to some women getting married was a little like volunteering for the draft. You did so, not because you admired the military or looked forward to the war, but because rightly, or at least inevitably, you loved your country, and because there was a great deal at stake.

The analogy, however, was mostly lost on Roger, and when he continued to frown through her explanations, Ellen broke off hopelessly in mid-sentence.

It was his turn to be hurt, and he struck back. He didn't want to trap her, didn't want her to feel forced into anything. If she didn't really love him, if she thought of him as some sort of roaring pansy who would march her around, then perhaps she'd prefer not to think about him at all. His words were just beginning to fall into cadence with his pride and his incomprehension, but Ellen was already crying, and what was the point? She assured him that she loved him. Apologized again and again for the poem. It was badly made. Didn't say what she really meant. Her regret was sincere, almost despairing. Apart from the poem, she was simply not able to convey to him what she had offered this one, halting, disastrous time and would not offer again.

It was the first and last time she willingly showed him anything she had written. For his own part, Roger had had two painful exposures to Ellen's poetry, and her subsequent reluctance to share it with him was an arrangement which satisfied his sense of propriety quite as naturally as the prohibition which kept him from following her into the ladies' room.

With their marriage, however, from the very first moment, fixed proprieties and intimacies somehow entered into flux. Pre-established safe-lines threatened—though uninvited—to dissolve, and late on the night of his wedding, Roger Talmage, no longer a virgin, and only mildly disappointed at the awkwardness of his first performance, lay awake nursing the sense of foreboding that had distracted him during the reception. Finally, rising up on one elbow, he looked intently down at his wife. There remained something startling and severe in this soft sleeping girl, something he was not prepared to accept yet apparently was unable to exorcise. He ran an experimental finger from the base of her breast over the rising and falling rib cage to the deep female curve of her waist, then carefully laying the palm of his hand flat against the vulnerable flesh of her stomach, retraced the same course, letting his mind slip quickly away from the sudden resolve that had brought him to his elbow—that he should pray over her—into warm, obliterating desire.

When she awoke, they caressed and struggled with an intensity that overwhelmed the awkwardness of their first lovemaking. Roger found himself swept far beyond the still measured space of his fantasies, and in this night and the nights to follow, his young wife's pale thighs against the pale sheets became a vision he would carry into the dreams of old age as the burden of what had been lost.

When children came, she would find herself, settle into the responsibility, the reward. But children came, and he was disappointed, though not in her performance as a mother. She showed the intense affection and pedagogical determination he expected of motherhood's call on a woman. Still, she was not settled, not at peace with herself, and the vague disappointment he felt only distantly mirrored her own. In some deeply withheld, inarticulable way, she felt disloyal to her family. The estrangement put the woman at fierce odds with the wife and mother, a struggle that flashed out regularly in petty explosions, followed always by disproportionate declarations of remorse. Roger, who did not easily lose his temper, was annoyed at this lack of self-control, and when with the passing of time his wife's dramatic swings of emotion seemed to resolve themselves into a kind of ironic aloofness, he was at worst relieved. She had become more remote, and in uncomfortable moments he recognized that the calm she displayed was shallow and cynically self-imposed. Nevertheless, it was calm. She had gotten herself under control.

Working late at the office on an April evening, he received a call from Ellen. With steel in her voice, she announced that she had had a difficult day with the children and was going to her room. He, she regretted, would have to see to their care for the rest of the evening. Then she hung up. Preoccupied with his work and on the edge of anger, he called back immediately, only to get six-year-old Allison on the phone. The child was obviously upset. She said her mother had already gone to her room and wouldn't open the door or answer her knocking. The baby was crying in the background. With no choice, he gave Allison instructions about herself, her little brother, and the baby, and then, after making her repeat them, hung up the phone and began to clear his desk. When he drove into the garage, he had fully formulated his anger, and as soon as the children were put to bed and the kitchen passably cleaned, he went upstairs to confront his wife.

Reaching the bedroom door, however, he opened it much more cautiously than he had intended. Nor was he prepared for what he encountered inside. The room was dark. While his eyes made their adjustment, he found himself wincing with amazement at the sounds that assaulted him. Wild sounds. The desperate, chaotic sounds of a terrible dream. When the room's contours emerged, Ellen was kneeling on the floor in a posture of what appeared to be prayer, though not posed serenely at the side of the bed as he would have expected, had he ever imagined her praying alone like this. Instead, she was rocking awkwardly back and forth on her knees in front of the open window and stammering out into the moonless night in nearly hysterical sobs and rapid conspiratorial whispers whose vehemence and unintelligibility made him physically recoil.

Amazed, his mind stuttered, then began to conjure urgent explanations: the woman raving on his carpet was not his wife at all, but some poor, deranged creature, who having lost her way into his bedroom was hissing out her fear and imagined betrayal into the darkness. He would have to call the authorities.

Roger closed the door of his bedroom with the absolute haste and stealth of someone who has committed a dangerous indiscretion. In the hall again, it occurred to him for the first time that perhaps his wife needed professional help. The thought embarrassed and unnerved him, but he held on to it, faced it, until it was he who was praying, apologizing for this monstrous excess in his wife's behavior, and pleading for her recovery. He was seriously frightened and willing to do whatever was necessary to help Ellen get control of herself again.

Most of the night he sat up in the living room brooding, praying, devising strategies. When he arose late the next morning, Allison was already in school and the younger children, excited by his presence so long after his usual time of departure, vied for his attention. Ellen, matter-of-factly busy and looking as unexceptional as if nothing at all out of the ordinary had taken place, served him his breakfast with an apology. She was sorry to have been so abrupt on the phone, sorry to have burdened him with the children when she knew how busy he was at the office; but the day had been terribly frustrating, and she had gone to bed with a headache. Could he forgive her just this once?

When she had finished she smiled dutifully and, anticipating—or perhaps not requiring—his forgiveness, went on with her work.

"I don't think," he murmured wrestling absently with the two-year-old on his lap and trying hard to concentrate past the eggs on his plate, "I don't think you can get there from here." It was nearly a week before he slept the entire night through again without waking at least once to reassure himself that his wife was lying quietly and sanely at his side.

When her mother was dying of cancer, Roger drove Ellen to the country-club development on the Monterey Peninsula where her parents had retired. Her father was not well and not able, nor for that matter anxious, to take care of a wife from whom he had been comfortably estranged most of their married lives. Roger stayed four days before returning to Salt Lake. He found each succeeding day alarmingly more painful. Not that he would mourn his mother-in-law. They had established no bond between them. Nor had she been close to Ellen. She seldom telephoned, never wrote, and even her interest in the children seemed to him more ceremonial than real. She was, by her nature and, as far as he could tell, independent of specific cause, an undeterrably angry woman, who stood resolutely aloof from the things and people he most valued. In their Mormon community, before she left it, she had cultivated an aura of rebellion and acerbic iconoclasm which, quite obviously, she enjoyed at the expense of her family.

For her part, Ellen was, as in almost all things, dutiful but ambivalent toward her mother. As a girl she had suffered from her parents' habitual fighting—the permanent climate of civilized warfare which made room only for combatants and camp followers. And because her mother was the more aggressive, the more articulate adversary, she had sided emotionally with her father, who rewarded her ever after by spoiling and exploiting her expansively.

Now, as Ellen's mother sat emaciated and distracted by pain in the garden that was her only remaining fondness, she seemed to Roger as proud and unreconcilable as ever she had been in her life, yet Ellen cared for her with an unselfconscious patience and concern that startled him. He was dumbfounded, not just by the expression of his wife's obvious love, but by the bare fact of it at all. In all their married lives he had never experienced anything like the unrestrained affection she inexplicably seemed to be squandering on an irascible old woman, whom he knew she had struggled not to hate, and who even now made no attempt to acknowledge her daughter's attentions.

On his last day in California, weary of his father-in-law's relentlessly political Mormonism, he stood alone at the kitchen window watching Ellen read to her mother who sat rigid, white fists clenched and trembling, in her metal lounge chair on the lawn. When suddenly she slept, Ellen covered the still tense arms and shoulders with a sweater and, folding her own arms defensively against the cool ocean breeze, wept silently over her mother's head to the golf course beyond and far out over the Pacific.

Solitary and unnoticed, Roger felt a voyeur's sense of guilty alienation. All at once he needed very much to be at home on his own high ground with his own people. But the long trip back through the desolate Nevada mountains only increased his jealousy and estrangement. Ellen was, he knew, a good wife to him. Moreover, she strove with all the ferocity lost in that old-fashioned word to be what he wanted. Still, her behavior toward him, now and as long as he could remember, had always been tempered by the almost palpable will that imposed it. It was as if she had taken him on like some sort of commendable regimen, a diet or an exercise program, not for his own sake or for love of him, but because it had been the right and proper thing to do.

He wanted to go away to somewhere clean and simple, somewhere absolutely barren of voices and complication, where he might pray his life with all its attachments clear and straight and tractable again. But he knew in reserve and in the end that the dark feelings which oppressed him were just that . . . feeling, emotion, self-indulgence. For what was he to pray? A chastened wife? Was he to protest this newfound love for her mother, to condemn his wife's sudden and unexplained capacity for forgiveness? Answers were easy and inevitable, of course, but like all answers that are merely right, they brought no peace. He was deeply offended, yet with no object for his anger but an absence. He possessed in Ellen a gift that had paled and disappeared in the possessing. She remained in many ways his obsession. He desired her as much as ever he had, but he did so—and this both shamed and puzzled him most of all—almost entirely in her absence. His intense affair with his wife proceeded nearly unabated, but only in his imagination, and always apart from her, as if he alone were living out their intimate lives together.

Even the older children were long since asleep, but agitation at the prospect of his wife's return kept Roger awake and led him finally to cross a border he had carefully avoided all his married life. He had never really entered Ellen's study—hardly paying attention to the tiny room at the end of the hall except to note occasionally, when the door was open, that she kept it strewn with books and papers in a disarray apparently and singularly immune to her compulsion for order elsewhere in the house. He accepted the room, as he did her writing in general, as useful not for its own sake—

involuntarily, he disliked any corner of disorder—but as a kind of therapy.

As he entered now, he did so with a sense of trespass that kept him standing nervously in the center of the room for a minute or more surveying the tangle on the writing table and reading miscellaneous book titles. When this initial disquietude had passed, however, he seated himself and reached purposefully for the notebooks which, unlike almost all other objects in view, lay neatly stacked and at right angles to the edge of the table. He smiled at the spiral-bound, wide-ruled paper as he turned the pages of the first notebook. He hadn't handled one of these since leaving high school, and it confirmed to him a latent suspicion that Ellen's retreat here was a kind of withdrawal into adolescence.

The pages of the notebook were crowded with illegible scribbling blurred over and over again by erasures. Occasionally he came across a page on which a single poem had been painstakingly written out, only to be spoiled again by marginal notes and new erasures, then carefully recopied on a second or perhaps a third page. He read some of these, but even after careful rereading, knew he must be missing the point. He found precious little to help him understand his wife, though in the swaggering, nose-thumbing rhythms into which the poems often fell and in their consistently acid tone and choice of words, he believed he clearly heard the sharp-tongued disaffection of his mother-in-law. It was the same dissenting sarcasm that had offended him in the published high-school poems so many years before and which apparently persisted unchanged and unmatured in the woman who kept his house and his nearly grown children just beyond the study door.

He started several other poems but, unable to get through more than the first few lines of any of them, began to be annoyed with himself and with the entire enterprise. It was not only somehow deceitful, it was futile as well. Flipping rapidly through the pages, he wanted to make a quick end of this and be gone. Then he was brought up short. "To Roger Across the Looking Glass," the title addressed him point blank from the page, leaving him no choice at all but to stop and examine the poem that followed. Checking backward and forward in the notebook, he found fully seven attempts at a clean version of the text, and when he had counted them all, he turned to the final still unamended, unerased version and without raising the notebook from the table, began to read.

If all our time, that never is,
(when all of space, ranged in those three
impaling ranks of "Let There Be,"
bears down through you to bury me)
had boiled to metamorphic fizz

that overspills the looking glass
and bubbles down its frosted sides
to make of tidy seconds, tides
and of the virgin minutes, brides
who loose their limbs in laughing gas;

or if our plaster point of view
had crumbled through the program lace
to filter softly into grace;
or had the gerund taken place
just one, sweet, saving once. Then you

and I and maybe even God,
instead of casting poisoned bread
and sleeping with the empty dead
in sovereign corners of the bed,
might well have kissed what we have clawed
or managed, somehow, through the blow
to touch the wound.

But no. The drain
extending down our pillowed plane
dispels the circle, drives us sane.
There is no orphic afterglow.

And so
I'll rest for now to write some more,
though writing more is counting sheep:
Perhaps there's watching when I weep?
Perhaps the dark my soul will keep?
Perhaps . . .

The poem, even in its seventh version, was still unfinished, but Roger didn't notice. When he had read it several times, he closed the notebook, yet remained motionless in his seat. Inside, he was as contracted and bewildered as if he had been struck viciously from behind. There was and would be no attempt at comprehension, but from that moment all of the vague temptations to prayer that had distracted him over the preceding weeks vanished behind a single, sullen preoccupation. Somehow he must see to it that these notebooks never fell into the hands of the children.

The narrow confluence of pain and of pleasure begins now to skate over Roger's senses like a blade, and he closes his eyes to concentrate on the deepening lines of intersection. Iridescence in his nerves grows, and as it does, the body locked under his driving embrace begins to change, to metamorphose. No longer Ellen, but instead his smiling receptionist, then the dark wife of a client, then yet another woman and another and another in an accelerating whirl drawing him surely, swiftly, steeply down into the singular, piercing, world-devouring whine of his genitals.

Afterward he washes carefully in the bathroom. There is no hurry. This still novel sense of control is by itself a wonder to be savored and admired. He does not want to surrender it too soon to sleep.

When he has brushed his teeth and buttoned his pajamas, it is well after midnight. In the bedroom Ellen is lying in almost precisely the same position in which he left her. Her eyes are closed, but he does not think she is asleep. It surprises him that she has made no effort to dress or to clean up, for Ellen is normally fastidious. The lapse, in fact, annoys him, and as he climbs into bed, the way she lies there across from him, garmentless and unwashed, strikes him as somehow defiant. The surge of anxiety is all too familiar, and after a time he reaches out for reassurance. Taking his wife's hand he whispers, "Goodnight, Ellen." And then, after weighing it for a moment, adds, "I love you." Her answer is barely audible, but comes immediately and with a certainty that confirms her wakefulness. "Thank you, Roger," she says, and the finality in her voice denies him any response. He can hardly say, "You're welcome."

For a while, needing to keep the upper hand, he listens to her breathing, waiting for her to give in to sleep. But in the end his own weariness seduces his resolve, and, rolling onto his side, Roger Talmage quickly loses track of his wife in the early morning darkness.

Living Oracle

> release: v.t. (1) to liberate, to set free from bondage or obligation. (2) to give up, surrender or relinquish, to let go or drop. (3) [law] to lease again.
>
> —American College Dictionary (New York, 1954)

Afterward, after the interview and handshakes and parting address, after taking delivery of a new Pentax camera with real leather case, extra lenses, and four special filters, after making one last visit for Kuchen and gratitude and stopping one last melancholy time at the Bahnhof for yogurt, he finally boarded a plane with the friend, whom he had not seen in two and a half years, and who had come halfway across Europe to join him. They flew to Berlin, and on the way he punched his old buddy gently in the ribs and quoted directly from the Instant Preparation Book in his bag. "Tomorrow," he said, winking puckishly, "is the first day of the rest of our lives!" His friend punched him back, and they laughed together silently.

They were, of course, both still bound by rules and oaths of solemn self-denial, but the stopover was costing them only $17.00 each, and if you didn't go to Paris or Rome or London on the way home from your mission, you ought, at least, to see Berlin.

A city like Berlin was alive with temptation, and they were determined, though their determination remained unspoken between them, to succumb a little, if just a very little, because, though still bound, they were also practically free, and freedom, after all, had to be observed, had to count for something. Freedom needed celebrating.

So they wandered the Kurfuerstendamm all afternoon, reading marquees, and staring at glossy photographs of nearly naked women, always too inhibited by one another's presence to declare themselves openly for any flesh-and-blood den of liberation, at least, that is, until they found a marquee announcing "Robin." Now, according to the marquee, Robin was British and a singer, and, according to her photo, she was a girl fully clothed, but so pretty, so prom-queen lovely, so exquisitely like Dorothy Collins on *Hit Parade* or like Donna Reed on *Donna Reed* that each boy stood there aching and yielding and making love to her, silently, of course, and privately, and very very chastely on a public sidewalk, not at all needing to touch or think or look past her incredible smile. A hundred bosoms, a hundred peek-a-boo behinds, a hundred measured yards of pure, white European thigh collected from half a hundred leering marquees resolved themselves there, dissolved into that one sweet, wholesome, ever so softly made-up, bright-eyed, high-cheekboned, prim, and oh so promissory smile. They looked at one another with no need to speak. Beyond any shadow of doubt, this was the place.

But when they returned, naive and impatient as they were, they arrived at 8:00 o'clock to find the nightclub still empty and unswept and not even darkened. A hard-eyed barmaid looked them over and informed them in condescendingly bad English that the first show would not begin until 10:30. They looked at each other, embarrassed, but they had waited two and a half years. They could wait another two and a half hours. And they did. Sitting in a corner, watching the empty tables and dance floor and the barmaids who, assiduous in their professionalism, carefully avoided watching them. He ordered Sinalco, an orange drink nearly void of sugar and as orange as chicken soup. His friend ordered mineral water, which was worse, and they paid the unbelievable tariff and didn't even flinch, and when there was absolutely nothing else to do, they ordered again.

They could not talk over the band and its amplifiers, so they listened helplessly while it played American songs with the singular original contribution of heretofore unimagined volume. 10:30 came, and it went. And then 11:00. The tables filled slowly, and the dance floor came alive, but at 11:20 P.M., he was exhausted. He couldn't face another Sinalco, and so turned to his friend to admit defeat. "Let's get out of here," he said. But at that very moment, at the precise outer limit of hope and endurance, the house lights went up, the awful music fell into sudden, blessed silence, and the house manager stepped to the microphone to announce in both German and broken English that the club's featured guest artists "Robin and She" were about to appear.

Robin. Now, there was a lovely name. Simple and lyrical. It sent a wave of fresh, sweet promise through the heavy cigarette smoke. Some things were worth waiting and enduring for. Some especially worthwhile things saved you only in the very last possible nick of time. He ordered a Coca-Cola.

But, as it turned out, Robin was not the young lady on the marquee. She was, in fact and to their unutterable astonishment, a *he*. A man. A balding, sun-freckled, middle-aged male, wearing a faded pastel tuxedo and wheeling a metal cart with an overhead projector on it. He waltzed the cart, literally, to the end of a long yellow cord and then trotted up to the microphone.

"Ladies and gentlemen," he said, "I'm Robin Rollins, and my beautiful partner and I are absolutely ecstatic to be here with you in the great city of Berlin this evening. The lovely 'She' will be out to sing for you in just a little bit. And let me warn you gents in the first few rows here. Beeeeee careful! She's the seventh wonder of the erotic world, the actual siren of myth and legend, the Lorelei direct from that famous Rock on the Rhine. Listen to her, and you're lost. Look at her, and you're a lecher. Touch her," he stopped, winked sleazily and raised his thumb in a blatant gesture, "and you turn to stone." Then he laughed, and the two discoverers in the corner looked at one another in amazement. They had been so taken in, so gulped up and swallowed by that photograph, that they hadn't even paid attention to the billing. The girl on the marquee was not the winsome 'Robin' whom they'd imagined and waited for, but, in fact, some generic, man-mesmerizing 'She.'

It was blunt, and earthy, and once again, of course, embarrassing, but there it was, or almost, and not, after all, entirely off the mark. They had found what, without owning up, they had set out to find in the first place. And so, a little more worldly wise and steamier of blood, they settled back onto their chairs to wait again.

Meanwhile, *Sir* Robin prepared the appearance of the crowning seventh wonder of eroticism with a graphic review of the preceding six. His talent was the knack of turning any line or squiggle or scratch drawn by any member of the audience onto the glass screen of his projector into a sniggering obscenity. The careful right angle drawn by a young man with glasses became the astonishing fulcrum of an outrageous and unnameable act. The shy ellipse traced by a very hesitant and embarrassed woman came to rest on the crown of a phallic enormity. The "boobs" named and drawn with pre-school skill by a grinning American soldier zealous to cooperate disappeared into a sensuous intertwining of toes. After three such wonders, they were staring at their empty glasses, but couldn't escape the commentary, nor the equally shameless laughter.

It took forever, but forever finally came and passed. The cartoonist switched off his infernal machine and, still laughing, stepped to the microphone. "Ladies and Gentlemen," he announced, "I give you She."

The lights faded. Curtains opened. A vague, female figure stepped quietly out into the shadows. An orchestra struck up. Strings soared and then were quickly swallowed in grinding rhythms from a piano and saxophones.

"That old black magic has me in its spell, that old black magic . . . " The voice was sweet and dark and genuinely magical. A spotlight blinked on, and the figure launched into action. There in the light, moving quickly, incredibly across the dance floor toward them came a woman . . . a woman fully twenty years and thirty pounds departed from the vision on the marquee. Her enormous hairdo was as stiff and bleached as salt grass in August, and she looked absolutely pile-driven into a dress that took your breath away in sympathy. That garment crushed her, forcing her relentlessly inward only to release the laboring flesh as pointedly elsewhere in extravagant paroxysms of femininity. The panoramic hips swept cosmically between the tightly ensnared waist and knees. Her bosom rose dizzily above, but contracted just as sharply beneath a neckline plunged far, far, far below her powdered neck and chins. She was a vision, a specter, a phantasm, and a living, crooning, cavorting erotic cartoon.

She carried a microphone and moved quickly along the first row of tables. "Those icy fingers up and down my spine . . . " She shivered in rhythm to the music and ran the fingers of her free hand through the stubble on the GI's head. He whooped and grabbed for her, but she had already slithered out of his reach and moved on to an older, more solid-looking citizen. Holding the gentleman's ears, she leaned over elaborately to kiss him on the forehead while he stared transfixed into the luxuriant hanging gardens of Babylon. In the next second she bounded away again, moving on, singing, working the crowd, kissing bald spots and foreheads, tousling hair, rubbing backs, bumping and dancing and grinding and dodging.

And then . . . then suddenly, she was directly in front of him, immense and voluptuous and incredible. "And down and down I go." She sank gradually, rhythmically onto his helpless lap, her fingers circling playfully around his head. He loved it. He hated it. His churning blood, the icy tingle in his spine, the electric charge in his trousers. His breathing stopped. He prayed his legs wouldn't collapse. He couldn't stand it. He couldn't wait. And . . . and then she was gone again. Gone before she was there. He'd hardly felt that woman at all. Hardly touched her. His mouth dropped open in amazement. It was . . . a hoax. All a hoax. She'd sung to him, sat on him, played with his hair, but it was all illusion, an imposture without weight or heat or even contact. She moved off, retreating through the tables. And as he watched her go, he recognized the voice in the sound system. It belonged to Doris Day.

When he reached the sidewalk outside, his friend was already there, already standing, looking at the photo on the marquee. You could see the resemblance, but that picture was from another world, another kingdom altogether, another mega-degree of glory. It might have been taken at a high-school sweetheart's ball or even a church dance, that is, if anyone had had the courage to ask out a girl so forbiddingly, so absolutely, unapproachably lovely.

On the way to the hotel, they walked in meditative silence, and when he broke it, he spoke out of preoccupation.

"Ever wonder," he asked too softly, "if things . . . I mean stuff that happens to you . . . ever wonder if maybe it means something?" His companion turned and stared at him uncomprehendingly, but he couldn't explain or phrase his question any better, any more precisely. He foraged through his mind and memory and mentally through the Instant Preparation. But nothing came. Nothing. He couldn't even think of a way to change the subject.

Space Abductors II

"Well, are the children watching their movie?" She looked up from her book.

He stood in the doorway and stared at the plastic basket between the dresser and the wall spilling over with unsorted laundry. "I suppose so. I don't know why they watch that stuff." He'd come upstairs to check for plumbing leaks in the open access hole behind the dresser. He should have checked long ago. But he hadn't. And now the laundry rose in his path like Everest. He sat on the bed instead.

"Tired?"

"Exhausted. Why do you ask?" There was suspicion in his voice. He saw himself on the way to the Revco or the Dairy Mart.

"Nothing, I just haven't seen you in a long time."

"Every morning."

"For fifteen minutes."

"And every night."

"Five minutes, unless you're tired and fall asleep early."

"I'm sorry." He didn't sound very sorry.

"Oh, it's all right, dear. I talk to you at night anyway."

"You do?"

"Yes. I ask you to stop snoring. And you're always very sweet and very apologetic. You always stop."

He grimaced, but didn't answer. He hated the thought that he snored. Snoring was geriatric. "We have Monday night," he said, changing the subject.

"That's right. Monday night with the children. You preside. And I conduct. You put the children to bed. And I clean the kitchen. The principal difference is you fall asleep in your clothes reading to Jennifer, and then she comes and wakes me to tell me you're snoring on her bed."

He was irritated. "Is there some particular point you're trying to make, Dianne?"

She didn't react to his irritation, and she didn't answer right away. She looked him coolly in the eye. "Do you have a headache, Marvin?" It wasn't until that moment that he noticed her shoulders were bare. "Jennifer's asleep and the others have their movie." She announced this after a few seconds of significant eye contact. She said it as if it were news.

"Oh," he replied uncertainly, making a fresh start. Then more clearly and in a tone of suggestion he said, "Oh! I think I'll get a quick shower."

"Good idea." She settled back into her reading, and the settling unsettled the liquid surfaces lying unrestrained just below the pearl-white silk. He watched dumbly with his mouth open.

In the bathroom he wondered why, after all the years and all the times, the same subterranean movement held him in the same subterranean thrall, and he wondered as well if it really was the same. He took a long shower, much longer than he'd intended, and thought purposely about the girl he'd seen in the video store, and turned down the hot water, and stood in the cool wet spray, flexing and breathing deeply and shaking his wet hair under the shower head. Some men were active into their eighties. Charlie Chaplin in his sixties had exhausted lovers forty years younger, waking them every two hours through the night like a brimming wet nurse. He'd read that in the Sunday Magazine. It was all in your mind. All a matter of attitude and self-confidence. He stood in front of the mirror. His body, though strategically padded like a sailboat or a trampoline, was nonetheless a testimonial to racquetball. You saw leanness through the bumpers and the blanket rolls.

He wrapped the towel around his waist. It still met and overlapped, though not as generously as it once had. He tucked it securely in, and shaved. He fluffed his thinning hair, and brushed his teeth, and flossed, and gargled twice, and trimmed the mustache, and clipped his fingernails, and then his toes. When he'd finished, he carefully recapped the solidstick and the aftershave and the toothpaste, and put them away together with the clippers and the scissors and the razor and the toothbrush and the floss. It was all in your mind. So he re-tucked his towel, and remembered Chaplin in his sixties and Robert Redford in *The Way We Were*, and he turned off the light and stepped out into the bedroom again.

She was still awake. Her book was in her lap and her eyes were glazed and rolling, but as he came into the room, she caught herself and shook her head and pushed up on the pillow a little.

"You didn't drown after all?"

"No."

"I'm glad," she said. "You never know about quick showers. There could be sharks." Sitting up and stretching, she turned down the blanket next to her. "Or mermaids." She smiled and bit her lip and switched out the lamp while he approached from the bathroom. It was all in the mind, thought Marvin, and in the blood, and in healthy, heat-sensitive skin. Like a Chaplin or a Redford, he dropped the towel at the foot of the bed and climbed slowly, gracefully across the open covers.

"Mom! Maaw-om!"

It was a split-second alert, leaving only the narrowest, action-packed, temporal margin before the door swung wide, and the hall light fell across the bed.

"Maawm, Robbie's being a jerk. He sticks his knees up right in the middle of everything so no one can see and if you ask him he just ignores you and he doesn't care about anybody and he's making an incredible mess and why do we have to see stupid *Space Abductors* anyway. We've seen it five times already and we hate it!" Standing fiercely in the middle of the room with her arms folded and her eyes puckered, Kimberly Anne Chisolm expelled her entire complaint in a single breath and at a high B flat that wavered siren-like on the edge of tears.

Dianne pulled the blanket to her neck and spoke with perjured calmness. "If you don't like the movie, you and Emmie can go up to bed, dear. It was Robbie's turn to choose."

"But he's being a jerk. He won't put his knees down."

"You tell Robbie that I said for him to put his knees down so everyone can see."

"He won't listen to me!" The girl's rising glissando underscored the stupidity of the suggestion. "He's a jerk."

"Your brother is not a 'jerk,' dear," the studied maternal voice flowed out upon the panicked semidarkness like frozen yogurt, "but if you can't get along, your father will come down and turn the TV off, and you'll all go to bed."

"Mom, he won't listen to me." Kimberly turned with a gesture of futility and started for the door, but stopped suddenly and turned back with puzzlement perched on her face. "Where is daddy?"

"He's . . . in the bathroom." The eleven-year-old girl looked up into the darkness through the open bathroom door and then back at her mother, who, for her part, clung resolutely to her silence and to the blanket at her throat until her mystified daughter had left.

By the time Marvin had climbed up from the floor on the far side of the bed, probed diagnostically at the spot where his forehead had struck the nightstand, and covered his nakedness with dark blue cotton percale, his wife was already in her bathrobe.

"She's right. He won't listen to her. They just boss him, and it makes him more stubborn."

When she returned, Marvin was still awake. He had lain there through the interim stretching and flexing and pinching himself, thinking "R," and fighting somnolent nature on behalf of the natural man. He was weakening, but he was not defeated.

"You really are tired, aren't you?"

"I'm just fine."

"We don't have to do this."

"Of course we do. Sometime. Or forget how. Buried talents are repossessed, remember?"

"You have to put them to the usurer's."

"Exactly."

"Am I your usurer?"

"The whole firm."

She giggled. "Well, then, maybe I can help out."

She kissed him on the nose, and then deeper while reaching under the percale to hook her hand under his raised knee and then on to the inside of the thigh. With a careful thumb and forefinger she took hold of the short hairs there and braced and pulled. Pain shot from his knee to his bald spot, and he roared up off the pillow.

"Awake?"

He was awake, and he grabbed the offending arm, forcing it behind her, and her, laughing, down onto the bed where he began to undo the buttons down her front with the fingers of his free hand. Like a bicycle, he thought, you never forget, but the compliment was extravagant, and she was already looking at him with forbearing patience in her eyes. He'd been twenty-nine years old and five years married before he realized why women's buttons were sewn on backwards.

"Maawm!" Robbie, like a gentleman, issued his first warning from the far end of the upstairs hall. "Mom! The girls are eating cereal in the family room!" By the time he entered, both of his parents were up to their chins in coordinated linen.

"Rob!" Marvin sat nearly straight up in bed and would have gone to his feet, but the cool air on his back made him lie quickly back down again. It was not possible, however, to rage properly and patriarchally when you were naked and prostrate before a glowering eight-year-old boy. He felt ludicrous, but he boomed at Robbie all the same. "If you can't get along down there, I'll come down and turn the damn thing off, and everybody'll go to bed. Do you understand?"

"But you're not supposed to eat in the family room."

"That's true." Dianne's preoccupation with domestic infraction was unfailing.

"You tell those girls to get that stuff out of the family room, and if I find one flake, one drop of milk, one dried-up crusted-over spoon or bowl in the morning, the TV goes off for a month. Do you hear me? And you keep your knees out of the way and stop fighting with your sisters, or I'll turn the damn thing off for two months." Marvin raised his head as high and dropped his voice as low as he could. "Now, go downstairs. Watch your movie. And leave us alone. Your mother and I are tired. We work hard. We need our sleep. And if you can't watch a movie together without barging in here every five minutes and waking us up to tattle on each other, then it's time we got rid of movies altogether and put you to bed at 7:30." He'd been looking for a sign that his anger had found a solid target, but in vain until Robbie's eyes widened at the prospect of a 7:30 bedtime.

"On Friday?"

Marvin drove the silver spike home. "Every single night of the week. Do you understand?"

"Yeeeees." The boy whined his capitulation and headed for the door.

"And don't bother your sisters!"

Robbie kept going.

"And don't you bother us again!"

"Don't worry," he was at the end of the hall, "I won't . . . until the blouse part."

"The . . . " Marvin shot up in bed, "Rob! . . . ROB!"

It was too late. The boy was gone.

"What is it, dear?" Dianne was looking at him incredulously. "What did he say?"

"Oh, it's that stupid movie. He was telling me about it in the car. He says there's a part at the end where this monster lizard tears the clothes off some woman and then there's a love scene . . . "

"With a lizard?" Horror rose in his wife's eyes.

"No, no. With some guy. Look," he assumed a defensively pedagogical tone, "I don't know about this. I thought you'd seen this movie. You let them watch it before."

"I certainly never let them watch anyone making love to a lizard."

"Well, it doesn't matter anyway, because I told him they couldn't watch that part, and he'd have to pause the machine and come and get me to check it out."

"So," she was thinking it over and smiling, "he stops a love scene down there and then rushes up here to stop another one."

"We should have a lock on that door."

"Maybe what we need is a pause button." She was grinning now. Near giggling. "Do you have any idea when he's scheduled to, ah . . . interrupt us?"

"You'd think they'd put locks on bedroom doors, wouldn't you? I mean, isn't it pretty stupid in a four-bedroom house not to put a lock on the master bedroom door?"

"Every time someone coughs or the house creaks, you say we ought to put a lock on the door, and every time I remind you, you say, 'I'll get to it.' "

"Well, can't you hire someone?"

" 'Thirty-eight-fifty an hour to install a door lock? Any idiot can install a door lock!' "

He knew she was quoting him. He changed the subject. "Rob says it's at the very end of the movie." He looked at the glowing digital display on the night table. Dianne's eyes followed. "It can't be half over yet."

"No," she said, biting her lip again and leaning back against the pillow, "it can't."

When he pulled away the sheet, nearly half the buttons were already undone. But the work, he suspected, would be double now. So they lay in the semidarkness under the tickless, blinking eye of the digital clock, and they loved with the familiar ingenuity of experience, talking and not talking, methodically reviewing the holds, familiar and forgotten, that had ever formed or compressed or ignited the narrow space between them. The room drew in close around and the world contracted like a gathering summer storm that circles and darkens and trembles with bursting humidity, but will and will not rain. And every second brought the monster lizard—and menacing child—closer.

"Crap!" Marvin heaved himself over on his back, "any minute now he's going to come dancing through that door."

Dianne looked at the clock. "I don't think so, dear. Not yet." She spoke in a still, small voice.

"Well, I can't perform under deadline pressure." He was lying rigidly staring up at the ceiling, and his wife moved over beside him and ran her finger across his forehead and down along his nose. There was something maternal in the gesture.

"You're not at work. You don't have to perform. We don't have to do this at all." She kissed him. "Anyway, it's your intentions I care about. It comforts me to know you still harbor indecent intentions."

He kissed her back in the comfortable corner where chin and neck merge and then whispered in her ear. "Yes, but faith without works is dead." He sat straight up on the bed. "And I'm not dead. Not yet. Look, what we need is a room with a lock, and the only room in the house that isn't a bathroom, and . . . " he looked at her quizzically, "I'm not really up for bathtub gymnastics, are you?"

She shook a bemused head.

"Well, the only other room with a lock is the garage."

"The garage?"

"Yeh," he confirmed in deadly earnest, "the garage! Except," he caught himself, "I don't exactly mean the garage. The Volvo." His face lit up with the brilliance of his idea. "We paid a fortune for that upholstered boxcar. It's got everything on it but an electric bidet, and if you put down the back seat, you can put a whole Cub Scout troop in there, or a block party, or a wrestling meet, or . . . "

"In the Volvo, Marvin?"

"Di, it's even soundproof!"

"You're serious?"

"Absolutely. We'll elope." He was at the closet rummaging around in the darkness. When he found his jeans, he began to put them on without underwear. "Look, I get dressed and go downstairs and get the car ready," he explained, hopping from side to side, trying to keep his balance with one foot in his pants and the other still groping for entrance, "and you get sort of dressed—don't overdo it—and go down and tell the kids that I have a headache from all the fighting and waking us up, and you're going out with me to the drugstore to pick something up, so they should finish the movie . . . "

"What about the sex-crazed lizard?"

"Finish the movie up to the lizard, and then just go to bed if we're not back, but we'll be back soon, so not to worry, and then you just come out to the garage where I await you, and . . . " he paused and spoke slowly for effect, "you-lock-the-door-behind-you. Haha!" He had his pants up and cautiously zipped and was pulling on a T-shirt he used for racquetball. When he got his head through, his wife was sitting serenely on the edge of the bed, smiling up at him.

"I admire your determination," she said.

In the garage the overhead light was burned out, and he didn't want to use the one on the garage door opener because you had to open the garage door to use it, and he didn't want to open the garage door—and then close it again—for nosey night people in the neighborhood to wonder what he was up to in the garage in the middle of the night opening and closing the door. So he groped his way to the Volvo and turned on the dome light. It was a poor work light, but it would be candlelight-romantic when the work was done. There wasn't room in the closed garage to put up the hatch at the back of the car, either, so he had to crawl in over the back seat and around the frame of the jump seat. Then things became difficult, because the jump seat needed to go into the very space in which he crouched in order to work on it, so that as he brought it over and down upon himself, he had simultaneously to wedge himself upward and around it, a mechanical inversion unforeseen by any engineer or by Newtonian physics and requiring almost transubstantial exertions. When he'd finished, he was sweating heavily. Putting down the back seat was easy, however, and when it was down, he turned and surveyed the vast open plain around him. It was hard as a rock.

He hoped against hope that the football blankets and pillows were still on the storage shelves under the camping gear. He could unroll the sleeping bags if he had to. He would do whatever he had to, and he set his jaw, but as he turned to look, the door opened, and his wife appeared on the threshold with the hall light behind her.

"I went to tell them," she said, "but they were all sound asleep in front of the television. I sent them up to bed." Backlighted in her translucent robe on the stair, she was an intimate phantom. "You've gone to so much trouble. We could stay here. It would be different." She waited for an answer. "The car light is kind of romantic." Still no response. "But it would be easier upstairs, wouldn't it?"

Marvin felt like a man pink-slipped on the eve of retirement, but he was too spent to protest. He needed a shower.

When he'd toweled off and left the bathroom for the second time, it was nearly 2:00 A.M.

They were both awake.

"When we were first married, sometimes we stayed up all night."

"Oh yes. We were showing off then. Pulverizing the national average."

"Do you think we've regressed to the mean?"

He thought a moment. "We've probably lowered the mean." "That's unpatriotic."

"It's treasonous."

"Can we do anything to make restitution?"

"We can try."

"No," she said, "don't try." And she knelt over him in the soft, transforming darkness and managed her own buttons in a ritual which after all the years and all the times, and the children, and the anniversaries, the payments, the policy renewals, the plumbing leaks and overdrafts and Monday nights and stretch marks and thinned hair and cellulite and geriatric snoring, which even after the long evening's debacle and the vision in the video store, drew him surely back out over the edge of adolescent fantasy rising magically and geyserlike toward a single, sweet soprano note ringing somewhere far back in his brain.

"Mom-meeee."

The geyser subsided with a sigh.

"Yes, dear?"

"Are you still awake, too? I can't sleep?"

"You need your sleep, dear."

"But I can't. I'm finishing my skirt. I'm doing the hem. I'll sleep in the morning. It's Saturday."

"What do you want?"

"I don't know what to do now." Kimberly Anne appeared at the door. "I'm almost finished."

Dianne, whose preoccupation with domestic infraction was superseded solely by enthusiasm for domestic enterprise, defected.

"Well, bring it in here. What do you need to know?"

"Can't this wait until morning?" Marvin glared at the ceiling.

"It'll only take a minute." She turned on the bed lamp, and her eleven-year-old daughter laid the skirt out across the foot of the bed.

"I have the tape in, and I've measured, but I don't think I have enough pins."

"Did you iron it first?" asked the naked woman hiding at Marvin's side with her neck craning up and over the leading edge of the covers. The ensuing technical conversation settled hypnotically down over her husband like deep, soft snow. His eyes ceased seeing. His muscles dissolved sweetly, one after another, into liquid twilight. His restless will swam round and round in slow, languid circles.

"Don't you want to take this into your own room now?" urged Dianne. She sensed the deterioration at her side.

"No, Mom, if I move it, I'll mess up. I don't have enough pins." The pretty eleven-year-old sat and made whip stitches according to instruction and looked down at her unconscious father. "Does daddy always sleep with his mouth open?"

"Yes, dear." Dianne craned to see and supervise from too far away in bad light. "In a little while he'll start to snore."

"Mom!" the little girl bleated reproachfully and looked up in shock, "that's gross!"

Dianne smiled a little guiltily and directed her daughter back to the hem. "I suppose," she said, "but you get used to it."

Mormon Tabernacle Blues

When Rachael Holbein married, she swore a vow of eternal happiness, and she was four fat children and thirteen smile clenched years into bliss before she broke it, conceding to herself, though to no one else, one dark evening, that heaven had defaulted its end of the bargain, giving her a husband in the very image of her father. He was a drunk. But a week of prayer and an afternoon of fasting, together with the ice-edged light of the gospel, brought her back to the saving realization that if there were fault, surely it was her own. She arose in church the following first Sunday and apologized to all those, especially her family, whom she'd offended in any way, and then set hard at work to remove offense utterly from herself and from any and all around her. She was unrelenting. She was everywhere, hovering early and late over the salvation of her own—and of everyone else. And in heaven's own manner, that strange higher manner which requires so much thought and agility to reconcile to the plain and rustic ways of men, her zeal was rewarded, for shortly thereafter the chief burden and torment of her life, her husband, was overtaken in the midst of his vagrant sins by a state gravel truck resolute in its decreed course. He broke cleanly with life, leaving in his stead and intact death benefits to his family which, had he lived, would surely have succumbed, together with his job, to his perversion. Moreover, these posthumous assets, being treasures merely of this life which could not be made liquid for the next, held, hidden within a gross loss of revenue, a net gain of income. Rachael grieved, of course, insistently, of course, but at the root of her grief there grew a kind of celebration. She saw her husband called on a mission of insurmountable sobriety from which indubitable justice she would some day claim him on evidence of her own vigilance and righteous industry. The Lord had put her in control. She would not fail.

But the reins of beatitude are intricate. Every pull or jerk of resolution leaves some leash slack and unattended. And while her children yielded without option to Rachael Holbein's grim determination, still, they moved on willful tangents of their own, dodging and sideslipping and making a mockery of agency . . . by using it. Her oldest daughter married a Catholic, a short musclebound man who wore a heathen cross on a silver chain through the hair in his open shirt. Her youngest left school and home and the Mutual Improvement Association to move to Steamboat Springs, Colorado. She sold sportswear Mondays through Thursdays, 10:00 to 6:00. Friday evenings and all day Saturday, she taught aerobics at the Scandinavian. Sundays, when she should have been in church (and her mother called to check), she was home in bed. But the remaining hours were unaccounted for. Rachael refused to think about those hours. Instead, she ground her teeth at night.

Sons were less trouble. Jared, the older and her chief earthly pride, had finished school and married a nice girl in the Second Ward for eternity. A general authority had married them, an uncle of a friend of the bride. Rachael hadn't recognized his name, nor found it subsequently in the church magazines. But she always looked. Jared took a job in St. Paul in a credit department where they made him assistant manager and then manager and then something else. He had a house and a riding lawnmower and a sprinkling system which rose up through the lawn like an elevator. And he gave his mother three grandchildren. She had only the three and ruefully suspected her married daughter and her married daughter's musclebound Catholic of unnatural practices. But what could she do about that? At least they weren't in St. Paul, which was $139.00 roundtrip away on the Greyhound. Jared never called if it wasn't a holiday, and when she called him weekly, right after the Tabernacle Choir on the radio, and she heard television cartoons already going at his house on the Sabbath and the children yelling out of control like Indians, she was afraid to say anything for fear he wouldn't call her at all anymore. He was like his father. He never talked back. He rarely argued. He just cut you off. $139.00 was a lot of money.

Only her youngest child, Roy, Jr., named after his father at his mother's insistence in order to spur the latter to a more exemplary life, was completely unlike his dad. Thank the Lord. And he was the only one left at home. He'd actually gone on a mission with the help of his brother and of the Seventies' quorum, and when he came back smiling at everyone and carrying his scriptures everywhere out of habit, he'd given a talk in church which Brother Crisp, the elders' quorum president, recorded for her on cassette, and which she played at narrowing intervals when she was feeling down or hopeless and remembering what sort of failures in life might never be compensated by any other success. It was a wonderful tape. So pure and uplifting, it made it all the more painful to watch her last, best hope of unblemished maternal victory slide slowly, steadily down into the sin of bachelorhood. Three and a half years home, and instead of settling down with an eternal mate, he dropped casually in and out of school, grew his hair, and rode on motorcycles. He put his scriptures away and his missionary suit, and now, when he took his mother to church, girls who only months before had smiled and blushed for his attention crowded closer to their mothers and stared blankly at his ponytail and studded boots . . . as if he were a Martian. Or a gentile.

She exhorted him morning and noon and waited up nights, but he only smiled at his pouting mother and took out the garbage or mowed the grass or fixed the faucet or the screen door. And, if the truth were known, for all her exhortations, deep down inside she was happy at this steadiness which, though its wrongheadedness broke her obedient heart, was all she'd ever really wanted of a man.

Moreover, she needed him at home, for just when the other children's departures had begun to resolve into calm, when their distance sometimes allowed her whole hours of forgetfulness and almost serenity, the final and fiercest trial of all was sent to crown her earthly struggle. Her father moved in. He was eighty-four, a retired railroader, and as in need of care as he was deeply resentful of it. He was as she'd always known him: angry, alcoholic, impossible, imperial. And evidently he was immortal as well. He had outlived by two decades the devout and abstemious woman who'd worked and prayed herself to death for his deliverance. And he survived to spite her, to refute daily her wasted convictions and repulse her martyr's devotions by his sodden longevity. Since his retirement he had sought as well to frustrate altogether the accusing finger of piety through a fiery conversion to the church of reason. He had become a disciple of science, and his room in Rachael's house was dominated by a stack of *Scientific Americans* four times the size of the pile of *Playboys* she'd once found under the dirty laundry behind Jared's bed. He studied those books with a libertine fascination.

Daily he read, and daily came down to assail her with the fiery darts of astronomy or genetics or evolutionary biology. "Listen to this," he announced at breakfast and at supper, reading aloud and gesticulating with his finger and concluding always with a ritual pronouncement: "That crap the church feeds you poor blockheads . . . it's all a crock."

Rachael winced and drew in her neck and tried to argue or didn't. She felt besieged, though her faith went entirely unscathed, for she understood next to nothing of what her father read to her. It was the pitch of his voice that upset her, and the malevolent glint in his eye. Roy, Jr., however, only grinned and winked at her when his grandfather wasn't looking, and this calming reassurance might in time have helped her to live passively, even contentedly with her father's openly impenetrable assaults. It might, that is, if he had not sensed her growing immunity and found a way maliciously and once and for all to impale her on the spired prow of scientific progress.

When he presented it to her, he was as transparently matter-of-fact as a little boy with a hand-buzzer. "Last Will and Testament." It was only a form from the office supply with names written in the blanks, but under "addenda," he'd copied out three apocalyptic sentences. In block letters. "All bodily organs," it read, "including heart, kidneys, eyeballs, et cetera to be donated to medical science for research and any other scientific purposes. Remaining remains to be cremated and scattered. No Sermons no praying no religious bunk."

She collapsed slowly back against the vinyl chair cushion, limp and spent as a gored balloon. "Daddy, I won't do it," she said, not looking at him. "I can't."

"Won't do it?" He stared at her with studied incredulity. "That right there in yer hand is my last will. My dyin' testament, 'n yer tellin' me as ma own daughter, ya ain't gonna do it. Well, if that don't . . . Jus' what the hell kind a daughter are ya?"

He had her. Clean through the heart. What kind of a daughter was she, after all? What kind of ill-starred, inadequate child? But she couldn't. She knew from the Sunday School and from the Relief Society: it was against the church. She looked it up in the *Mormon*

Doctrine to be certain. Her immortal soul ached over the short paragraph. She couldn't. But every morning and every evening he came to her table with the same sanctimonious demand, and he glared at her through a martyr's burning eyes and read her chapter and verse out of the *Scientific American*. And every day she winced at his footstep on the stairs and died a little inside, feeling desperate and wondering desperately if her Redeemer might not take her first before her father as penance . . . and reward. She prayed unceasingly.

And when the answer came, it came from heaven. It was Sunday, and she was listening to the Tabernacle Choir and looking in the notebook by the phone for Jared's new, unlisted number when a slip of paper fell out with the name on it and number of Brother Rolley Boone who lived not two blocks away by the garden apartments and taught in the junior high school. Brother Boone was a Seventy, an elder in Israel, a faithful, every-Sunday bearer of the priesthood, and—it came to her suddenly with the force and clarity of scripture—he was a teacher of science. She was beside herself. That very afternoon after the sacrament meeting, she took Brother Boone aside to unburden herself to him of her dilemma and her inadequacy and to beg him for help and deliverance.

Rolley Boone smiled. He couldn't help himself. He put his hand on her shoulder and told her she mustn't worry. There was room in the gospel for all the truths of science and then some. If Brother Bimmer—he named her father formally by his name and a title she'd not heard pronounced in his behalf in years—if Brother Bimmer needed convincing that gospel laws were in harmony with nature, and that preserving the human body for its literal resurrection made absolute, sure-fire sense, then he thought he could supply that assurance from the perspective of science itself. He'd thought these matters through. He'd be glad to help, glad to talk with her father.

Had Rachael been lighter, she'd have floated the three blocks home like a balloon. Before leaving she invited Rolley to meal after daily meal till he agreed to Saturday supper. It was a long time to wait, but on Saturday he would be entirely free; on Saturday he could stay late to reconcile the mysteries of science and theology for her father.

Through the week she made plans, and when at last she led Rolley Boone, late but arrived, into her dining room, there awaited him a meal for a spiritual prince. No ingredient unrefined, no rind, nor crust, nor lowly dripping untransfigured by her art.

"This is Brother Boone, Daddy."

"Evenin'." The old man, bewildered by extravagance, eyed him carefully, looking for a hook to hang suspicion on. Rolley meanwhile was expansive.

"Good evening, sir." He offered a confident hand. "Hi there, Roy. How'r things?"

Rachael seated her guest across from her father and asked Roy, Jr., for the blessing. Then she served. The pale Boston lettuce in her bowl glistened in lemon and sugar and a river of heavy cream. Cloud-white rolls steamed and shrank under sweet and maple butters or orange-blossom honey or deeply maroon boysenberry jam. She gave them ginger ale to drink, poured over crushed, frozen apricot nectar. And then she fetched the meal. Northern fried chicken, fat and full and audible. It snapped when you bit it like tortilla chips, but this was no tortilla. It was, she said, a Norwegian recipe as rich as shortbread. The smell alone was aphrodisian, and the men fell to eating almost before it reached their plates. She brought out beans in a silken, ivory sauce alive with bits of bacon, and broccoli afloat in muted cheddar. And she said she'd never understand how some women served up vegetables with a little salt and nothing as if a bare naked bean or Brussels sprout were some kind of meal for a man. She whipped the potatoes with whipping cream. And nutmeg. And she warned them to wait for the gravy, which was her mother's recipe, and put up annually in jars for occasions, and was the stroke that made the meal. She was right. And when she'd filled their plates and made a second round with fresh rolls and ginger ale, she sat to watch them eat.

"Brother Boone is a scientist, Daddy. He's a science teacher, and I thought he might be interesting for you to talk to."

The old man was chewing in the deliberate, preoccupied manner of old men and infants, but he opened his eyes and then narrowed them again around an ice-blue beam of recognition. So that's what this was all about. She could almost see his jaw set around his chicken.

"Yes," said Rolley innocently over a forkful of broccoli, "your daughter tells me you're interested in science, too. She says you're quite a reader."

Howard Bimmer didn't look up from his plate. "I read some."

Rolley was not certain where to go from there, but he thought it was important to establish some common ground and a congenial atmosphere before he got off into cremation and organ transplants.

"I don't know how you fellows stay so slim. If I ate like this all the time, I'd rotate on axis." It was a professional joke which no one actually got, but Rachael laughed hopefully, and Roy, Jr., grinned and said, "Me too," and reached for more potatoes.

"*The Scientific American* is a wonderful magazine." Rolley turned his attention directly to Bimmer. "I subscribe myself . . . at school. It's an education."

"Yep." The old man chewed and stared at his plate.

"And what never fails to impress me is how the really solid discoveries in science always seem to fit so marvelously into the gospel plan."

"Is that so?" Bimmer was looking up now, chewing only with his front teeth and staring narrowly up at Rolley from under clouds of eyebrow. Rachael bounced nervously up to fill the serving dishes and to get more gravy for Roy, Jr.

"Yes, sir!" offered Rolley brightly. "It's amazing."

"Well then," said Howard Bimmer, starting slowly, "meybe y'ought ta tell thet to ma daughter there. Seems like she thinks a little science is gonna get her kicked right outa that gospel plan a yers 'n sent straight ta hell."

Rolley laughed comfortably, amiably. He took a drumstick in his hand, bobbing it lightly between thumb and forefinger for emphasis. "Brother Bimmer, sometimes people are frightened of things they don't really understand. That's human nature. But there's no need to be frightened of the truth."

"Y'don't say?" said Howard Bimmer looking tactically impressed, "and the damn sure scientific truth is that when yer dead, yer dead. Finito! Kaputt! Ain't no one 'r nothin' gonna bring ya back."

"Well," Rolley leaned back to regroup, "I'm afraid I'd have to disagree with you there, brother." His tone was carefully, cheerfully apologetic. "I'm sorry, but you see the reality is . . . that view is just not scientific."

"The hell it ain't!"

Rolley pulled back the drumstick he'd been waving and, to gain time, bit into it thoughtfully. "You see," he began again, and then, still chewing, leaned forward to confide in his antagonist. He placed his elbow directly in the broccoli bowl. Roy, Jr.'s eyes grew large and fixed on Rolley's sleeve. The horror-stricken Rachael all but cried out. Yet she bit her tongue. This was no time to interrupt. "The thing is," intent and oblivious, Rolley was getting down to business, "nothing ever really dies or disappears. Not absolutely. Not ultimately. Nothing comes from nothing, Brother Bimmer, and nothing goes there, either. That's the beauty of it. And it's not just religion, no, sir! It's science. It's the first law of thermodynamics. Everything is preserved." He smiled hard and at close range.

"Science, huh?" The old man eyed him with disdain. "Well, tell it to that chicken yer chewing on. Tell her how the Lord's gonna haul all them original chicken parts outa yer gullet 'n liver 'n yer gluteus maximus 'n reconstruct her particle perfect in all'r glory. 'N you, mister. I s'pose you think thet when yer six feet under, he's gonna gather you up too . . . outa the bellies of a hundert thousand worms 'n grubs 'n tree roots 'n whatever else's discovered yer nutritional value, so's he can reestablish you on this the American continent with ever last hair, 'n tooth, 'n ever last friggin' molecule in place. Ain't that right?"

Rolley was suddenly, abruptly adrift, unsure where they were headed, but he was both learned and artless enough to nod concession.

"Yep!" the old man exulted, "that's what they teach you blockheads. But I don't s'pose you can tell me whether he's gonna reestablish you with or without that poor damn chicken yer eatin', or maybe you get to keep the white meat which is particular low in cho-lestrol, 'n the chicken gets resurrected all in dark. Maybe there's a lesson in there on the valiance a chickens," he laughed villainously, " 'n what happens to them worms 'n grubs and all them poor damn tree roots when some chicken eats 'em fer breakfast 'n fer dinner yer great granddaughter feeds the same damn chicken to yer own damn grandkids and not a hair or a particle a you or a that chicken or a them worms neither gets lost. What about that'n, Brother Boone?" He sat back with a nasty air of satisfaction. "Maybe," his eyes lit up with mischief, "the Lord God'll jest resurrect the lot of ya in a big box like Betty Crocker sellin' Bisquick with a book a recipes pasted ta the top: two cups 'n plain water gets ya worms, dirty water 'n ya get grubs; add eggs, it's a chicken, and if you puff it up with enough baking soda 'n decorate the damn thing, ya get Homo Eerectus Assininus hisself settin' at some table eatin' his own genealogy with biscuits 'n gravy." Bimmer stopped to laugh again, but with his mouth closed this time. He guffawed slowly in deliberate, nasal puffs as rich in derision as they were void of mirth, and he glared triumphantly across the table at Rolley, who blinked disorientedly back, unsure of what he'd heard and of whether or not he'd been directly and intentionally insulted. Rolley's own mouth was ajar, and his forgotten fork hovered awkwardly and uselessly above his plate.

Rachael, meanwhile, who had long since stopped hovering to listen and oversee the battle, was growing rigid with impatience. Why did Brother Boone hesitate? This was the moment, if ever there had been one, to thrust in his sickle with terrible swift might, and to reap an unregenerate sinner. This was the moment to set her pigheaded father straight, humble him, quote him chapter and verse, expose his perverseness and his heresies. But Rolley Boone just sat there at her table and blinked and thought and blinked some more, still holding his fork ridiculously in the air. And when finally he'd rediscovered it, set it down, and brought himself, introspectively, to finish chewing up the mortally apostrophized chicken in his mouth, he turned to her father and said, as if he were really saying something: "Nope." He pushed out his lower lip just as if that puny, bare naked "Nope" were some kind of genuine answer. And it got worse from there. "I don't think that's what the Lord has in mind," he went on, "but you raise a good point." Rolley sank into thought again, snagged in the great food chain of being, re-reviewing the question. "A good point." He shook his head while he spoke. And he smiled bravely in retreat. "I'll have to think about it."

Rachael wanted to pour gravy down his back. Her hand and the pan she carried in it began to shake. The whole damn priesthood was nothing but a pack of men. If there were a lower, meaner, more worthless organizing principle in the entire universe, she couldn't think of it. Her obdurate sot of a father, far from having been brought low, sat as high now and as haughtily on his chair as if he were perched on his whole stack of *Scientific Americans*. Her own son, meanwhile, looked and ate blankly on as if nothing had happened.

And her deliverer, her expert, consulting specialist was a flat-out fraud. "You've got your arm in my dinner, Rolley Boone!" The flames that reddened the bungling impostor's face and neck were balm to her cheated soul.

She didn't serve dessert. When Roy, Jr., asked, she announced icily there was none. But she left a hot pie out in the middle of the sideboard for all with eyes to see and noses to smell. The look in her arctic eyes froze their tongues and every attempt at sociability and, not long thereafter, sent the amiable Elder Rolley Boone sledding for home in bewildered, perhaps even unconscious disgrace.

Later, before bed, she took the pie to the table and cut it for herself. What she didn't eat, she threw out.

In the morning her father came down to make his coffee in her kitchen and to drink it on Sunday in front of her at her table. She looked up at him across the polka-dot formica and asked, "Where do you want them spread?"

"What?" He jerked his head toward her.

"I said, where do you want us to scatter them?"

He stared back and narrowed his eyes.

"Your ashes, Daddy. Roy doesn't care. He'll put 'em on back of his motorcycle and scatter them anywhere you want. So where do you?" She looked away at the place in front of the back door where the linoleum was broken and curling. The radio was on, and the choir had just begun gently to raise its sacred strain from the crossroads of the West.

"Hell . . . " The first word out of his mouth was reflex, but a generation's worth of labored silence crowded into the narrow space before the next: " . . . how should I know? I haven't thought about it." He seemed stunned, but he remembered to be angry. "Do ya have ta have everthin' spelled out fer ya?"

She abandoned the linoleum. "Yes, Father!" She roared the words out in a barely audible, hissing whisper and stared him down. His thin, contrived, male anger was no match for her rage. "Yes, I do!"

In the evening he seemed older, ten years older, as if the morning's sudden triumph had broken a dam inside him, released some long pent-up flood of life and living to send it rushing downward through an open channel. She sat in her kitchen and watched an old, old man trudge off to bed. He had his laundry bag. Probably, he had a bottle. But the impulse to leap up and intervene drained away as quickly as it had come. Let him, she thought. Let him. Her mother had said to her once and wearily, that, at least, a man who drank in bed could not fall down and hurt himself. At least, he was quiet. There was wisdom in that. And humility. And a deep, aching comfort in quiet.

The Righteousness Hall of Fame

Damon sat puzzled in the front seat of Ernie Block's yellow Rambler wagon, his short legs straddling a new aluminum canning kettle. The back was full of firewood.

"Hey, Damon, sorry. I had two restorations and an emergency extraction this morning. No time to unload." Ernie divided all his days and hours into billable procedures. "But believe me, when you see what we've got here, you're absolutely going to forgive me. Sometimes, old buddy . . . sometimes, I'll tell you, I really think there's a guiding hand out there."

He checked his mirror, and when the blockade of split poplar and maple stacked high behind them failed to yield to his stare, changed lanes anyway . . . or tried to. The nautical bray of an eighteen-wheeler sent the car wincing and reeling back into the center of the highway. Damon felt sweat on his back. But Ernie punched the Rambler into passing gear, leaned into the wheel and, like a starship pilot counting down seconds into hyperspace, nodded intense, rhythmic encouragement to the engine. At the very last moment, he pulled the wheel sharply to the right, careened across two lanes of traffic and up and out the oncoming exit.

At the stop sign he grinned triumphantly at Damon, who collapsed a little in his seat belt and attempted a smile. Ernie made a right turn and then less than a quarter of a mile from the highway made another onto what appeared to be a private road. There was no sign. Not even a mailbox. But the car ascended a perfectly maintained lane and a half of new asphalt winding scenically up the late winter hillside through oak and ash and tulip trees still stark against the black earth and remaining islands of grey snow.

Damon assembled his thoughts from the diaspora of relief that followed their deliverance from the interstate. He didn't like being a passenger, not in anyone's car, and riding with Ernie, whose attention soared distractedly over wide kingdoms and dominions, was an act of wanton self-endangerment. Yet it was precisely the recklessness in his friend that also inspired trust. Damon liked Ernie. Couldn't help it. Couldn't help liking a man who treated ideas, as he treated eighteen-wheelers, with passing gear and competitive enthusiasm . . . who would interrupt a procedure, for instance, and sacrifice an entire rubber dam just to have Damon explain one more time the difference between "transcendent" and "transcendental" . . . or who cheerfully kept solvent patients and real income waiting while the chronically penurious scholar expounded some fine point in his *Meta-Critique of Spiritual Materialism*.

"Whew!" Ernie would say, "That's wild. But it just absolutely makes sense, doesn't it? I mean, it's brilliant. Ya know, a guy like you oughta be doing research full time and finishing your book. It's a crime. The wrong people have all the time and all the money."

Damon couldn't have agreed more. Times were hard at the college. Enrollments sagged, and the students who came seemed uniformly pre-med, pre-law, and/or preoccupied with money and business. He hadn't had three Greek students in three years, and upper-division course offerings on the evolution of theism or even on New Testament history might as well have been framed in black and published as obituaries. Untenured colleagues had been let go and not replaced, and he, consequently, filled his sorely underpaid pensum teaching "Intro." to crowds of underclassmen whose only pleasure in his course was having found one that filled a requirement.

There had been a time not long before when he'd have won these conscripts over with stagecraft and collusion, thrilled them with iconoclasm, fed egos and encouraged nascent rebellions—*us* against the establishment, your parents, other pharisees—only in the end to burst the very bubble on which the class was riding and to drop them down to earth again sadder and wiser and probably nearer their homes than they'd been when it all began. But Damon was tired of clever stratagems and of round trips through radicalism which ended, however victoriously, at McDonald's on the mall. The truth is he did have something radical to say about philosophy and about religion, but it was something that could not be performed in fifty entertaining minutes from the lectern. It required absorption and pathos and attention span, and as he revived old jokes to revive drooping eyelids in his classes or as his own lids drooped over the vacuous papers queuing endlessly on his desk, he realized he'd lost his forum. Perhaps forever. The quality of his work life was suffocating under the mindless quantity of his work.

In church—and Damon scandalized certain colleagues by going religiously to church—he found no solace. In fact, there he encountered the same fate his younger colleagues had met at work. He was let go. Sunday School teachers do not enjoy tenure, and the religious flame that fired his own pedagogical imagination seemed to fire its more anxious institutional keepers after the manner of bricks. Their interest was solid, but inelastic, and they replaced Damon Boulder with a younger man whose unquestionable skill was, in fact, the very one Damon had put so resolutely behind him at work. He now sat with the class and listened in guilty embarrassment while this new talent departed radically, veered off unexpectedly, incited revolutions, but all in the carefully covert service of accommodation. Depression wound itself round Damon Boulder like Morley's chain, and there remained to him, or so it sometimes seemed, only his unfinished book and the improbable enthusiasm of his dentist.

As the car pulled near the crest of the hill, the road turned sharply to the right again, and evergreens, planted in carefully cropped pairs, began to appear on either side. In the distance at the end of the tightening columns of shrubbery, there was suddenly an elaborate iron gate and a tract-colonial gatehouse of salmon-colored brick.

"Where are we?"

"Hey, you'll see." Ernie winked at him, and brought the car to a slow, rolling halt in front of the gatehouse. A uniformed guard appeared, a man too old, too serious, and too carefully starched and pleated to be merely underemployed. He looked military, and he eyed them with open suspicion.

Ernie rolled down his window. "Hi, this is Dr. Damon Boulder. And I'm Ernie Block, B.S., M.S., D.D.S., and," he looked over at Damon and winked playfully, "P.T.A., retired. Professor Boulder and I are expected inside." Ernie turned his grin back to the security man, who, however, did not pass them through, nor even respond, but mustered them as methodically as if following some internal checklist. He walked the length of the station wagon, disappearing behind the woodpile on Ernie's side of the car to re-emerge on the other side headed in the direction of the gatehouse. There he reached up and pulled a clipboard from somewhere under the eaves and, returning to his original point of surveillance, traced down the board with his finger.

"You Ernest Block?"

"Yes." The fun had disappeared from Ernie's voice, and he sounded tentative, but the information (or perhaps it was the tone) seemed this time to satisfy the sentry. He stepped back a pace and waved them on with a slow, sideways gesture of his head.

"All right," said Damon when the gate was behind them, "I think I'm ready for an explanation."

"Him?" Ernie shrugged his shoulders and his eyebrows at the same time. "Who knows? But, hey, they're expecting us."

"Who's expecting us?"

"You'll see. You'll see."

The road descended from the crest of the hill across a meadow and into another stand of trees. When it emerged on the other side, there was grass all around them and then, dead ahead on a rise in the middle of a vast rolling lawn . . .

"The promised land!" Ernie announced this as if it were self-evident, but Damon only blinked and squinted like someone who has missed the point.

"You mean this is what you've brought me out here to see?"

The object of attention was a group of large, two-story buildings arranged three to either side and one at the far end of an open quadrangle. They were new buildings, or new enough to seem foreign and plopped down on the barren grass, and they were built of the same salmon-colored brick and in the same pop-Georgian style as the gatehouse a quarter mile behind them. As Ernie guided the Rambler into the quadrangle, Damon thought of office complexes near the beltway with names like "Executive Commons" and "Free Enterprise Greene." Long white columns, square and spindly as linguini, rose to meet the giant portico that swept the entire length of each building directly at the roof line and hovered protectively over the view from the second floor. There were grand double doors, paneled and weatherproofed and surmounted by a central Palladian window, and in front of each building stood a white oval sign on a squat brick foundation: "The Hamiltonian," "The Madisonian," "The Federalist." Various other "-onians" and "-ists" followed, all heralded in patriotically antiquarian script, but Damon had turned his attention back to Ernie.

"All right, I give up. What is it?"

"Hey, Damon, it's a city on a hill. Might be Zion!" Ernie was obviously having great fun, grinning and gritting back his love of explanation for the sake of mystery. So Damon, who would have liked to press the question, shrugged instead and fell silent. But he was not a patient man, and he was irritated.

The car turned down a sloping drive toward a parking lot behind one of the buildings. Damon was surprised at the depth of the structure and to find another entire story on the downside of the slope. In fact, from the rear the building seemed enormous. Ernie parked the Rambler some ways off from the building in the nearly empty lot. There was plenty of space near the rear entrance, but Damon guessed from his guide's expression and from the way he stood back, hands on hips, and looked things over before striking off that the walk across the parking lot was intended to impress him with the scale and grandeur of it all.

Inside they found themselves in a long hall. Large windows at regular intervals on the left opened onto a clinically polished gymnasium. Ernie stopped at the second window and pointed across the antiseptic vastness.

"Training room's over there." He whispered in apparent deference to the stillness. "Free weights, Nautilus. Anything you'd ever want." At the next window he explained that the locker area had both a sauna and a steam bath.

"The pool's at the other end." He gestured down a hallway forking to the right, then continued on until he came to a tiny door in the right-hand wall. Turning back to Damon, he raised two knuckles, tapping gently at a spot just above the miniature entrance.

"Squash," he said, and there was an especially reverential hush in his voice.

"Oh, squash," replied the round and sedentary Damon in a tone just high enough to sound knowledgeable. Ernie's eyes switched to high beam.

"Do you play?"

Caught in a snare of his own making, Damon shook his head. He didn't even eat squash. But Ernie just grinned.

"Hey, you'll love it."

At the end of the hall was an elevator, and when they had entered Ernie punched the two unlighted buttons.

On the main floor he held the door and pointed across the foyer to an executive dining room seating "two hundred" with a "fully automated, full-service kitchen." In the other direction he reported offices big as hangars and an even more sublimely automated "executive" washroom. "State of the art!" he summed up solemnly with a wink and released the elevator door.

At their last stop Ernie led Damon out of the elevator and down a long hall toward a door marked "CONFERENCE." They walked silently, side by side, on the Wedgwood-blue carpet, and it occurred to Damon that, since passing the gatehouse some time ago, they hadn't seen another human soul. Not one. Not anywhere. And for a fraction of a moment a shadow fell over both his curiosity and his irritation, so that when Ernie, holding him confidingly by the shoulder, reached out and pushed open the heavy conference-room door, Damon started and looked up as blankly as if he'd been sleepwalking.

"Well, it's about time!"

The voice was familiar.

"Come in here, you two!"

The tone and even the volume were familiar. Damon blinked and recognized B. Harriman Hunsaker—"President Hunsaker" to the members of Damon's congregation; in fact, to all the congregations in the region. He was a leader and past leader and friend and perennial advisor to past and present leaders, whose voice from a pulpit and through a P.A. system was as familiar to everyone as Sunday morning.

"Where have you been?" The question was anything but reproach. Hunsaker beamed across the room at Damon like a proud parent. And he rose, greeting Ernie with a conspiratorial wink, to take Damon's arm at the palm and at the elbow and to pump it firmly once, and then again, and to narrow his smiling eyes in intense, patriarchal greeting.

"Been hearing good things about you, brother, good, good things."

Damon was mortally astonished. Oh, not that Harriman Hunsaker had heard of him. He'd suspected that. Lately, he'd prided himself that he was known. But as a heretic, of course, and as a willfully uncorrelated troublemaker. What "good" things could B. Harriman Hunsaker possibly have heard?

"I'm told you're quite an intellectual. Out of the best books, eh? Doctrine and Covenants 88, isn't that right? Well, believe me, I envy you. Heaven knows there are too few of you in the world, brother. And too few people who appreciate you. You wouldn't know it to look at me, hard-nosed old business man and church bureaucrat, but I've always admired the life of the mind. And Brother Block here tells me you're writing a book. Is that right?"

Damon was still stiff with astonishment, but he was able to nod.

"He tells me it's brilliant. Says it's the first systematic treatment of the theo . . . " He knotted his forehead and tried again: "theo . . . "

"The theo-empirical foundations of revealed religion," Ernie dived in eagerly to recite the memorized fruit of his labors over Damon's teeth, "and it is brilliant. Absolutely! If we can just get him to translate it into English."

Damon, who was acutely uncomfortable, tried to prune back Ernie's extravagance. "I'm afraid Brother Block gets carried away, but as a preliminary sort of study, I think it could make a certain contribution."

"Well, I think it's marvelous!" Hunsaker took the reins again. "And I want you to tell us about it. All about it. Oh, not here. Not today. Not in ten superficial minutes. Today we have other things on our mind. Business. Details. Today we'll have to be a little superficial. A book like this one of yours needs time and serious attention, a seminar maybe, or a lecture series. That's what I have in mind. I don't think there's a man here who wouldn't count himself lucky to take part in something like that. What do you think, brethren?"

Hunsaker looked away, and for the first time Damon became aware there were other men in the room. They were seated senatorially around the immense perimeter of a very long, very polished conference table stretching away a dozen feet or more across the carpet. On the table were papers, and folders, and a ledger, and there were yellow legal pads in front of each of the five men, who nodded and grinned in response to Hunsaker's question, and who now stood to greet Damon and to shake his hand.

"Professor Damon Boulder, the man we've all been hearing about. He's a scholar. And," Hunsaker winked the same playful wink Ernie had performed at the gate house, "he's a brother."

"Damon, this is Gordon Hawkes. Gordon is our security specialist. Formerly C.I.A."

A little bewildered, Damon surrendered his hand to a vise grip at the end of a natty plaid sleeve.

"And this . . . this is Stan Picker. Maybe you've already met Stan. He's on the high council."

In fact, Damon recognized most of these men, though he knew only one of them by name.

"Stan is our comptroller, numbers man. The best, in fact. A regular genius. But don't let him scare you." Hunsaker bent to Damon's ear and made a show of covering his stage whisper. "Long-windedest speaker on the whole council. Puts his own wife to sleep." Brother Picker blushed, and the others in the room laughed a comfortable, collegial laugh. "Stan and Ned, here," moving around the table, Damon accepted a third hand, "are in business together. Family Home Investment Services. Maybe you've heard of it. These fellas work wonders, really, positive miracles, and Ned is the wizard of real estate. Right, Ned?"

Ned, whose last name Damon missed, seemed very young though his hair was already as sparse as it was blond. He wore rimless glasses on thin wire frames, and radiated a scrubbed, nordic innocence.

They rounded the end of the table and headed up the other side.

"Walt Dwyer, marketing and public relations. Walt did those inspirational inserts for the *TV Guide*." Damon hadn't seen the inserts though, of course, he'd heard about them and about the cassette tapes as well.

"And this is Mason Sorenson. Mason is our legal eagle. Keeps us on the strait and narrow." Damon accepted Sorenson's hand, and nodded with involuntary deference. This was the man he knew by name, though he didn't really know him personally. He was one of those familiar strangers who sit on the stand at conferences, and who are introduced among the first rank of dignitaries, yet who rarely speak, or pray, and who never conduct. Bishops and quorum leaders brought him notes or whispered messages. Presidents and counselors conferred with him behind discreetly cupped palms waiting for a nod or a shrug before going about their business. He was a presider, though a not entirely official one, and he wore the strict clerical vestments of his office. The slate-grey suit was just light enough to be distinguished from black, but no lighter; his shoes shone with a hard brightness; his socks, if he crossed his legs, would, Damon knew, not only match, but be flawless ebony and as smooth and taut as seventeen-year-old skin; and his pure white shirt under the muted cranberry tie was a broadcloth so heavy and tightly woven it allowed no hint, no suggestion of underwear. Gold cuff links, simple and luminescent as a prelate's ring, caught the eye and conjured ancient offices and ceremonies while the zippered leather scripture case he carried even now was so immense, so oiled and polished to so deep and Abyssinian a hue, it seemed worthy of the golden plates themselves. Mason Sorenson wore unannounced power like a carefully fitted topcoat, and Damon, whose own relationship to authority was necessarily voyeuristic, had long since marked his name and his influence. As he now took his hand—"It's very good to meet you, Brother Boulder"—he felt a sense of initiation.

"Well," announced President Hunsaker, moving back to the head of the table. "It's time we got down to business. Sit down, brethren. Damon, you just take a seat in the middle there, and, Ernie, you sit down too. Brother Boulder is wondering why we've asked him here today. Perhaps he's even a little bit concerned. He doesn't know yet that we've brought him here precisely because his own important concerns as a scholar and educator are the very ones most on our own minds right now. You see, Professor Boulder, we are troubled men. Yes, deeply troubled about scholarship in this country, and education, about the teaching of religion and values and honor and patriotism. About the dark prospects for freedom's holy light in this land of prophetic promise."

Damon, who wasn't at all sure he liked the direction of President Hunsaker's reassurance, furled his eyebrows.

"Oh, I know. I know what you're going to say. The world today is full of hand wringers. People who complain. People who criticize. But where are the people who are doing something about it? And that's just it, Damon Boulder; that is precisely why you're here," he shifted his legs underneath the table and folded his arms with particular gravity, "because it's time we stopped complaining and started performing. It's time we put our money where our mouth is, became doers of the word and not sayers only. And . . . " he leaned forward slightly, "indeed, we are going to do something . . . something very decisive, I promise you." Hunsaker unfolded his arms and put his hands on the table. "But, of course, when you want to be effective, what do you need to do first?"

After a moment it became evident he expected an answer, but Damon had no idea what he was talking about and the others were all cautiously silent.

"Ernie?"

Nervous, Ernie Block leaned back and hemmed. "Well," he began, "considering the importance of this whole thing, which I think pretty much everyone is probably agreed on, the first thing, I think, you've absolutely got to do is ahh . . . ahhh . . . is ahhh . . . to set goals. I mean," having found a trail, he struck out bravely, "short term, intermediate term, and then, of course, you have your big picture. Now, for myself I like to use the seven basic . . . "

"Yes, of course," Hunsaker intruded pre-emptively, "but before you set a single goal, what will the wise man do first? Gordon, you tell us. What is the first necessary step?"

The security man didn't hesitate. "I would consult with an expert in the field," he said and leaned forward intently to place an underscoring elbow on the conference table.

"And that's just what we're doing, isn't it? We're consulting with an expert, a scholar, a distinguished teacher of religion and values, a man with degrees from the finest universities who's dedicated his life to teaching young people in this country the theo . . . theo . . . "

"Theo-empirical foundations." Ernie dived in for the save.

"Exactly. Brother Boulder, you see here at this table men who have decided to make a difference, determined, resolute men, but before we take action . . . first we need your counsel and assistance."

Boulder was still astounded, and before he could begin to collect himself, Hunsaker blindsided him from yet another unexpected direction.

"Now, what do you think of our little place here, Damon?"

The professor struggled for an answer.

"It's a . . . it's certainly . . . ahh . . . colonial."

"Isn't it? Did Ernie tell you it's a Williamsburg?"

"Uhh, no . . . no, he didn't."

"No?" Now Hunsaker seemed surprised. "Well then, Ned, you tell him."

"Delighted!" The real-estate wizard's tenor was rapid and melodic. "Till last September this was corporate headquarters for HH&H Incidental."

Damon's eyes glazed.

"Heritage Health and Hospital. You know. Incidental coverage."

"They run spots on late night TV," clarified Stan Picker.

"Anyway, George Weeder—he's the founder and chairman of HH&H—George had it built in authentic Williamsburg. The guy's a stickler. Did you notice the brass on the lampposts outside?"

Damon shook his head.

"Well, you should. You really should. Exact reproductions. Really ought to take a look at them. There's twenty-thirty thousand in W.B. brass on those lampposts alone. And then there's the door-knobs. And the foot scrapers. And that's just for starters. I mean, we're talking real wood chair rails here, parquet, crown molding everywhere you look, simulated beamed ceilings in the dining room, the club room, and half the executive offices. And every last nail and knothole absolutely one hundred percent authentic."

"Show him the site plan, Ned." Hunsaker coached from the sideline while Ned with epiphany in his eyes reached under the table to produce a large rolled drawing he spread out in front of Damon Boulder.

"Three hundred and seventy-two acres, over two hundred of 'em wooded, and enough left for half a dozen golf courses. Drainage is fantastic. We've got two paved access roads, seven buildings, three outbuildings, an underground air-raid shelter, an artesian well, an emergency power generator, an emergency septic system, and, believe it or not, a trunk line to the sewer paid for by the county. The only thing we don't have up here is neighbors, and if we get any, we've already made good neighbors out of 'em with the most advanced security system in this part of the country. Right, Gordon?"

The security specialist came up off his elbow. "Nothing like it for three hundred miles."

"Well, what do you think now, Damon?" Hunsaker began again at the beginning, and though Damon Boulder could find nothing entirely appropriate to say, this time he spoke less guardedly.

"It's a . . . amazing."

"It is amazing, isn't it? And would you believe me, Professor Boulder, if I told you that we represent a group of investors who have just purchased this amazing facility?" He leaned forward in an intense way that made Damon nervous.

"I . . . I'd be surprised, I suppose, but I certainly don't have any reason not to believe you."

Hunsaker smiled a tight, satisfied smile and continued in a voice dramatically lower and more deliberate.

"And would you also believe me if I told you, Brother Damon Boulder, that we've bought it," he paused and narrowed his eyes, "just for you?"

There was a very long silence. Ernie Block grinned, and the other six stared at Damon with the open curiosity of observing scientists.

"Of course not." Damon anticipated some looming joke, and he forced a chuckle through his answer. But no one else laughed.

"I think you are in for a surprise, professor."

"I told you, Damon." Ernie couldn't contain himself any longer. "The minute I heard about it, I knew it was perfect for you."

"What was perfect for me?"

"The Foundation."

Damon stared clear glass blocks of incomprehension at Ernie and then at the others while a look of bemused good will made its way around the room.

"He means our 'Freedom's Holy Light Foundation,' Damon." Hunsaker was expansive with explanation. "He means an institution dedicated to research and teaching and to the promotion of revealed principles in our inspired constitutional republic. Now, how does that sound to you?"

There was another pause as Damon began to gain ground on his bewilderment.

"This is going to be some sort of research foundation?"

Hunsaker nodded. "And what would you think of the opportunity to devote yourself full-time to your studies and your writing?"

"Here?"

"Yes, of course. Here."

"And you would pay me for that?"

The president's bemusement was waggish.

"Well," he demurred, "modestly, I'm afraid. We are not—as they say—made of money. But, yes! Of course we would pay you."

Befuddlement still contorted Damon's face. "Why?"

"Because," Hunsaker answered with the barest tinge of impatience, "a research foundation would hardly be a research foundation without researchers, would it, men like yourself, Professor Boulder, with the skills and background and credentials for genuine, bona fide research? Can't have a legitimate scholarly foundation without legitimate scholars. Isn't that right, Brother Sorenson?"

Mason Sorenson, whose sandstone features had remained untouched by the general amiability at the table, nodded officially.

"That is correct," he said.

"So you see, Damon, we need you. You are exactly what we need." His tone became pedagogical. "You know, brethren, sometimes the veil is very thin. Sometimes you can almost see a guiding hand out there. Even adversity has its purpose. Now, I had a toothache. Worst toothache of my life. And I'm embarrassed to tell you I fought that adversity, resisted it. Absolutely refused to go to a dentist. Ask my wife. But the Lord's purposes will not be denied. He put poor Jonah in the belly of that whale, and he put such torment in my tooth, I had no choice. I had to go—and when I did, when finally I yielded to those fierce inner promptings, the trial I'd been resisting all along turned out to be a blessing, a revelation." He rolled his eyes in self-admonishment. "As I was explaining our little project to Brother Block here—through that infernal rubber dam and a pound and a half of soggy cotton," Ernie's grin broadened, "and as he was telling me all about Brother Boulder's book and about certain troubles down to the college, well, I think it came to both of us in the same precise instant."

"Right," Ernie confirmed as gravely as his grin would allow, "Absolutely!"

"Now, Damon," the speculative metaphysics in Hunsaker's voice fed rapidly down into business, "you have a need, and we have a need; you have an ambition, and we have an opportunity here; you have a dentist, and I was prompted to seek out that same fine dentist. Whoever the guiding hand hath thus brought miraculously together, well, they had just ought to get on with the program. Now, that's the way I see it. Don't you? Don't you agree with me, brother?"

Damon had during Hunsaker's discourse, as he did customarily during all such homilies, attended principally to his own thoughts, and the word in the sermon upon which his mind now fixed itself was the word "opportunity."

"Please, let me get this straight. You would like me to come here to do my own research, and to write my book?" He paused. "Without any strings?" He paused again. "And you would be willing to pay me?"

"Of course," Hunsaker amended, "Of course, we would like you to get involved in the program of the foundation, too. After all, there are concerns that every red-blooded American . . . "

"Your own research, Professor Boulder," Mason Sorenson's measured voice cut off Harriman Hunsaker in mid-sentence, "your own book. You would have certain administrative duties, of course, but otherwise you would be free to pursue your related studies as you deemed appropriate."

"Why, yes, of course, absolutely!" Hunsaker picked up again quickly with course correction in his voice. "Now, some of us are aware, Brother Boulder, of an incident in the Sunday School last spring. Unfortunate. Truly unfortunate, but I think the problem is simple enough. A man like yourself, a sophisticated scholar and educator, is out of his element in a Sunday School class. There are likely to be new members there or investigators or just a whole lot of people who don't understand these things. Milk before meat, as they say, milk before meat. And I'll tell you something else. Yes, let's admit it. We've got plenty of milkmen in the Church, don't we? Plenty of dairy stores with yogurt and ice cream and every known variety of cottage cheese. But where, I ask you," he pointed a demanding finger at a spot directly between Damon's eyes, "where can a man sit down and sink his teeth into a big, juicy, prime American beefsteak? Where? Think about it. Think about the opportunity here. We are going to build us a real steak house," he winked playfully across the table, "a millennial mansion for meat eaters, and Damon Boulder is going to be master of the menu, guru of the grill, presiding bishop of the barbecue." The president was delighted with his compounding metaphor, but his pleasure paled against the incredulous sensation Damon Boulder suddenly felt at hearing his own long-standing irreverence reflected colorfully back to him out of the very mouth of authority. He must, he thought, be dreaming.

"Well, I'll have to admit, that if you're serious about this, I mean about funding a center for independent research, I'm certainly not without interest . . . which is to say . . . well, in fact, I'll be honest with you. It sounds almost too good to be true. I don't want to get mixed up in any screwball propaganda thing."

"Of course not." Hunsaker's sympathy was adamant.

"But to have the time off . . . to have the leisure for work . . . " The men around the table laughed, and Damon, when he realized what he'd said, laughed too. "I mean to really work at the work I want to work at, that would be a dream come true. That's the sort of thing a person could make sacrifices for."

"Sacrifices, Brother Boulder?"

"Well, all I mean is that it wouldn't have to be a lot of money."

Hunsaker sat back like a satisfied examiner. "Now let *me* be honest with *you*. We've been counting on the willingness of a man like yourself, a man of your caliber and commitment to make certain sacrifices. And I see we haven't misjudged you." He smiled gratefully, but then a new concern seemed to cloud his expression. "Tell me, Damon, will we find others as well? Oh, I don't mean a lot of others, but a few good men?"

Damon closed his eyes for a moment and then spoke with the hushed, heartfelt intensity one expects only of someone much younger. "I attend a lot of conferences," he said, "and I can't tell you how many times I've sat up half the night with colleagues dreaming about just such an opportunity. If you truly mean what you say you mean, I know scholars . . . fine, capable men, but disheartened. Discouraged. I think they would jump at the chance."

"So, you see, brethren?" Hunsaker panned wide eyed round the room. "You see how perfectly things fall into place? This is no accident. Of course not. There are times when the very word 'accident' is a sin against the spirit. Brother Damon here has been directed to us. He's the man of the hour to help us build an army, a spiritual strike force for moral and educational rearmament in this country."

Damon winced at the metaphor, but succumbed almost as quickly to a certain glow of testimonial recognition which lighted the faces at the table. "If I can really be of help," he said with uncharacteristic humility, "I've always tried to honor my callings in the Church."

Hunsaker, Stanley Picker, and Mason Sorenson all, and all at once, shot up in their seats, in fact, almost out of their seats.

"Oh, this is not a church calling."

"Not actually."

"Not officially."

"Not at all." Sorenson's particularly eschatological baritone took up the rear. "We represent," he explained with re-established composure, "an entirely independent foundation of which the Church, as a matter of general policy, neither approves nor disapproves, even though our aims and intentions might be perceived as consonant with those of that organization. We are, in a word, entirely independent."

"Oh," said Damon in a chastened tone. He looked puzzled. "I suppose that's all to the good, isn't it? I mean, for an independent research foundation, but if the Church is not involved, then who's paying for all of this? This place must have cost a fortune, and the upkeep, and salaries. When you start talking about an 'army' of scholars . . . "

"Well," Hunsaker demurred, "perhaps I got a little carried away. Perhaps a platoon would have been more like it. Or a squad, maybe. We are not—as they say—made of money."

"But," Boulder pointed to the site plan still spread out on the table, "we're still talking about a great deal of money here. Who would buy a place like this and just donate it for scholarly research?"

"Oh, don't you worry about the money!" Stan Picker, the numbers genius from Family Home Financial, broke in. "There is always enough money for the right kind of investment. Big money. Believe me, money is no problem. And who said anything about 'donations'?" He looked around. "Did anyone here say anything about donations?" The room was cheerfully silent. "You see, Brother Boulder," Picker intertwined the fingers of his hands and leaned confidingly on his forearms, "when you go into the donations business, you enter into competition with the Lord himself. I mean, it's all his, isn't it? All the wealth, all the resources. All his. And when a man makes a donation to the Lord's Church, he's only yielding up a small return on the Master's eternal investment. But if that same, tax-deductible donation was to go completely unearned to some worldly cause or other, even our own Freedom's Holy Light Foundation, now that would be a diversion of funds, wouldn't it, a misappropriation. Reaping where we have not sown, leveraging where we've built no equity. That's welfare, Brother Boulder, pure and simple. It's the dole. And I don't need to tell you what the authorities of the Church think of the dole."

"No, I suppose not," Damon conceded.

"When you understand correct principles, Brother Boulder, most of the so-called charities in this world are taking the daily bread right out of the very mouth of God. No, sir, the Church does not look kindly on the worldly donations business, and we look at our business from the same eternal perspective as the Church. This is not going to be any free hot-lunch program up here. We pay our own way."

"You can't expect to set things right in the world," Hunsaker summarized from the end of the table, "if you begin by setting a bad example."

Damon shook his head uncomfortably. "I sincerely hope you don't expect to pay the rent from my book."

There was just the very briefest of deep silences before good natured laughter broke out. Brother Picker was particularly amused, and even Mason Sorenson smiled.

"No. Not from your book, Damon," Hunsaker assured with a broad smile, "but I think it'll make a certain contribution, all right. You might want to look at it as a sort of 'loss leader.' "

This time the laughter and the joke were lost on Damon, whose concern gave way to puzzlement. "But how . . . "

"Now, that's the question," Picker broke in again, "the very question we asked ourselves. How'r we gonna do it. And, I'll tell you, I was a skeptic myself. Added up the numbers. Added them again and again. Just kept looking at the numbers. Couldn't figure how in the world we were going to pay the piper. But, you see, that was just the problem. My mind was set on the things of this world. I'd forgot the power of inspiration until Brother Dwyer over here," he pointed, "who'd gotten himself in tune with the spirit, reminded all of us that, in fact, we have got us a product here, an incredible product, the most amazing, marvelous, fantastic product in the entire world, which people are just dying to get at, and just absolutely selling their souls for lack of, and all we've got to do to market this amazing product is find just exactly the right way to package it, which in fact we had already found without even knowing it. And so the whole time we'd been sitting smack on top of a gold mine and too blind to see it."

"Product?" Damon repeated, no less puzzled than he'd been earlier.

"Absolutely!"

"And what is it?"

Brother Picker pursed his lips and bobbed his head up and down reflectively. "When I tell you, you'll be embarrassed you didn't see it yourself. Really. When Walt told us, we were all embarrassed. Isn't that right?"

Guilty grimacing and head-hanging circled the table, but Damon was undeterred.

"But what is it?"

Picker prolonged the suspense yet a little longer, smiling mysteriously across the table.

"It's righteousness," he finally said. "Do you have any idea how many people in this country are hungering and thirsting after righteousness? Right this very minute?"

"No," Damon admitted. Suddenly it was he who was staring uncomfortably at the table.

"I said you'd be embarrassed, didn't I? These things are so close to us, brother, yet without the spirit, we're blinded to them. Did you know that in Colorado there are training centers where executives, corporate leaders, important men of means and influence pay out perfectly good money to be trained whole weeks at a time in the pernicious doctrines of secular humanism?"

Damon winced and looked helplessly toward President Hunsaker, but the patriarch only nodded gloomy corroboration.

"It's true, Damon. I'm afraid it's true."

Damon looked back down at the table.

"But what choice do they have?" Brother Picker went on. "Think about it. What choice do they have? There are plenty of centers for teaching the philosophies of men with all the enticements and allurements the world has to offer. You bet there are. But where, I ask you, where is there a first-rate, executive-class corporate training center for the doctrines of righteousness? Where?"

Finally the connection melded in Damon's forehead. "Let me guess," he said and put his palm on the site plan, "here . . . it's going to be here?"

The answering emotion in his interrogator's smile spread like a brush fire to the others, so that soon everyone in the room was explaining excitedly and all at once.

"Seminar rooms, ballrooms, executive dining."

"We're putting in an eighteen-hole golf course."

"Total fitness center."

"And squash!" Ernie added with insistent enthusiasm.

"We've got full limo service to the airport."

"And here!" A finger descended out of nowhere onto the site plan. "Here's where the heli-pad goes."

"Luxury-class dormitories."

"First cabin all the way!"

"Absolutely!"

"Horseback riding."

"Survival training."

"Genealogical archives."

"Counter insurgency."

"Crash courses on the Constitution."

"Gordon's setting up a rifle range."

"Small arms competitions."

"Prayer breakfasts!"

"Martial arts!"

"Scripture chasing!"

"And every inch . . . " Hunsaker's voice rose over the clamor, "every last centimeter, absolutely 100 percent authentic Williamsburg. Do you see, Damon? Do you get the vision of this thing?"

"We're not talking just any companies here." Stan Picker was still flushed with excitement. "We're talking strictly Fortune 500 with massive training budgets, incentive programs, executive furloughs, community outreach."

"He's right, Damon. Listen to him."

"There is a field here so incredibly white and ready to harvest, it's blinding. And that's not all, not by a long shot."

Damon's mouth was as dry as Saudi Arabia.

"I think you should tell him, President Hunsaker. I think he should hear it from you."

Hunsaker drew himself up and spoke with ecclesiastical solemnity. "Damon, do you realize that people in this country have built temples of homage to baseball players, and football players, to stock car drivers and rodeo cowboys and even movie stars? In Wisconsin there's a memorial to beer drinkers. Can you imagine that? And Brother Dwyer tells me," his voice and his face darkened with evident distaste, "there's even talk now of a Rock 'n' Roll Hall of Fame. Isn't that right, Walt?"

Walt Dwyer pushed his lower lip gravely upward and nodded confirmation. "In Cleveland."

"You see. A hall of fame for every fool and every folly under the sun, but where . . . where, I ask you, is the Righteousness Hall of Fame?"

For the second time in as many minutes, Damon found himself pushed to the brink of revelation, only this time the vision truly stunned him. "Here?" he asked weakly.

The answering smile was triumphant as Hunsaker rose from his seat and walked around to Damon's side to point to the site plan himself. "This is the place!" He indicated the building at the head of the quadrangle. "Here is where we will honor the unsung field generals and quarterbacks and designated hitters in the great contest between revealed free-market Christianity and godless atheistic Communism."

Hunsaker explained elaborately that every graduating class from the "Freedom's Holy Light Foundation" would nominate potential inductees of proven character and accomplishment for submission to a blue-ribbon panel of referees including well-known church men, business leaders, prominent figures in the sports and entertainment worlds, a successful inspirational novelist, and two past winners of the Mrs. America contest. Stan Picker offered to get Damon a copy of the list, but Damon declined, and the briefing continued. Winners would be honored with a genuine Williamsburg brass plaque recounting their contributions and achievements and including, across the bottom, a plate inscribed with all the names of the nominating class.

"Why that?" Damon, not knowing where to begin, began with the immediate.

"A good man wants to know who his friends and supporters are." Hunsaker winked.

"And friends and supporters," Picker added without winking, "want to be associated with a good man."

"Or a powerful one," Damon amended under his breath, but he let it drop and went on to another question. "You're going to make this place into a tourist attraction?"

"Oh, heavens, no!" Hunsaker laughed.

"Quite the contrary," said Mason Sorenson.

"Admission will be strictly controlled!" Gordon Hawkes spoke with a clipped military intensity. "Very strictly controlled!"

"But, a Hall of Fame? How are you . . . I mean, why . . . ?"

"You really don't understand, do you, Boulder? Can't say that I blame you." Hawkes mellowed. "You lead a very sheltered life, you know. Most Americans lead a sheltered life. It's one of the dangerous luxuries of our system. It spoils us, lulls us to sleep. But there are forces out there, believe me, I know, powerful forces, that are already plenty worried about this little operation up here. For years they've had it their own way. They've infiltrated the government, the schools, the corporations, and even the churches . . . most of them . . . with a steady stream of amorality, humanism, collectivism, anti-individualism. They've seriously undermined the whole vital structure of the American system. I've watched it. Smelled it. Read the reports. I've been on the battle line myself for twenty years. And I'll tell you something scary, Mr. Boulder, the very agencies this country relies on to keep it strong and free are infected. Subverted. Why do you think I left? They're useless against the disease out there. Worthless."

"Isn't that just a little dramatic?" Damon made no attempt to hide his skepticism, but Hawkes remained unruffled.

"You think I'm paranoid, don't you, Boulder? I wish I was. Unfortunately, seven thousand five hundred and thirty-three documented cases of subversion and infiltration in just the last four years is not paranoia. That's hard cold conspiracy, Doctor, and I think it ought to bother you just a little bit that the evidence never makes it onto your TV screen, or into your paper. Why doesn't your congressman speak out, or the president? Don't you think there are reasons? Seven thousand five hundred and thirty-three documented cases. I wish I was only paranoid. Paranoia would be a pleasure, believe me. But in the real world out there, some of us have to play the cards the way reality deals them. That's my job, sir, and I intend to do it. And I'll tell you something else. Right here on this hillside, we've got the answer. Right here. Many are called, Professor Boulder, but few are chosen. To succeed, you need only a small, dedicated organization giving energy, stability, and persistence to the struggle, an organization with all the unseen threads of leadership in a closed fist. Do you know who said that? Do you?"

Damon didn't know.

"They tell me you're a scholar, Boulder, and I'm willing to take their word, but I don't think your scholarship goes far enough. Lenin said that. And for sixty years he's been right. Dead right. It's just now we're starting to use those very same tactics in the cause of free-market republican democracy and of decency and common ordinary righteousness. We're not a big outfit here, but we're tough. We're not powerful, not yet, but we have the drive and savvy and street smarts to train up a network of committed leaders. And if anyone is wondering whether the collectivists are worried—well, you can just bet your bifocals they are. We are a dedicated, disciplined para-missionary organization here, and we are about to turn the tactical tables on the Bolshevists. At this very moment, I guarantee you, they have only one thought—to infiltrate us, and one goal—to neutralize us."

"And Brother Hawkes is here to see that doesn't happen," President Hunsaker intruded with a reassuring hand on Damon's shoulder.

"And you believe all this?" Damon's voice, though still pinched with skepticism, was less shrill and less insistent. The question sounded almost like a question.

"I don't know much about these things, Damon, but none of us has had Brother Hawkes' considerable experience, have we? If we're going to make mistakes here, well then, we had darn well better make them on the side of caution."

"So you get yourself the most advanced security system for three hundred miles."

"Exactly."

"And you admit only top executives from certified Fortune 500 companies."

"Yes."

"And you set up your Righteousness Hall of Fame for generals and general managers and general authorities."

Hunsaker stared blankly.

"What about the people?" Damon translated, but there was still no answer. "Doesn't any of this strike anyone as just a little bit elitist?"

Harriman Hunsaker let go of Damon's shoulder and stepped around him to an empty chair. Easing carefully down, he turned the chair slightly toward Damon, and then, placing his hands firmly at the end of each armrest, brought his great head up slowly to look Damon Boulder directly in the eye.

"Of course it does," he said, "I'm just absolutely stunned, Brother Boulder, at how alike we think, you and I. Those were almost my very words. Isn't that right, brethren?"

"Why, yes . . . yes, they were," confirmed Stan Picker.

"Almost exactly," said Mason Sorenson.

"Elitist!" repeated Harriman Hunsaker thoughtfully. "And what about the people? Why, there must be thousands of them. Tens of thousands. Ordinary people living extraordinary lives of quiet inspiration. How do we, vulnerable as we are and with limited resources, how do we include, how do we acknowledge and honor all those good and righteous ordinary people? And, do you know, I was stumped. Yes, I was. And discouraged. And almost ready to concede defeat, and then just when it seemed hopeless, Brother Walt Dwyer over here, good Brother Walt who is so quiet and so inspired and so tuned in to the spirit, Brother Walt called me up and solved the whole thing."

Damon looked over Hunsaker's shoulder at the smallish man at the end of the table, who, in fact, had spoken only two words since their introduction, which now seemed hours past. He seemed an unlikely oracle, but his TV Guide inserts and his cassettes were famous.

"Walt," Hunsaker prodded, "tell him."

Dwyer's face took on an obliging air. "Direct mail!" he announced softly. His voice was boyishly ethereal. "Direct mail is the answer! We can't bring everybody here. Brother Hawkes says it's a security risk. It's certainly inefficient. And just like you said, Brother Boulder, it's kind of arrogant, isn't it, to expect everyone to come here? Not everyone has the time off or the money. No, the secure and effective and really fair way is the ancient way of old, the scriptural way. Go ye out into all the world."

"Mark 16:15," said Harriman Hunsaker involuntarily.

"Mormon 9:22," added Stan Picker.

"D&C 84:62," concluded Dwyer in a tone and cadence of confirmed enlightenment. " 'And unto whatsoever place ye cannot go ye shall send,' that's what it says, Brother Boulder, that's the secret. 'Send.' Plain as home-made bread. We have the product, we know the market, and we use the latter-day technologies raised up for that very purpose. Direct mail. It's the right approach, and it's right there in the scriptures."

Hunsaker, whose eyes had never left Damon, reached over now and took hold of his sleeve. "The Freedom's Holy Light Foundation Righteousness Hall of Fame," he paused for breath, "is going to be a Hall of Fame without walls, Damon. Do you understand? Big as all outdoors, big as the postal system."

Damon tried unobtrusively and unsuccessfully to free himself. "And just where are you going to hang your brass plaques?"

Hunsaker reddened with enthusiasm. "Now there is an intelligent question. Did you hear it, brethren, a very important question. Walt, tell Damon where we're going to hang our plaques."

Walt Dwyer reached silently down to the floor beside him and drew a dark grey attaché case up onto the table. In pregnant silence he opened it and carefully and ceremoniously drew from within a small rectangular plate. "We'll hang them right here," he said modestly and then handed the plate to Harriman Hunsaker, who in turn handed it over to Damon. Damon squinted at the small piece of plastic and drew it up toward his glasses. There amid miniature columns and crenelations in ornamental relief he read his own name, "DAMON BOULDER, Ph.D.," in tiny raised letters.

"What is it?"

"It's a scale reproduction." There was just a shade of pride in Dwyer's hushed voice. "Actually, it's an exact, color-monitored, caligramerged supraduction of an original from Cooperstown. Altered, naturally, for text and religious imagery. And, of course, you recognize the name." Dwyer paused and everyone grinned. "But details are precisely to scale. The injection mold is computer-driven. It's designed for full, fully personalized production."

Damon sat squinting for a moment, his mouth half open. He turned the red-gold rectangle over in his hand and then turned it back again. "And you're going to send these things out to people?" he asked slowly.

"Of course not," Hunsaker was still glowing. "When someone's been officially inducted, we'll hang his plaque right here in the Hall of Fame where it belongs."

"That plaque you're holding," Stan Picker broke in, "is exactly three by five inches. Now, we need a little space around it for hanging, but we figure that the smallest wall—that's 8 by 12 foot—in any of the smaller rooms on the second floor will comfortably handle 718 plaques. Most of the interior walls, the dividers, are 16 feet deep and only about a third of them have doors. That's 958 plaques without and 801 with. Twenty rooms, two sides, adjusting for the windows at the ends of the building, comes to 26,504, and when you add the room ends, adjusted again, it's 38,414. Mind you, I'm still not even taking the two conference rooms into account, or the hallway which is nearly 140 feet, double-sided, minus the doors and the stairwell, of course, or the vestibule by the elevator. And if you start to think moveable partitions in the rooms, believe me, the numbers'll climb right off your calculator." Stan paused for a response, but Damon only blinked like a rabbit transfixed by oncoming headlights. "Remember, we're talking strictly second floor here. The whole first floor is completely reserved for full-size, full-service inductees from the training seminars."

"Oh," said Damon, heading off another awkward pause, "I see."

"Right!" confirmed Harriman Hunsaker. "Damon's beginning to see the scope of this thing. Thirty-eight thousand. Just for starters. That's not exactly elitist, is it, brother? Every plaque mounted right here at the Hall of Fame, every induction certified, and every inductee honored in the comfort and security of his own righteous home." He turned to Walt Dwyer and held out a hand, into which the spiritually attuned public relations and marketing specialist placed a large glossy folder drawn from the grey attaché case. Hunsaker laid it in front of Damon and opened the authentic Williamsburg cover to reveal a large color photograph. "Damon Boulder, Ph.D." There was his name again in bold Roman letters across a heavy brass plaque mounted on a white wall.

"A Standard for the People and an Ensign to the Nations," read the next line. Damon looked again. It had been too small to decipher on the plate still in his hand. "Inducted on this day . . ." the date was the current one ". . . for valiant service as a scholar and a teacher and a champion in the cause of American freedom and righteousness." There was more, but Damon looked up from the folder with one eye narrowed in psychic pain.

"Looks real, doesn't it?" Walt Dwyer was asking with anticipatory enthusiasm.

"Yes," Damon conceded and opened his eye again.

"Looks like brass?"

"Brass," confirmed Damon.

Dwyer paused and looked knowingly at the others around the table. "It's a blow-up," he said confidingly. "Very high resolution. No air brushing. It's all mechanical. Absolute cutting edge technology."

"And what about this?" Damon pointed to the unmistakable fronds of a Boston fern clearly visible in the right foreground of the photograph.

Walt Dwyer smiled. "Standard double exposure," he said, "N. B. D."

Damon looked perplexed.

"No Big Deal," interpreted Stan Picker. "But you're right. It's a nice touch." He picked up where Walt Dwyer had left off. "Now, that's an eleven-by-fourteen glossy. Ready for framing. Look inside the back cover, and you'll find two eight-by-tens snapped in there." Damon opened the back cover. "Great family gifts. We thought about pre-framing, but it bumps the price up, and shipping's a hassle. Take a look at the whole package."

Damon leafed through the pages that separated the snap-in, ready-for-framing photographs inside the front and back covers. They began with a certificate of award to the inductee which included, across the bottom, the names of those who had made the nomination. In his case the list began with Ernie Block and appeared to include all the men at the table. There followed several pages in full-color praise of the "Freedom's Holy Light Foundation Righteousness Hall of Fame" and its programs and featuring aerial photographs of the Foundation buildings around the quadrangle, a close-up of the genuine Williamsburg brass detail on the lampposts, portraits of the Founding Fathers, of J. Edgar Hoover, of Paul Harvey, and of a grinning B. Harriman Hunsaker. There was also a page devoted to the blue-ribbon panel with pictures of churchmen and business magnates, sports heroes in uniform, a television announcer, a successful inspirational novelist at his typewriter, tie loosened and white sleeves rolled up, chewing thoughtfully at the temple of his glasses, and two beamingly interchangeable former Mrs. Americas. On almost every page were highlighted passages from scripture together with excerpts from the Constitution and, near the end, the entire text of the Declaration of Independence. Hunsaker's portrait was on the facing page. The final three pages were perforated tear-out sheets, the first two being pre-printed, pre-personalized press releases for the inductee's local newspapers and bearing "Director of Media Relations" Walt Dwyer's facsimile signature in royal blue ink. The last tear-out was a numbered form for the inductee's own nominations to the Hall of Fame with instructions for documenting his selections and with space on the back for listing the names and addresses of additional references. A pre-addressed, all-postage-paid envelope was attached.

"The whole basic package goes for just $39.95," Picker continued. "There are add-ons, of course, but conceptually we're going for the little guy, the really broad market. Like Walt says: D&C 84:62. There's a field here totally white and totally ready to harvest. Believe me. Just take 'honor thy father and mother,' for instance. I mean, birthdays. The father who has everything. Right? And anniversaries."

"We do a discount for couples," added Ned.

"And a group plan."

"Churches, clubs, family organizations." The wizard of real estate filled in the options.

"We're working on a group program called 'The Reciprocation in Righteousness Nominating Plan.' "

"We charter the organization with regular dues, and we give them a nominating quota."

"But initially we just go with quality mailing lists."

"Direct mail. Let the customers identify themselves."

"Then we network."

"Then television with operators standing by."

"The possibilities are tremendous!"

"Incredible!"

"But what," Damon's voice was testy and accusatory, "has any of this got to do with me?" He almost stood up.

The visionary enthusiasm surging round the room drew up short, and attention gathered itself awkwardly toward the locus of dissent.

"Why, you're our scholar, Damon." Hunsaker, looking perplexed, invoked the obvious. "You would research . . . and teach."

"Teach what?"

"Why, the theo-empirical foundations, of course. The red meat and potatoes of revealed religion."

"To executives?"

"We discussed that."

"Fortune 500 executives?"

The president nodded.

"For profit?"

Hunsaker raised his eyebrows.

"Or not for profit then," Damon corrected, "a very profitably not-for-profit business-school of the prophets, right?"

Hunsaker was obviously turning Damon's phrase over carefully in his mind. "Perhaps that's not an altogether unfortunate way of putting it," he offered cautiously. "You just may have something there."

"Yes, I'm afraid I have. Sorry, gentlemen, but I'm not interested. I've no doubt you've got this thing all worked out. You may know your market and your product and your technology. But obviously you don't know me very well. I'm a scholar. A serious scholar. Not a huckster. And I am certainly not about to be trotted out for show and tell. I'm afraid you'll just have to reap your incredible white harvest without me."

Hunsaker looked grave. But not shocked. Not even particularly surprised. He seemed to be on the edge of something, and his eyes gravitated to Mason Sorenson who sat stone-faced across the table and stared coldly back. Finally, however, the lawyer nodded his head in a gesture of apparent permission.

Hunsaker forged ahead. "Damon, we are a nonprofit organization for research and public education. Such an organization enjoys certain tax advantages vitally necessary to the performance of its mission. You, on the other hand, are a scholar with the background and credentials to assure any interested party about the seriousness of that mission and about our competence to carry it out."

"You mean the IRS," Damon annotated dryly.

"I mean any interested party." Hunsaker was irritated. "It is every bit as true as you yourself admit, Professor Boulder, that your scholarship alone is not likely, not at all likely, to bring in the kind of money needed to support it, and since we are neither practically nor morally in a position to beg for charity, we have chosen here the higher path of self-sufficiency. Our ways may not always be your ways, professor, but your presence here and the presence of others like you is part of a plan for your own salvation. It is that plan, sir, and only that plan, as far as I can see, which will make it possible for you to carry on your important work as it should, indeed, as it must be carried on. We have asked you here out of nothing more or less than sincere respect for your ideals and your work and your good intentions." He paused, and a great sadness filled his eyes. "But, obviously, you are not willing to offer us that same confidence and respect. It's a pity. It's a pity because we have such an incredible missionary opportunity here. Together, we just might have made a difference. I wonder . . . excuse me, but I wonder if your impressive education hasn't made you a snob. It pains me to speak so bluntly, but I think that of all people you are the real elitist here."

Damon felt a little ashamed. In fact, he felt a lot ashamed, though he suspected, not very obscurely, that it was his shame he was most ashamed of. Hunsaker, meanwhile, saw the vacillation in his face.

"Perhaps we need to give you some time to think about this, Damon. You are not here by accident. I'm certain of that. And I believe you'll yet find it in your scholar's heart to throw your lot in with these good men here, who, though they lack your worldly sophistication, still share in your noblest ambitions. Perhaps . . . " his voice was hushed and intense, and when he paused the silence in the room was enormous, "perhaps we might speak alone for a moment before you go."

At this invitation the other men began to gather papers and fill their briefcases. One by one they excused themselves, shaking Damon's hand with lingering missionary intensity and sincerely admonishing looks. "Think it over, brother." And then they were gone. With the exception, that is, of Mason Sorenson, who still sat at the table, and of Ernie Block, who was Damon's ride.

"Ernie," Hunsaker smiled diplomatically, "could you wait outside for just a moment?"

A little embarrassed and a little disappointed, Ernie left the room, but the inscrutable lawyer remained sphinx-like in his place while Damon and President Hunsaker began their talk alone.

"Let's be practical for a minute, can we? The truth is that with you or without you there will be scholars here," Hunsaker's tone was matter-of-fact, "teachers, writers, researchers, men with educations and opinions. My wife has a brother-in-law, in fact, and then Brother Picker knows someone, and Gordon Hawkes has given me an entire list of 'reliable' people."

"I'll bet he has." Damon didn't try to disguise the disdain in his voice.

"Who knows, you might even approve of one or two of them, perhaps, or . . . well . . . well, I thought you'd be the one to show us how to go about finding the right people, but . . . " He looked at Damon over the top of his glasses. "You can't choose up the teams if you don't play the game, now can you? Oh, I suppose," he heaved a sigh of concession, "there is a certain romantic attraction to being a voice in the wilderness. Seems kind of heroic. Adventurous even. But the truth about wilderness is . . . it's damn lonely." Damon, who'd been looking down at the table, looked up. "And it's hell to make a living out there. Oh, but I think you already know about that; don't you, Damon?" Boulder didn't respond, but his face was taut with attention. "You've got to be careful about wilderness. It's a thankless calling. Look," Hunsaker leaned forward and placed a fist on the table, "I'm going to make a confession to you. You see, I know one of the trustees at your college, an old business friend, very good man, very discreet, and I'm going to confess to you, I asked that good friend what the salary range would be down there for a professor of religion." He looked guiltily down for a moment, then resolutely up into Damon's eyes. "I hope you'll forgive me for doing that, brother, but the truth is we were afraid we might just be wasting the time of a man with your background and accomplishments. Oh, I know we shouldn't be so sensitive, but when you have a dream, Brother Boulder," his voice became intense and confessional, "well, you just don't like to . . . to be laughed at."

In spite of himself, Damon protested. He didn't care who knew what he made, and he certainly wasn't going to laugh at anyone.

But Harriman Hunsaker had already raised a lecturer's finger and bobbing it rapidly up and down gave his jaw the set of exhortation.

"I'll tell you this, brother, I was shocked by what I heard. I was stunned! A man devotes himself to scholarship. Earns the highest degrees from the best universities. Dedicates his life to teaching word and precept to our precious young people. And what do we pay him?" He sat for a moment shaking his head sorrowfully, and when he began again his voice was flat and overcast. "It just tells you something fundamental about our society, doesn't it, about what's happened to values in this country. Teachers are the guardians of the very future of this republic, and they might as well be on welfare. Hell, they'd be better off on welfare!" He turned to Damon with apocalypse in his eyes. "Do you have any idea the kind of money a man can make doing absolutely nothing whatsoever at all in this country? Do you?"

Defensive instinct shook Damon's head.

"Well." President Hunsaker straightened up. "Well, forgive me. Forgive my language. Sometimes I get so angry I lose control. I'm ashamed. But that's what this is all about, isn't it, about teaching values and ideals and limits in this marvelous, glorious, deeply endangered country of ours. Of course," he leaned back, "don't think you'd get rich here with us, either. 'Seek ye not for riches.' Real ideals are going to take some sacrifice, Brother Boulder. We're not in this for personal reward, are we? Of course not. But I can tell you this." He made a final cut up field and headed for the goal post. "We still have *some* sense of values around here. We still know enough to know that in the vineyard of the Lord, the laborer is worth his hire. And I think we can do a little better by you than those skinflints down to the college."

Hunsaker reached into his suit coat and drew out a matted silver ballpoint pen with a digital clock and a calendar in the shaft running parallel to the clip. "Goodness, it's after five o'clock. My wife will have my scalp." He took hold of Damon's elbow with his left hand and then reached over with the right to scribble a figure on the yellow legal pad lying on the table in front of Damon's seat. His handwriting was oversize and unequivocal, and when he'd done, he leaned back to let the number penetrate for a moment. Damon sat bolt upright in his comfortable chair. He felt sweat on his back.

"You think on it, Damon. Pray on it. I have a great deal of faith in you, and I sense that this may be one of the most important decisions you'll ever make. Day after tomorrow, you give me a . . . No, by golly. Day after tomorrow you just come right on down to my office in town, and we'll talk details. Maybe even draw us up a plan for a lecture series on the theo-empirical foundations." Damon stared at the paper. "It's time we did something about my education. No one, least of all Harriman Hunsaker, is going to be saved in ignorance. The glory of God is intelligence—Section 93, verse 6—and it's time I got started. It's time we all got started."

In parting, he shook Damon's entire arm again, gripping palm and elbow, and smiling into the very roots of Damon's eyes.

On the way out of the building, Ernie stopped the elevator on the main floor.

"Hey, old buddy, you just got to see this before we leave."

He guided Damon through a louvered door into a bathroom upholstered floor to ceiling in Harris tweed. The mirror frames and the faucets were ebony and antique brass and the fixtures a milky, synthetic alabaster with cirrus plumes of white and gold and tarnish green. When Ernie placed his hand over the handleless faucet, water began to pour from the tap. Then he moved his hand to the left, and as he did, steam rose from the sink. "Hot!" he announced in the thrall of rediscovery, then reversed direction and the steam thinned and disappeared. "And you haven't seen anything yet!" He bounded to the nearest stall and, holding the door wide open, dropped down directly and fully clothed onto the elegant commode. Then, making a California stop, he leaped as quickly to his feet again. And as he did, the deep churning, thrashing sound of mountain waters burst forth from the cabinet behind him like a beer commercial. "No hands, Doc! Really!" He raised his own as evidence. "Absolutely state of the art!"

Damon smiled, and Ernie led him down the hall to an open office at the front of the building. It was indeed as big as a hangar with an entire wall of built-in, honey-oak bookcases and a glass-top desk the size of Ernie's station wagon.

"What did I tell you? Sometimes, old buddy, you gotta believe there's a guiding hand out there. Things come together, and you know this can't be just some accident. Look at this! Only office I've ever seen in my life has as many shelves as Damon Boulder has books. Did you see these?" Ernie opened a sliding panel to reveal another entire complex of drawers and shelving, but Damon wasn't paying attention.

He was standing close behind the desk looking out the window where the sun was setting, and long shadows trailed across the interminable lawn. Groves and tree lines in the distance raised slender, hopeful fingers into the salmon sky, and even the tangle of freeway and developments and industrial parks in the valley far below seemed softened and transfigured. The silence was nearly visible, and Damon Boulder tried hard to concentrate past the smell of genuine leather rising from the high-backed executive chair on which his arm rested, past the weight of the sheet of yellow legal paper, folded twice and then again and tucked carefully into the inside pocket of his jacket, and past the diaphanous evening to a small shrill voice grumbling irascibly on somewhere very deep in the pit of his stomach.

Borrowing Light

Then, the rain fell steadily on glass
grey walks and on the pale fire maple red,
the sodden gold of failing summer's end,
but one was only six, though claiming more,
and one was six feet two in uniform
with ribbons underneath his coat for charming
six-year-olds. In shy solemnitude
they peered beneath the raised lapel. And then
we heard them whoop, and saw them run and whirl
in celebration on the drowning lawn,
for both were six, though one was six feet two
in uniform . . . and older than we knew.

Dear Michael,

You still owe me a letter. Telephone calls don't count. Especially not collect. But I'm writing you anyway and sending you this poem because Sister Something Smith or Smith Something, whom I sort of remember, but you wouldn't remember at all, of course, because you conveniently never remember anybody, came to see me at work. I don't know how she knew where I work. I didn't ask. In fact, I didn't think about it at all until just now writing. But she was actually very nice, and she asked about you and about Allison, and she gave me this poem. It's from mom. I think it's about uncle Hank, and about you. Mom sent it to the Ensign, or whatever they called it then, in 1969, and Sister Smith something was an editor. She says she liked it a lot. And she recommended it, but they wouldn't use it in the magazine because it wasn't uplifting, and they were paranoid back then—that's not the word she said, but it's the one she meant—about discouraging anybody or sounding disloyal. So they didn't use it, and they sent it back, but she knew mama from school, so she asked her if she could keep her copy, and mama said okay.

I think it's beautiful. But it makes me sad. The Ensign or whatever they called it was right. It isn't uplifting. It's like everything about mama now. Maybe it's good there are so few things left. All the hours she spent at the end of the hall writing, and sometimes I wonder if she tore it all up or burned it at night when we were asleep or just threw it away, because she knew it was sad, and she didn't want us to have to read it someday and go through it all too.

Allison told me that mom and daddy used to fight about Hank. He'd say she wasn't grateful and didn't understand anything, and mama would say he was right; she wasn't and she didn't, and she didn't care. To be honest, I can't imagine her talking back to him like that, but I was pretty young, and maybe I just can't imagine me or Allison or anyone else, except you, of course, talking back to my father. I wanted to ask about Uncle Hank—we never talked about him—and even about the fights and what mama was supposed to understand, but I couldn't get up the nerve. He gets so angry, and you don't know what's going to set him off. But there's no one else to ask, is there? You were only six. And Allison and I never knew anything anyway. So I pulled myself together and tried it. I guess it wasn't so bad.

He was in the den watching the elections, and I took the poem in and sat on the end of the couch and just handed it to him. He looked at it and started to read with one eye on the paper and the other on David Brinkley, but then he kind of stopped and started over again and really read it and stared at it for a while. He actually took the clicker thing and turned off the TV. He seemed kind of upset and asked me where I'd got it. When I told him that Sister Smith Something gave it to me, I think he was relieved. I don't know why, and I know that doesn't make any sense, and I'm probably wrong, but I think he was deeply relieved. He told me it was probably about uncle Hank from the Vietnam war. Uncle Hank came home on furlough the last time in the Fall of '68. He remembered it rained a lot. I said I'd thought that's what it was, and he agreed I was probably right, and then we just sat there and stared at one another as if that's all there was to say. I waited for him to pick up the clicker thing and for David Brinkley to take over again. But it didn't happen.

"Your uncle was a very brave man. He did what had to be done." It sounded so standard, so predictable. I'd never, ever heard him really talk about his brother, but when he did, it was like I'd heard it hundreds of times before, always exactly the same, and somehow I couldn't just sit there and nod and say "yes, sir" one more time. So I didn't. I looked the other way and told him I'd always thought that his brother's dying was a complete waste because no one I knew thought the Vietnam war was even worth fighting. I can't believe even now that I said it. And the truth is I didn't exactly say it that way. I mean I didn't say "complete" waste. I'm not even sure I said "waste." I had to repeat myself a couple of times. But he got the point because the air between us was like at dinner after her funeral. You remember, I know. We all remember. And he looked at me in the cornered way he looked at everybody then, and I felt as sorry as then, and as angry and as terrified. Where is David Brinkley when you need him? But the world didn't end. He didn't even yell.

He just looked cornered and really tired, and when he talked, he said something which, because I don't know how to take it, or even if I really disagree with it, or know how to disagree with it, I'm writing to tell you. This may take a while, but you're so smart—and not just in your own humble estimation—and so independent, and you always have an answer for dad, which I never do, and so I'll leave it to you to have the answer this time too.

He said that he knew what people said about the war, and that from where we are now Hank's life did seem wasted, but where we are now is lost. We don't believe in who we are any more or what we stand for or where we're going. And no matter who you are or what you have, when you don't believe in it, you're right.

I argued. I said I believed in who I was, but you can't push those things on other people, and you can't destroy people's lives and country for your own personal idea of what's right. He just smiled a kind of bitter smile and asked me why not. He said there are plenty of people in the world already paying out endless innocent lives for a lie. Why should it be so wrong to sacrifice not just yourself but your brother as well or even a million perfect strangers for the truth. Unless the truth doesn't matter. Unless it's a joke.

I said what was true for me might not be true for someone else. And he laughed and said if a decent person couldn't decide that some things are worth sacrificing even other people's lives for then I was probably right. Truth was probably just the name that everyone gives the particular lies they tell themselves.

That wasn't what I'd said. He was putting words in my mouth, but when he asked me what else my kind of truth could mean, I didn't know. I couldn't explain. I just kept repeating myself. He had me trapped. He knew it, and I knew it. But then he turned around and conceded my point anyway. Maybe I was right. Maybe there is no truth for everybody. Maybe two and two have a right to be three or nine or sixteen or anything anybody sincerely wants them to be. But if that's true, if the truth is that there is no truth, and we've all been liars all along, then the problem for us is we've become very poor ones now, and sooner or later bad liars have to get out of the way of liars who still have the courage of their convictions. He said "convictions," but I've been thinking about it (I've even written it all down), and what he really meant was "delusions," wasn't it? "The courage of their delusions." It was all there, Michael, all thought through and worked out, just waiting like a trap for me to ask him, so he could lay it all out for me: what I was really thinking and not thinking, what it really meant, and where it would all lead. And I can hardly believe how terribly close to terribly cynical my upright, patriotic, God-fearing, establishment father has come. How close to thinking his brother died a better death because he died a bigger fool. All of a sudden, I want to go downstairs and shout at him that I was wrong and he's wrong. I want to argue. But I can't. I can't find the arguments. I feel them. But I can't find them.

I asked him how mother felt. You couldn't tell from the poem exactly. It was sad, but not really bitter. He looked at it again and read it and shrugged and said that, in fact, she was bitter. There'd probably been other poems, and she'd argued with him more than once. Picked a fight, even. He was honest about that, at least. Although who knows who picked the fights. He said she always felt strongly about things, but didn't really understand them; in fact, he sometimes thought she felt absolutely everything, took everything personally, but understood nothing at all. She wouldn't let him explain things. Wouldn't let him in. For the first time, I think, he was trying to explain to me and to apologize. I really think he was, but didn't exactly know how, and I didn't know how to let him. He said he liked the poem, but when I offered to make him a copy, he just shrugged. He didn't really appreciate poetry, anyway. We all knew it. He never got past John Wayne movies and happy endings. When I got up to leave, he got up too. He kissed me. For the first time since . . . I suppose since the last time I let him.

I went upstairs, but first I stood in the dining room for a long time and watched him. He'd turned on the elections again. He sat on the couch and looked at the TV, and I don't know, but I think he was crying, or maybe I would just like to think he was crying. Maybe I fantasized it. I remember mother so clearly. I remember her so pretty and so nervous, doing our hair on Sundays and upset because we were late. I remember French toast and the brown pumps with the white sidewalls and the open study and the locked bedroom door and the tears and tears and mysterious, interminable tears. I remember it all, but I don't remember mama. I never knew her.

You don't know anyone until you're in junior high, and then only girlfriends. No one I know ever really knew her mother until she was married herself and mad at her husband and kids. But I wish I'd known mama. I wish I'd sat on her bed and told her secrets you could never tell your mother. I wish one of us, even poor daddy, had known her soon enough and well enough to stop her. But she was too old, too. Or too big a fool. Sometimes I cry in front of the television.

I hope you like the poem. I think it's beautiful. But I would probably think it was beautiful even if it was shit. What do I know? My father never got past westerns with happy endings. At least you knew uncle Hank. At least you got to yell at him and chase him around on the lawn. You saw inside his coat. And got all out of breath with him and muddy and rained on. Boys do stupid stuff. Boys get all the breaks.

I went to church last Sunday for the first time in two years. Not here. A ward across town where nobody knows who I am. I kind of liked it. No one fawning, or pumping your hand, or whispering on the other side of the chapel. It was all very straightforward. The teenage boys stared. No one else even noticed I was there. Please write again soon. And don't be so cynical. Maybe you can tell. I can be cynical now all by myself.

Love,
your little sister

Whole Life Premiums

When Harold Potter turned sixty-five, he sold Fairweather Hardware, which he had purchased from Newell Fairweather in 1953. He sold it to a national chain at an exponential return on investment. He also sold the family home, a salmon-colored, brick ranch with two additions, a flagstone barbecue, and a vinyl-sided aluminum tool shed on a full three-quarters of an acre of bluegrass and fruit trees. The buyer, an orthodontist with six children and an unabated gleam in his eye, paid Harold's asking price without a quibble. Harold, in turn, bought a two-bedroom condo on the edge of the newly redeveloped Mayfield Country Club. He didn't play golf. Nor did he intend to, but the management kept up sixteen acres of trimmed and tree-shaded lawn directly outside his new back door while the garage door—measured by the odometer in his Oldsmobile Cutlass—was a mere 2.7 actual miles from the house in which for twenty-two years he had raised his family and his standard of living. He would shop at the same Pick 'n Pay, eat lunch at the same Dairy Queen, and, most importantly, go to church in the same chapel he had attended for well over two decades.

Harold was a practical man of disciplined habits who, before he moved, resolutely conducted a "garage" sale on the front lawn of his old home. There were bunk beds and boxing gloves, plant stands and tennis rackets, broken baby walkers, collapsible flannel boards, four-by-eight-foot sheets of marine plywood, gas masks, an entrenching tool, bales of peat moss, hundred-pound bags of soy meal, institutional-size cans of date crystals, yeast, and powdered potatoes, a wheat grinder, a completely unmolested exercise machine, skis for every season and element, and appliances, familiar and exotic, operable and nearly operable. And whatever there was, he sold . . . to neighbors, to wily second-hand dealers, to brazen-elbowed bargain addicts, and to entirely unsuspecting passers-by. He closed it out . . . all of it . . . right down to the inevitable flotsam of paperbacks and paper dolls, 45-rpm records, unmatched galoshes, tole-painted tie racks, ornamental grape clusters, and recession glass that gave his post-sale lawn the look of stadium seating after a rock concert. When he had swept this residue into three-ply, thirty-gallon bags and deposited it, twisted and tied, on the curb, he called—as had been stipulated in the sales contract—for the hardware store delivery truck to come and remove the remaining essentials together with certain valuables to his new home on "On The Greene."

This divestiture took place in 1977 and coincided directly with the onset of payouts on thirty devout years of whole life premiums. It marked as well the establishment of a "living trust" which was to be the final, practical monument to a life of resolute, shirt-sleeve industry, casting into legal concrete Harold's deep disdain for taxation—even with representation—and his nearly religious abhorrence of the government's stealthy incursion into the American pocket. There were, he knew well enough, freeloaders abroad in the land, and the dangerous thing with freeloaders was an invidious talent for organization that did not come naturally even to the notice of the self-reliant. "Damn 'em," he would say, sometimes even in church, though there only within the cloistered security of the high priests' meeting, "before you even know what's happened, they've got ya so wrapped up in their welfare nets, they'll just strangle ya to death with good works." Then he would shake his head and roll his eyes toward the acoustical-tile ceiling while others nodded or grimaced as time and hard experience had variously instructed them to do.

When all was finally moved and settled, Harold even sold the Oldsmobile Cutlass. It was only two years old, but he let it go at 20 percent off blue book to his son, who, having settled finally into real estate, needed more representative transportation. There was, of course, still his wife's Nova, which would do until he'd decided on a van or four-wheel-drive. He wasn't in any hurry. He would take his time choosing just the right vehicle for fishing and for traveling west to visit his daughters and his grandchildren.

The one remaining item listed on the three-by-five card in his shirt pocket was a trip to the new mall in Beachwood. There he bought flowers for his wife, Sylvia. They were cut flowers, expensively out of season, and since it was neither her birthday nor their anniversary, the gesture might have seemed crazily out of character to anyone who knew Harold Potter merely well. But to someone who knew him well enough to know him as his wife's husband, it was an act of schooled pragmatism.

Sylvia Potter was a deeply rooted woman who on account of the move, and of the sale, and of certain disagreements over the terms "necessary" and "valuable," had not been speaking with her husband much. In Harold's preemptive judgement she dithered and agonized so extraordinarily at the prospect of any of life's inevitable changes that he had long since embraced the entrepreneurial wisdom of dispensing with the agonies of permission to begin instead and more productively with the afterglow of forgiveness. For all her fervent resistance, Sylvia was a forgiver, as generous of heart as of proportion and as adaptable in retrospect as she was inflexible toward the future.

The flowers predictably undid her. She hugged her discomfited husband who, even in private, shied at being embraced with the light on. She made him a dinner his doctor would have forbidden him, and after the dishes, when the rates went down, called her oldest daughter in California to describe the special greenhouse window, the step-in utility closet, and the coordinated wallpapers in the new home.

In the morning Harold, who rose early to attend to his bladder and his prostate anxieties, sat alone with a bowl of Grape Nuts at the old dinette in his brand-new kitchen and checked the last item off his list. Then he drew out a fresh three-by-five card and began a new one. Sprinklers chattered in slow-arcing circles on the fairway outside.

"A smart man knows when it's time to hang it up," he thought, "and he's ready. He doesn't piddle around wondering what he wants to do, or what he ought to do, or how in the hell he's going to pay for it. A man who knows what he's doing, knows when he's done." He put "transportation" at the head of his list and mapped out a decision path: passenger van or off-road, eight cylinders or six, standard or automatic, purchase or lease, domestic or foreign. He penciled in question marks above the last items in each of the last two categories, but left them there for the sake of symmetry. Next he planned an itinerary. He would begin with the GM dealer and the A.M.C./Jeep outfit on the far west side. Then he would catch lunch with Rolley Boone at the DQ. And in the afternoon he could go to the big Dodge dealership in Pinell. He planned Ford for the next day, the Bronco and the E-150 conversion, and, as an afterthought, got the phone book and wrote down the address of one of the foreign dealers, the German one, not the Japanese. Then on a new card he wrote LIBRARY in large letters. He put his empty cereal bowl in the sink, found the red-and-white nylon-mesh summer cap from Snap-On Tool, yelled goodbye up the stairs, and set out.

At the end of three days, he'd combed over five different dealerships, engaged and frustrated as many salesmen, talked casually but pointedly with a dozen service mechanics, written out post-interview notes, and gathered enough sales literature and initialed price quotes to half-fill the rectangular plastic dish tub next to him on the seat of the Nova. At home he spread it all out on the floor of the den, first by manufacturer, and then he broke it down into subcategories for evaluation. On Friday he went to the library with seven pages of cross-referenced notes in a spiral notebook. The lady at the desk showed him where to find the back issues of *Road and Track* and of *Car and Driver*. For reports that were older than six months, she had to show him how to use the microfilm machine, but after he got the knack of it, it went almost as fast.

When he was finished, he went back to the reference desk again because a young fellow in wire-rimmed glasses with whom he'd struck up a conversation had told him that one of those magazines —he lost track of which—was in the pocket of the American car makers, while the other was paid off by the imports. If you wanted the straight, unbiased poop, you had to go through the *Consumer Reports*. Harold did.

After he had worked through the last issue and extracted the last report, he gathered his work systematically around him. Assigning numerical values to all non-numerical assessments, he carefully reduced his seven pages of field notes, plus his new pages of library notes, to a single sheet of comparative, bottom-line tables. Then he surveyed his work with a sabbath-like sense of closure. Mission accomplished. Clip and clear and complete. It was good work. He would take it home and show it to Sylvia over supper. The answer fairly leaped off the page at you. Even she would easily see in those figures what the final family vehicle must be.

He pulled into the garage five minutes before suppertime, but instead of going in, went back outside and around front to see if the management had planted the shrubs delivered the day before and set out according to his explicit directions. They were in all right. Not exactly where he had marked them, but in. And at least the maintenance people had cleaned up after themselves. He opened the door. But Harold Potter did not step inside. In fact, he stepped backward. Then he looked to the side. Then back again. He must be at the wrong unit. There were children all over the floor, two large boys crawling at high speed and chasing one another round and round a coffee table while a smaller child, a girl, crouched on the table and pivoted on her knees, following the chase and shrieking.

The coffee table seemed to be his, but seconds passed before he recognized the children and nearly a minute before anybody noticed him.

"Grandpa!" The chorus was deafening, and the children ran toward him, but stopped a little way distant.

"What are you doing here?" he demanded in a tone far more astonished than grandfatherly.

"We flew!"

"We came to visit!"

"Grandpa, can we go to Sea World?"

"Mom said, if you said . . . "

In the middle of the clamor, a bedroom door opened, and his wife with his oldest daughter in tow appeared on the landing at the head of the little stairway.

He stared at them with his mouth open.

"She came to see the new house, dear."

"We wanted to surprise you, Daddy."

He took his cap off. The skylight over the landing made it easy to see that her face was swollen and red. "Well, you managed that," he said, "I'm surprised, all right."

"Mom, ask Grandpa if we can go to Sea World."

"Be quiet. We just got here. The kids want to go to Sea World, Daddy. I kind of promised them. If it's okay?"

Harold shrugged, and the children cheered, and his wife and daughter came down the stairs into the living room. She hugged her father, but without really looking at him, and then she hurried off in another direction.

"Mom showed me the upstairs. It's wonderful, and I love the skylight. But I haven't seen the kitchen yet. This is it over here, isn't it?"

As they all followed her into the kitchen, he looked at his wife with a question mark in the folds on his forehead, but she only frowned back and shook her head and waved him off. The question would have to wait.

In the kitchen they admired the greenhouse window, and tried out the microwave, and then, one at a time, walked in and out of the walk-in utility closet.

"And this is your den?"

The children, who had followed them back across the living room, crowded in and stood on the piles of notes and literature carefully sorted out on the floor.

"This," he said slowly, watching the children mill and shuffle, "is the God-forbid room."

"The what?"

"Now, Harold," his wife scolded.

"The God-forbid room. When you're my age, real estate salesmen say 'Well, of course, this is a den, but God forbid anyone should get sick or fall down and break something and can't use the stairs. God forbid, of course, but think about it. A room on the first floor.' "

"Daddy!" his daughter protested.

"No, it's a real selling point." He smiled a grim and irritably artificial smile and ushered his grandchildren off of his work and out of the room.

"Oh, look what you've done, kids!" The reprimand was as effective as it was timely.

It was after six, and there was not enough food in the house to feed so many for dinner, so Harold went to the Kentucky Fried, and his grandsons went along for the ride and "to help." They fought over the front seat. He made them both ride in the back.

At dinner around the crowded dinette, Harold relaxed a little. It was not unlike like old times with all the children at home. He told about his research, about the whopping lies car salesmen tell, and explained how you get a wary young mechanic to tell what he really knows without asking him outright. Then he went to the den and got the yellow sheet with his results.

"Pass this to your grandmother, son," he said, seating himself again. He assumed, of course, that his daughter would look it over too before she passed it on.

But before she could, the youngest reaching to take it and pass it along, tipped over her milk and burst into tears. Her mother rolled her eyes and pulled herself to her feet. It had been a long, exhausting day. Quickly she mopped up the table and hurried off to run a bath, so that they could get the children to bed. Sylvia rushed off too to find towels and sheets and pillowcases. When he got his document back, wrinkled and unread, it had escaped the milk, but was spotted nonetheless and translucent with Kentucky Fried fingerprints. He sat in the den recopying it and reconfirming the figures. Then he watched the news on television until the house grew quiet.

When he re-emerged, the boys were asleep on the hide-a-bed in the living room, and his wife was just shutting down the kitchen and turning out the light.

"Where is she?"

His daughter had gone to bed with her daughter in the spare bedroom. She too was exhausted.

"All right?" he said, looking expectantly at Sylvia.

"Shhhh." She put her finger to her lips.

"All right?" he demanded again, when the bedroom door was closed behind them. "Why is she here?"

Sylvia Potter drew in a deep breath and then let it out again.

"She and Gerald are having problems."

"Problems?" He knit his forehead and glared at her. "What kind of problems?"

"Well, I'm not sure. It seems to have to do with money and with . . . well, marital things." Harold looked quickly away. "Gerry's not being very reasonable, I'm afraid."

"Oh?" he said. His tone demanded to know more.

"She says he's impossible." She looked away, too. "She's talking about divorce."

"We don't get divorced in this family!" He raised his voice. She raised her finger to her lips again. "Shhh. She'll hear you."

"She was married in Salt Lake City . . . " he laid it out for her in case she'd missed the point, " . . . in the temple."

"I know that. I was there, which you were not!" Sylvia Potter was still whispering, but there was irritation in her whisper now and an old reproach. "She may have been married in the temple, but right now she's in your spare bedroom, and she's talking about divorce!"

He sat on the edge of the bed, staring at the shoes on his feet which he had sat down to take off. "Well, what does she think she's going to do? Live here?"

"I don't know," his wife shot back, "but we're her family. Where else would she go?"

He had no answer. He didn't sleep well, nor did Sylvia, and in the morning she said, "Just a few days. That's what they need. To calm down and think things through, and then he'll call or she will, and we'll put them all on a plane again."

He listened.

"Young people have a lot of pressure. They need a rest from each other. She hasn't been home in three years. And Gerry works too much. She says he's been working Sundays. She hardly sees him."

"A man can't just work when he wants to!"

"That's what I'm saying, Harold!" Her voice echoed the exasperation in his own. "He has his career. And she has the children all day, and these things just get out of hand, that's all. Sometimes people need a crisis."

"A what?"

"A crisis, dear, a shock. Sometimes it's the best thing to make them think things through and decide what really matters."

"What matters is taking care of things that need taking care of when and where they need it. That's what matters."

"Well, I do think they ought to go see the bishop or a counselor. I think you should tell her that. And I think you should tell Gerry when he calls."

"You know what I think?" He looked at Sylvia as if it were her fault. "If she's having problems with her husband, I think she's in the wrong place. He lives in California."

"Harold!" There was exasperation but no surprise in her voice.

It was Sunday, and they took their grandchildren to church to be admired by Sylvia's friends.

"They've gotten so big."

"It's only a short visit. She needed a break. She tries to do everything herself, and she's so exhausted, poor thing, I told her to stay home this morning. They are big, aren't they. We haven't seen them for ages."

In the afternoon they called their son and his family to come over and celebrate the surprise visit. On Monday Sylvia took everyone shopping, and Harold went off to look into transportation again. He spent the entire day looking over a Japanese "Land Cruiser" which he hadn't liked before he ever saw it, and liked even less after driving it, poking through the engine and the tool kit, talking to two separate mechanics, and, finally, discouraging the irritatingly good-humored salesman. When he got home, he found the living room boiling again with children and his daughter as red-eyed and as forcibly and fragilely cheerful as on the night of her arrival. Sylvia seemed near tears as well.

In the kitchen near the telephone, there was a note for him to make two calls, one to his son, and another to Zink Putnam. Zink had worked for Harold for fourteen years, and now he was the assistant manager at the store, the transition man. Dinner was on the table, but afterward, he went into the den. He called his son first.

"Dad."

"Yes."

"I need to talk to you."

"Your mom gave me your message."

"Dad?"

"Yes."

"I should have called sooner. I was going to say something last night, but . . . I mean, well, it was a celebration."

"What is it, son?"

"I really don't how to tell you this . . . "

What he didn't know how to tell his father was that the real estate business into which he had finally settled was itself sinking and near collapse. The strip center the company had developed and promoted was floundering in disputes with contractors and the zoning board. Investors had exhausted their patience.

"They're suing, dad."

"Suing?"

"For non-performance and . . . "

"And what?"

"And for fraud."

There was a very long silence.

"How much?" Harold asked grimly after his son assured him that this was not just some mistake nor, unfortunately, all that simple.

"$146,000."

Harold's mind whistled out loud, but he kept his mouth under control.

"Will they settle?"

"Yes, I think so."

"Well?"

"My part would be . . . at least . . . $38,000." He pronounced the figure in a fading whisper, and his father had to make him repeat it.

"Do you have it?"

"Dad, I don't have a nickel. I can't pay you what I still owe you on the Cutlass. Right now, I don't even know where my next mortgage payment is coming from."

After he'd hung up, Harold sat for a long while in front of the piles of transportation research he had re-sorted and re-organized in the wake of his refugee grandchildren. Then he went up to bed to lie awake another night next to his wife and to think.

He had promised on the following day to take his grandchildren to Sea World, and he did. He got up early and got gas in the Nova and coupons for discount tickets from the Pick 'n Pay. He brought home food for a picnic. Prices at the concessions were always open robbery. He took a brochure his wife had saved from the junk mail and sat and studied it while everyone else finished breakfast. He put other things out of his mind.

The children had to crowd into the back seat, but he warned them that if they fought, he'd turn the car around and take them straight back home. His daughter sat pre-emptively in the middle. Her youngest sat on her lap. It was a clear, hot day, and the humidity soared ahead of the temperature. By noon, tired and sunburned, he returned with his grandsons to the Killer Whale show, which they had seen once already. The women had gone on to see penguins, but the churning blue water made the air seem cooler at the whale show, and the great flying sea monsters fascinated Harold. After lunch he guided the boys back again to talk to one of the young ladies who smiled and answered questions and kept people from feeding popcorn or plastic O-rings to the denizens in the holding tanks out behind the exhibit.

"How do you get an animal that size all the way from the ocean to this little pond in a cow pasture? He sure didn't swim here."

"No," the smiling girl conceded.

"Can't fly."

"No."

"Well, then, they must come disassembled with Japanese instructions for putting 'em together."

She laughed. "No."

"You got a swimming pool on wheels?"

She laughed again.

He tried to imagine an eighteen-wheeler converted into a giant bath tub hauling down the interstate with those huge fish doing loop-the-loops behind the sleeper. He tried, but it was beyond conception. One flick of a monster tail would send the whole shebang pouring all over the highway.

"How do you do it?"

The magic, once discovered, did not strike Harold Potter as magical. As best he could figure out from what she said, they drugged the whales to keep them quiet, loaded them into a semi, braced them, and covered them with wet pads or blankets to keep them from drying out. Then they hauled them overland in a big hurry. It was easier, if no less bizarre and somehow also unsavory, to imagine those enormous creatures trussed up and doped like kidnap victims, speeding through the night five hundred miles from salt water in a kind of giant, predatory marine ambulance.

The whale show was marvelous. Clearly, this was all very good business. Harold was no sentimental, Sierra Club kook. But it bothered him a little all the same.

The afternoon lingered like a hot soup lunch in August. And by the time the children had seen the last show a last time, climbed over and through the last playground contraption, stained the last front with the last begged-for snow cone or bomb pop, they were nearly as exhausted as their keepers. On the way back the boys fought despite their mother's desperate attempts to stop them. Harold, however, had no place to turn around and go straight back to. When he pulled up at home, they were asleep.

At supper no one ate. When the youngest spilled her milk and burst into tears again, her mother burst into tears too. Sylvia shepherded them both off to bed, and the boys wandered out to the living room and fell asleep sprawled over the sofa fully dressed and black with dirt. When his wife came downstairs again, Harold helped her wake them and herd them toward the bathroom. Together, they opened the hide-a-bed and turned it down, brushing out the dirty socks and the graham-cracker crumbs. The boys left their shorts and shirts and underwear in a wet pile on the floor of the bathroom. There was a pile of laundry at the foot of the stairs in the living room as well and another across from the utility closet in the kitchen. Sylvia put away food and put cups and knives and Tupperware bowls into the dishwasher while Harold brought things in from the car. They didn't speak.

"How long," he asked when she finally followed him into the bedroom, "is this supposed to go on?"

She ignored him.

"It looks like a damn laundromat around here. You can't even sit down and somebody's sleeping under you. This is not a motel."

"Well," his wife turned on him, angry, "if you hadn't sold my house."

"Your house? Oh, I love that! Now, it was your house. Well, why don't you tell me just how many mortgage payments *you* made on that house? Why don't you just tell me that?"

Sylvia didn't back down. "She is my daughter. And she has every right in the world to be in my house. I do live here, don't I? Or do I have to show you a utility bill with my name on it?"

"She's just like that damn whale back there. That's what she is. You haul a poor dumb animal a thousand miles to do what it could do a thousand times better at home. Why isn't she home, her own home where she ought to be working this thing out. What good does it do her to sit around here and bellow and blubber at our four walls?"

Sylvia didn't answer, and he could see in her eyes and white face that there was trouble. He turned to find his daughter standing stiffly in the hall just outside the open door.

"Well," he set his jaw, "maybe it's time I said it to you. If you're having trouble with Gerry, why in the world are you here instead of there with him, working it out?" She just stared. "You don't run away from problems. I thought we taught you better than that. You face them." He tried to soften his voice. "Now, don't you think you ought to call him and go home?"

When finally she answered, her voice was calm, almost weary. "He doesn't want me, Daddy. He's not interested! Go ahead. Call him. He's not even there!" Now the tears came. "Would you like me to tell you where he is?" Her voice broke, and she turned and hurried into her bedroom, closing the door behind her. Half an hour later he could hear her sobbing, and after another half hour he got up and went across the hall. He knocked on her door.

"Yes?" she said, wide awake.

He went in and apologized, and then he sat uncomfortably on the edge of her bed and held his grown daughter in his arms in the dark while she cried all over again.

When he got back to his own bed, his wife was waiting.

"How is she?"

"She's okay," he said, and then with resolve, "She's going to be just fine!" He was mumbling as he rolled over on his side to go to sleep.

"What, dear?"

"Nothing!"

"Tell me, Harold!" she insisted, and Harold Potter rolled over in bed again and onto his elbow, glaring at his wife through the darkness.

"I said . . . " he spoke slowly and very deliberately, punctuating each word, and with no attempt to moderate his voice, "I said 'that no good son of a bitch!' Now, is there anything else you'd like to know?"

When she declined, he heaved himself back over onto his side again. But he didn't sleep. He'd forgotten how.

At breakfast Harold and Sylvia Potter sat alone in the kitchen neglecting their Grape Nuts. The children were still asleep. It was too early even for cartoons, so you could hear the chatter of the sprinklers on the fairway. Harold had his yellow transportation balance sheet. He was folding it lengthwise.

"Now what was that you wanted me to read?" asked Sylvia, looking up hopefully from her silence.

"Never mind," he said, "it doesn't matter." He folded the paper again, then tore it in the opposite direction and deposited the halves in the wastebasket under the sink.

Later, he went down to see Zink. He went at lunch time and invited him for a milk shake at the DQ.

"They're letting me go," Zink said as soon as he'd sat down at the table."

"What?"

"They're letting everybody go. They're closing her down." Harold's eyes were wide as half dollars. "The company's decided to build a real big one over by the belt route. If they kept us, they'd just be competing with theirselves."

"That's right," said Rolley Boone, setting his burger and shake down on the table and sliding in behind them. "I heard it this morning. They're going to close the hardware and build out by the beltway."

Harold was in shock.

"Discount?" He finally asked, and the anger in his question announced to all the world that he knew what the answer would be.

"Discount," confirmed Zink.

Harold Potter sat, as was becoming his habit, for a long time in silence. "Newell Fairweather opened that store in 1936. It burned down in '49, and he rebuilt it. I been there day in and out for twenty-four years, through the recession of '58 and the discounts on Mayfield and the . . . " He set his jaw. "And we turned a profit, dammit, met every damn payroll, paid every damn bill, and turned a profit, and now after exactly one month, they're going to close it?"

Zink nodded.

"Jeeesus Christ!"

"What?" Rolley, who had been looking glumly down the street at the hardware and shaking his head, looked up.

"Nothin'." But then Harold Potter raised his finger at his friends. "You work your ass off, and you pay and you pay, and every year they get their hand down deeper in your pocket for the freeloaders and the crooks and the damn politicians, but when an honest working man needs something, where the hell are they then? You just tell me that. Where in hell are they then?" He raised his voice loud enough for everyone in the DQ to hear, but nobody answered. Nobody knew.

Conference Report

"You just watch your tongue, young man." Carmen Stavely was scolding her grown-up son. "Your father and I aren't sending you all that money just to educate a smart mouth. There's still a thing or two in this world you don't know yet."

Walter, Jr., who was driving, pulled up short of the parking lot and smiled the smile his mother had waited half a year to see.

"Come on, Mom, conference is duller than Demerol. Let's play hooky and go to McDonald's."

"McDonald's is a Communist plot to destroy the health of this nation."

"Mother!" he despaired, "Where do you read these things?"

"Just never you mind, but I know what I know. After the meeting I'll take you home and give you something fit for human beings to eat. Right now we have a conference to attend."

"I don't think it's healthy, Mom. I think conference is drug related. It's the opiate of the elect. Really. Did you ever look around in there? Five hundred people sitting bolt upright on steel folding chairs with their eyes wide open and bawling kids climbing all over 'em, and it's so noisy you couldn't hear a bomb drop," his voice narrowed to a revelatory whisper, "and every other one of 'em's sound asleep. It's not natural, Mom. It's like mass hypnosis or something. It might even be a Communist plot."

Carmen folded her arms over her tiny chest and scowled.

"Well," he surrendered, "I guess you're right." He released the brake pedal and headed the station wagon into the parking lot. "It's probably not a plot, after all. Actually it's a religious art form. A sort of ancient, ascetic ritual. The Hindus sleep on nails. The Catholics, the real ones, anyway, wear hair nightshirts. And we have conference."

She reached over and punched him sharply in the ribs. "You just keep on, young man, and see where it leads." The truth was, she loved to hear him talk nonsense. Loved to read his funny, irreverent letters. Loved him. And all the while she worried about him terribly.

"There's still a thing or two in this world left for you to learn, Walter Stavely. And it won't hurt you to sit with your clever mouth shut for an hour and listen."

"Sure, Mom." He parked the car and climbed out, then went around to the other side and opened the door for his mother. "But, I think, if you're going to let Dad out of conference, you really ought to have me stay home and keep him out of trouble. Who knows what he's growing out there behind the tool shed?"

"Your father's old enough to look out for his own salvation, but as long as you're my responsibility, you'll be in church where you belong."

Walter, Jr.'s brothers and sisters were already there practicing with the combined youth chorus, and he knew he had as much chance of getting out of conference as out of judgement day. They walked through the parking lot and into the building where Carmen Stavely drank in the admiration of the other ladies for her oldest boy's height and good looks and fresh haircut.

"He's just home from college," she said again and again, "just for a week or two." And she took his arm and pressed relentlessly on toward the chapel.

"All right, Mom," he whispered when two of the ladies had passed safely out of earshot, "have it your way, but don't wake me up unless I snore."

"You just pay attention, and you'll stay awake enough. George Showalter's being called into the Stake Presidency today. He's a marvelous speaker. He's a marvelous man."

"If he's in the presidency, he's a clone."

"He's a what?" She straightened with indignation.

" 'Clone,' Mother," and he spelled it, "means exact genetic replication. It's our own version of what the Catholics call transubstantiation."

She stared at him blankly.

"It means, Mother, that if you've heard one, you've heard them all."

"Those men are called by the spirit of revelation."

"Well, it sure isn't the spirit of imagination. They could send all the resumes to me and save the spirit a lot of commuting time. I've got the profile down cold."

"I don't know what you're talking about."

"Let me guess. He's got ten kids and the oldest is five and his wife's expecting. Right?"

"Don't be ridiculous. Brother Showalter has seven children, and his wife is certainly not expecting."

"But she drives a nine-passenger Chevy Malibu wagon, doesn't she, with an inspirational cassette player, a two-years' supply of loose Cheerios, and in place of a hood ornament there's a handmade plastic centerpiece?"

She was glaring at him now. He repented.

"I'm sorry. I exaggerated the part about the centerpiece. Let's see. The guy's not a dentist. They put dentists on the high council. And if he were an accountant, he'd be stake clerk. Plumbers make Scoutmaster. Lawyers work on Sunday. And professors apostatize. I guess that leaves business. This guy isn't by any chance a successful business type, is he? A district manager, maybe, or a managing director, or even a corporate vice president?"

She was so furious he knew he'd hit pay dirt.

"Brother Showalter is a humble man, which is not anything I can say for you, right now. You're cocky. You think you're just something extra, don't you?"

Walter rolled his eyes.

"Your grandmother saw it when you were just little. She wrote it in the cover of your scriptures. 'Be thou humble, and the Lord thy God . . . ' "

"I know the scripture, Mom. I know it."

"That's the problem." She shook her head glumly. "You only know it. And the truth is you don't know anything."

Now he was irritated.

"Look, Mom, I'm sorry I know the type, but stake counselors are correlated all over the world. I'd recognize one anywhere." He thought a moment and then launched into a reckless improvisation. "A two-button suit, and a little round belly, that sags," he searched for a rhyme, "while he brags, like a bag full of jelly." That wasn't clever; it was vicious, and he knew it. If he had wanted to shock his mother, he'd succeeded. When they found seats down front where she could hear and see her children, she sat next to him in polar silence and with structural steel in her spine.

"Damn!" he thought. He didn't mean to upset her. He never meant to upset her. But she drove you to it. She worried tenaciously, indiscriminately, absolutely, and about everything. She worried about money and his father, which were probably worth worrying over, and about her children and their education, both how to provide it and how to prevent it. She worried about the weather and about air quality, about polluters and conspirators and multi-nationals and Communist plots at McDonald's. She worried about fluoride and salt and enzymes and fat and additives and refined, white sugar and about every mouthful of food that went into or failed to go into the heedless mouths around her. And above all she worried about heaven. Oh, not for herself. There was no time for that. She was conductor-in-chief on the train to glory with a half-dozen reluctant, backsliding passengers she was bound and determined to deliver if she had to get them there on her own back and more dead than alive. His mother loved him to complete, grim distraction, and it made him crazy. Sometimes it made him vicious. But he didn't want to hurt her. She had burdens and pressures enough. More than enough. And it didn't ease his conscience any to know that in the sensitive matter of his orthodoxy, her agonizing was probably on target.

Suddenly the electric organ threading prelude music in and out of the general conversational roar stopped, and conference began. The opening song. The prayer. The announcements. And then Walter Stavely, Jr., watched the noisy, wriggling congregation slip as steadily as habit down into a dense, golden narcosis. Occasionally, here and there—you could see it in the eyes or in the tilt of a neck—a listener rose momentarily to the surface of consciousness to see if anything was going on, but then, disappointed, sank again and as quickly back into the shadowy depths. Only the restless and resisting children showed unabating signs of intelligent life. Meanwhile, Walter sat next to his angry mother in an attitude of I-told-you-so condescension. He would be right about the new counselor as well.

And he was. Called to the pulpit, George Showalter wore a black executive suit, beamed a polished executive smile, and spoke in ringing executive tones. "My dear brothers and sisters," he boomed from the bridge while unbuttoning his suit coat to relieve tension on his prominent middle. "I am truly humbled here this morning . . . " The tone and rhythm of his humility were nothing if not self-confident, and he recounted the events of his recent elevation in the sort of numbing detail usually reserved for biographies of sitting presidents or cinema sex goddesses.

"And I was right down on Mayfield Road in the center lane, and I stopped for a light at Richmond by the Triple A there and the Dunkin Doughnuts, and I said to myself, George Howard Showalter . . . "

What he had said to himself sitting and waiting in the front seat of his new Cutlass sedan through the red and the left-only to the green was that the imminent reorganization of the stake in which he lived was going to affect his life. He sensed it. And when he got home from the hardware store and went in to Marion, his wife, who was standing at the electric can opener fixing his lunch, she said it was a funny thing, but she'd just been thinking about the reorganization, too. So they'd both been thinking about the reorganization at the same time, which struck Brother Showalter as especially significant.

"And I pondered that," he said. "And while I was eating my soup with some cottage cheese and a tomato slice which, to tell the truth, I'm not real fond of cottage cheese, but I'd been trying to lose a little weight, you see. And it occurred to me, brothers and sisters, that only a few weeks before on a Saturday in that very kitchen it had come to me that I really ought to lose some weight and get myself in shape and take more time off from work maybe, because it just seemed somehow like there were changes coming in my life, important changes. And I needed to do something to get ready. Now, of course," he straightened up and smiled modestly, "with 20/20 hindsight we know that all along the Lord had been preparing me to accept this tremendous new calling."

Walter, Jr., shifted his weight back and forth and resolved that in the future he would treat cottage cheese with more theological respect. He also decided to tell his mother he had so resolved. When he looked over to gauge her current approachability, he was surprised to find the armor plating completely vanished from her frame. She was leaning gently, almost gracefully, forward in her seat, her face shining and absorbed. In fact, when Walter, Jr., looked around the hall, he saw consciousness. Entire swarms and schools of consciousness . . . risen to the surface and treading lightly there on fins of rapt attention. He did not entirely believe his eyes.

"It reminds me," Brother Showalter was saying, "of a time some years ago when I was holding down four different jobs in our ward, and home teaching nine families on a route that covered 116 miles, and I was serving as Scoutmaster as well because, when the bishop called me, I said 'yes' before he even told me what he wanted." Showalter shook his head at his own folly while a light ripple of laughter flared and dwindled. "But I wasn't sorry, brothers and sisters. I'm always glad to do my small part." He paused to drain any traces of light-mindedness from his expression. "And, you see, it was just then that something remarkable happened. Something I was truly not ready for. Suddenly, I was called into the bishopric. But way down deep inside I knew . . . knew I wasn't the man for that job. You see, I hadn't really prepared myself. Hadn't really magnified my callings. I could have done more, far more for those Boy Scouts, spent more time, showed more concern. And I could have done more for those families I home taught, studied my scriptures more diligently, been more attuned to the spirit, could have taken those callings, all six or eight of them, far more seriously. I'd been a slothful, light-minded, unprofitable servant, and I knew it. And I knew the Lord knew it as well, but here he was calling me up like Jonah to the bishopric. It just didn't make any sense." He paused again and bit his lip introspectively. "Yet who was I to question the wisdom of the Lord's anointed? At a time like that, brothers and sisters, you look back over your whole life. You ask yourself the hard questions. And what was it that came to me in that dark hour? Was it the academic successes, the graduate degree from a top-ranked university? Was it the impressive job offers, the rapid rise in a major company, the substantial raises one right after another? No! No, of course, it wasn't. Was it the awards, the professional and civic recognition? Was it the admiration of men in high places? No, I'll tell you. It was none of those things. When the chips were down, it was the little opportunities for service in the gospel that came flooding back to me—to call me home. The encouraging word I had given. The hand of friendship I had offered. The golden missionary opportunities taken at their tide. You see, it's only when we do the work of the Lord that all the rewards and honors and all else whatsoever can be truly added unto us. So of course I'd take that job. I'd let my laxness be a lesson to me. I'd do better. That call was a summons to repentance, a marvelous, generous opportunity to bring my life into order. And so perhaps you will understand just how humbled I feel here today to know the Lord has offered me that same marvelous opportunity for repentance one more marvelous time. Oh, I have my faults, brothers and sisters, just as some of you may have faults, but every advance we make in this wonderful kingdom is a promotion toward perfection."

He paused for a moment and looked uncertainly around.

"I don't know. I hadn't intended to do this, but the spirit is so strong here this morning I feel . . . somehow I feel I ought to share this with you. Did you know, brothers and sisters, that if you were to go out and visit any of those nine families over 160 miles that I used to home teach every month, and if you asked them, they'd tell you, 'Brother Showalter was the best darned home teacher we ever had.' Now, can you believe that? Can you? Did I do that? Why, of course I didn't. You and I know better. And do you know what else? If you went to any of those boys I had in my Scout troup, they'd tell you George Showalter was the best doggoned Scout master they ever had . . . ever. Now, isn't that astounding? Did I do that? Did I? Of course not. That wasn't me. That was the Lord working through Brother George Showalter when he knew it not. God operates in mysterious ways, and I guess . . . " he winked at his audience, "I guess George Showalter is a pretty mysterious operation."

Walter, Jr., smiled incredulously. For some minutes he had been trying to name whatever it was that he was witnessing. Was it a feat of self-promoting humility or of self-deprecating arrogance? He didn't know. He couldn't tell. He shook his head, and when he looked up again, the speaker, George Howard Showalter, a man he'd never met nor seen before in his life, was staring directly back at him. Their eyes met.

"Well, I see some of you agree with me." Showalter grinned. "Maybe some of you are pretty mysterious operations yourselves." He winked and looked away. "But, seriously, dear brothers and sisters . . . "

Walter, Jr., steeled himself for a seriously boiler-plate finish. And he got it, though administered gradually over a period of nearly eighteen in-conclusion-ary minutes.

"And in that same humble spirit," began the final final-cadence, "I pray my modest presentation here this morning may touch an aching heart or lift a yearning soul, for if I've touched or lifted just one, well, then, how great will be my joy . . . and yours . . . in the endless eternities above . . . "

After the benediction people streamed forward to congratulate the new counselor, and to shake his hand, and praise his eloquence. Walter, Jr., meanwhile, stood in place with his mother and waited for the aisle to clear before taking her out into the foyer where they would wait for his brothers and sisters. She was beaming at him like a winter sunrise, and she took him by the arm and squeezed.

"Well, what did I tell you?" she said, nodding and goading him with her bright, black eyes. "Didn't I tell you? Sometimes, it's a crying shame a person can't just stand up in the chapel and applaud."

She seemed lighter, full decades of worry and trouble lighter, and he accepted her excited hand in his own and squeezed back.

"Yes," he said, and he meant it, sort of. "I suppose sometimes it is."

Thelma in the Sky with Diamonds

Skirting along the wall with a wary eye on the dance floor and on his unprotected flank, he wasn't watching where he was going, and he nearly ran into her.

"Excuse me." The tone was not even remotely apologetic.

"I haven't seen you here before." She smiled.

"I've never been." He didn't smile. He didn't look at her. Not at her summer dress, not even at her summer cleavage. He seemed irritated.

"You don't like Special Interest." She spoke carefully in a tone somewhere between question and statement.

"No," he confirmed, "I don't like Special Interest. And I do not like the common obsession for which 'Special Interest' is a poorly veiled euphemism." He turned and glared at her. "I did not, in fact and in case you are interested, come here to propose marriage to anyone, or to contemplate marriage, or even so much as to develop a wish to have the desire to contemplate marriage. I am single." He announced this as though it would come as a surprise to her. "And despite admonitions and edicts from on high, I consider that state to be a source of blessing and good fortune lesser in degree only to the happy state of those women of my acquaintance fortunate enough to be equally and entirely unmarried to me."

She blinked and stood silently, staring at the dance floor. In the dimmed light, her hair had the hard luster of freshly filed copper.

"Do you like to dance?"

"No."

"Oh." She tried to mirror his curt matter-of-factness in her own voice. "Why not?"

He glared again.

"Because I don't like to!"

"Oh," she said, and then, after a moment, to break the silence, "I love to dance. I never understand people who don't like dancing."

"I didn't say I don't like dancing."

Disorientation filled her eyes.

"As a matter of fact, I very much like dancing. I have tremendous admiration for the dance, and that, of course, is why I don't do it."

"Oh," she said.

"I don't walk on tightropes either. It happens that bad tightrope walking carries its own immediate penalty, which explains the extremely low rates of attempted tightrope walking, but I assure you, in the next life there awaits a similar punishment for bad dancers who, believe me, do no less violence to the laws of physics."

She tried to smile, but her amusement was so tentative, so clearly insecure that he moved to illustration.

"Look at that," he said, and he pointed to one of the couples on the dance floor. The man was tall and balding. With his head thrown back and his elbows raised high, he bobbed vigorously up and down in precise, aerobic rhythm to the fox trot while the woman, much shorter and softer, rose and fell and visibly perspired in his churning wake.

"A fellow like that should be dragging a sulky, not a partner."

She smiled guiltily.

"And look there."

She leaned to follow the trajectory of his arm, and for the first time he noticed the full waves of surprisingly sun-red hair. He could smell her hair spray.

"Who?" She craned her neck.

"Right there," he recovered. "With the boots."

She giggled in an earthy alto. The man in tall boots was dancing at a stiff arm's length with a woman half a head taller. Talking animatedly and distractedly, he met only every third or fourth beat of the music while his bewildered partner struggled to keep track both of his feet and of his conversation.

"But it's not really how you look, is it?" She turned and straightened up, and he found himself looking directly into the canyon at the brink of her dress. He was a little stunned. Weathered perhaps, freckled, probably settling, but this was an amazing, postcard landscape all the same—a gently eroded natural wonder welling up at whatever unnatural forces of stitchery held the dress together. And the dress . . . A dress like that with a neckline like that would draw attention anywhere, but in the Church . . . at a church-sponsored dance? Suddenly he felt acutely self-conscious. People must surely be watching her, and if they were watching her, they were watching and drawing conclusions about him. He cast a glance over his shoulder and tried to look as though he were looking for someone else.

"I mean it really isn't how you look, is it?" she was saying. "It's how you feel."

"Excuse me," he said.

She repeated herself. There was no avoiding her, but it was a long, awkward moment before he found his way to a clever answer. "That is a line from a popular pornographic novel, you know?"

She winced and blushed. "Well, I didn't know. I certainly haven't read it."

"Neither have I. My students quote it to me. They think it's profound."

"You're a teacher, aren't you?"

"Obviously."

"And your students read books like that?"

"My students hardly read at all, but they're resourceful. They find someone who can read, and he marks the meaty passages for them. Then they pass around dog-eared, annotated editions."

"Oh, that's nice," she said, but was immediately unsure, "or is it?"

"It's efficient. No wasted thought." He smiled for the first time and raised one eyebrow in a gesture of resignation.

They stood for a long time watching the dancers until a breathless cha-cha sent the short talker in the high boots lurching arhythmically into the path of the tall bald man counting his relentless, athletic way across the floor. The collision was made-for-television perfect. Both onlookers bit their lips and snickered helplessly through their noses. Now people really were looking at them.

"So," she said after she had recovered, "if you don't like Special Interest, and you don't like to dance, so how come you came to the Special Interest Dance?"

"Excellent question."

"I thought it was good."

"But I'm afraid the answer is not logical; it's political."

"Are you running for office or something?"

"I'm not running for anything. I'm running from."

"From?"

"From Carmen Stavely."

"Carmen?"

"Oh, it's not just Sister Stavely. There are others, but she is my principal tormenter. There is an as yet undiscovered allergic malady latent in the married women of the Church which is triggered by the sight or sound or perhaps it's just the smell of an unmarried man. It sends them wild. A kind of vicarious feeding frenzy. And the only way to cool down the mania is to give in to it. Or, at least, to appear to. I came here this evening so that Carmen Stavely will leave me in peace for a while."

"Carmen is a dear. She's my friend."

"Your dear Carmen," he closed one eye and narrowed the other, "is a relentless busybody."

"She means well."

"She means business. Everyone else's business."

"Carmen told me," she looked away smiling guiltily, "I should talk to you when you came."

"She what?"

"She said I should talk to you."

"You mean you are the reason she drove me to this feed lot. I mean. Excuse me. I didn't mean . . . I mean . . . "

He stammered and squirmed, and she watched with transparent pleasure for a moment before she released him.

"She just said I should talk to you."

"Well, you've done your duty. You've talked to me." He turned to go, but had no idea where.

"And it wasn't very easy, you know?" she said, raising her voice a little.

He turned back. "What wasn't easy?" There was irritation in his face and in his voice again.

"Talking to you. You're still real angry."

"I am not angry." He spoke with the measured coolness of extreme anger.

"It must have been a long time ago."

"What?" He glared cold incomprehension at her, but he knew exactly what she was talking about. He was astonished.

"You're still real angry, though."

"I am not angry!" He almost shouted. His voice broke an octave.

"I'm sorry," she said quietly. They stared at one another for a moment, but she was no match for him. She turned away. "Would you like some punch?"

He stared at the side of her head.

"No," he said, finally looking off across the dance floor. She looked in the other direction. They were silent for a long time.

"Is it still green?"

"Green?"

"The punch. It was always green. When I was young, I thought it was doctrinal."

She looked trapped. He liked that. She had no idea what he was talking about.

"I think it's red," she apologized. "It has a pineapple ice mold, but it's not really very good. It's sweet."

"Well, then it's the same punch. Different color, but the same. The policies change, but never the doctrines. The same yesterday, today, and tomorrow. As it was, as it is, and as it will ever be. That's a comfort. Color aside, there's still only one true punch."

She smiled uncomprehendingly, and he smiled back. He was sorry, too.

He got the punch, and they left the dancers and the phonograph music, the streamer-festooned basketball standards, the paper-covered tables and metal folding chairs, the laden trays of cupcakes and Rice-Krispie treats as well as an alerted network of watchers behind, and wandered out into the foyer.

"How did you know?" he asked when she had settled herself and her billowing, pastel dress on the faded brown sofa. He handed her her punch, self-consciously watching it recede toward the spectacular panorama at the rim of her dress. "How did you know I'd been married?" He sat down a conservative distance away on the sofa and turned slightly and uncomfortably toward her, aware as he had not been for years of the acute angle at which his stomach, when he sat, plunged over his belt. "Well?"

She only shrugged and smiled. Her face was still pretty, but hardened by eyeliner and too clear and monotone to reconcile with the varicolored vistas below. He'd always hated make-up.

"I didn't think anyone knew. I certainly didn't think Carmen Stavely knew."

"I don't think she does. She certainly didn't say anything to me. And Carmen's not one to hide things."

He laughed out loud. "No, ma'am, not Carmen. But then how did you . . . ?"

"Oh, I've been angry before, too . . . sometimes."

"You mean you've been married?"

She bit her lip and nodded. "Oh, yes." It was more a sigh than a statement, and she smiled again, but uncomfortably.

"Well, for me it was all a very long time ago. Ancient history. I'm amazed you could tell." He took his handkerchief out and began to clean his glasses. "Is there anything else you could tell?"

"Well, only . . . " she hesitated.

"Go ahead, go ahead."

"Only that it was her idea. To break up, I mean."

He put his glasses back on. "I'm really very impressed. How do you do it?"

She shrugged again. "I don't know, really. It just seemed like it."

"Well, you're right. She saw the light and put me out to pasture. A very bright woman."

"Is that why you loved her?"

He looked up sharply. And then he shrugged. "I don't really know. I suppose. She was a liberated woman. Very. As a matter of fact. Way ahead of her time, and of me. Of this place. And especially ahead of the Church. And I minded, yes, but I didn't mind really. She wasn't wrong. Not a little. But she wasn't all that right, either. She was not patient. So she divorced them all, the time, the place, the Church. And me. Last of all, but not least, she divorced me, too."

"You haven't forgiven her."

"Well now, she abandoned me, didn't she? And historically the abandoned are a vengeful lot." He forced a grin and busied himself untying and refolding the handkerchief still in his hand which he had used to clean his glasses, but which during the short speech just delivered and delivered who knows how many times before but never vocally, never to anyone outside his head, he had tied into knots. "And then, of course, there is the small matter of the boy."

"You have a boy?"

"Oh, you haven't already figured that out?"

"No."

"Good. That's a point for my team. Yes, I have a son. Do you have children?"

"No," she replied quickly and with a tone of apology. "No, I don't."

"Well, don't moon over it. Children are worse than wives and more mystifying."

"Oh?" she said, surprised, "Why is that?"

Seeing the interest in what despite artistic emblazonment really still was an attractive face and feeling uncomfortable at the ever more personal direction of their conversation, he took a chance. "Look, would you mind if we talked about this somewhere else? This place has all the atmosphere of a . . . a car lot." Discretion overtook him just in time to censor the word "used." "Maybe if we went for a ride, we could just talk. And I could buy you a root beer without pineapple ice mold."

She was willing to play hooky, and so they went out the back door and across the parking lot to the corner next to the lawn tool shed where he had parked his car.

"It's new, isn't it?" she said as he opened the door and she settled elaborately in. "I love the smell."

"Brand new," he conceded. "It's a celebration."

"Really! What are you celebrating?"

"The fact that I can't afford it."

"No," she insisted shrilly, like a woman used to being teased, "I mean really."

"Really," he said. "You see, I'm considering changing my employment. If I do, I'll be able to afford it, which is surely reason to celebrate. And if I don't, well, then, this is my way of consoling myself."

"Oh," she said, not at all sure of his point. "It's cute. It's Japanese, isn't it?"

"Yes, I'm afraid it's a little intimate, but I promise to stay strictly on my side of the hand brake." That, of course, was a little brazen, but she didn't seem to notice. She was still mulling over what he had said before.

"Would you go to another college?"

"No!" he said too loudly and then said it again in a calmer, more controlled voice, "No."

"What would you do?"

"Well, in fact, I am flirting with free enterprise, or more precisely, tax-free enterprise. But it's all very complex and improbable, and you really don't want to hear about it." The truth was he didn't want to talk about it. "Would you like to hear some music? The radio is stereo." He turned it on and the seat behind them filled with sound.

"Oh!" she said, and out of the corner of his eye he could see her recoil a little. The volume was reasonable, but the music raging in the back seat was the Bartok Concerto for Orchestra, the first movement. It was impressively the wrong music. He turned the volume way down and pointed to the tuning dial.

"The buttons don't work, but you can use the dial and find something nice."

"Are you sure? I don't mind . . . "

"Sure," he said, trying to sound free and open minded. "Anything's fine!" But the truth was that all the buttons along the bottom of his new radio were preemptively tuned to the same classical station.

While he drove, she located what he thought must be a "beautiful music" or a "golden oldie" or maybe even a "soft rock" station. He had read these terms as he had read everything cover to cover in the weekly newsmagazines, but he had never listened and had no hooks to hang them on. She turned the radio still lower.

"You were going to tell me about your son."

"My son? Well," he thought for a moment, "My son is now a young man of glowing good health, considerable charm, good looks, estimable talent, and almost no accomplishment whatsoever."

"Oh dear!" she said, and he was surprised at the genuine alarm in her voice.

"Raised by his mother, he's declared his independence from me by rejecting all those things and values which she has rejected. His declaration to her, on the other hand, was to spurn her formidable ambition. He has, in consequence, completely paralyzed himself with independence."

"Oh my."

"Oh, I don't wish to deny a share in the blame. I've seen him too seldom, and too anxiously, and learned too late that you've got to bring up a child six full fascist lanes to the right of the way he should actually go, so that when he grows up, he'll depart from it no farther than is necessary to become a reasonable, moderately useful and acceptable human being . . . and still be able to think he's some kind of hard-nosed, self-emancipated radical. Bring 'em up reasonable and you drive 'em into the hungry maw of insanity. That's the mistake."

Dismay had anchored itself sympathetically in her eyes.

"How old is he?"

"Twenty-two."

"And . . . what does he do?"

"You mean, besides nothing? He writes Rock and Roll songs."

"Really?" she said. And there was a note of hopeful pleasure in her voice.

"Oh, yes," he countered, "really. But he doesn't sing them, because the last I heard Rock and Roll music was still tonal. And he doesn't play them, because he's not a player, which would entail practicing, but a writer, which evidently doesn't. And he doesn't sell them or send them out, either, because not everyone appreciates his special sensibility. So he pins them on his wall and listens to records and waits for the millennium or the lottery or whatever it is that he's waiting for and meanwhile consumes enormous amounts of food and creates enormous piles of laundry, and . . . " he was extremely angry, "and that is it, that is my son." He paused and tried consciously to lighten his tone, but it sounded accusatory all the same. "If you met him, you'd probably like him. People do." He looked grimly through the windshield. "Even I do."

"I'm sorry," she said weakly, knowing it was the wrong thing to say. Nor was she surprised when he turned to her with righteous incredulity to ask why she, of all people, should feel sorry.

"I don't know," she said and shrugged. "No reason, I guess, but I can't help it. I just do."

He pursed his lips and shook his head.

"I'm sorry," she said again.

They crossed above the interstate.

"Have you read any of his songs?"

"Yes."

"Did you like them?"

"I do not appreciate Rock and Roll," he explained, not wanting to, but feeling coerced and that integrity required it, "I do not approve of Rock and Roll. It offends me."

"Really," she said without intimidation. She seemed genuinely perplexed.

"Not morally, of course. Musically. It's like bad Victorian theatre, full of sound and melodrama signifying either nothing, which is bad enough, or next to nothing, which is worse."

"Oh, but really, I like it," she argued, and then cautiously softened her stance, "some of it, anyway. Listen, I love this one." She reached down and turned up the radio. When the chorus began, she joined in, singing softly, but unself-consciously.

> Picture yourself in a boat on a river
> with tangerine trees and marmalade skies.

"With what?" he injected, but she only smiled and waved him off.

> Somebody calls you, you answer quite slowly,
> The girl with kaleidoscope eyes.

He looked at her incredulously and rolled his own.

> Cellophane flowers of yellow and green,
> towering over your head.
> Look for the girl with the sun in your eyes,
> And she's gone.

She finished breathily near the top of her range and stopped to listen to the refrain. It was noisy, and repetitive, and nonsense. It didn't help.

"I rest my case," he said when it was over.

"I love it," she said.

"It doesn't mean anything. It's just noise."

She smiled, unrepentant.

At the Dairy Prince, he went to the counter and ordered two root beer floats. When he emerged again, she had left the car and was sitting at the picnic table on the little strip of grass at the side of the building. The neon red of the sign clashed with her copper hair, in which it was strangely reflected. She was an incongruous woman. He liked her.

"Now tell me about you. You were married, too?"

"Yes." She seemed deeply interested in her root beer.

"A long time ago?"

"Yes, I suppose."

"And what was he like?"

"Oh, he was a baseball player. An outfielder. He was a very good hitter."

"Professional?"

"Yes."

"And big?"

"Uh-huh."

"And muscular and handsome?"

"Yes," she conceded.

"And rich?"

"Well, not rich exactly, but . . . "

"But well off?"

"Yes, I guess so."

"Then why . . . "

"You mean, why the divorce?"

"Yes."

She looked at her root beer again. "Because he hit me."

"He what?"

"He hit me." She didn't look up, but she knew he was staring at her. "I mean, he hit me a lot."

"He hit you? How long did you stay with him?"

She shrugged and looked deeper into her root beer. "Two years. Two and a half, maybe."

"Why?" His voice soared with incredulity.

"I don't know, really." She was stalling, and he scowled at her with teacherly impatience.

"I guess I thought he needed me. He sure needed something."

"But you left?"

"Oh, yes."

He seemed to be waiting for an explanation.

"He broke my tooth. This one." She pointed to her second incisor on the upper left. "It's capped. I looked awful. I couldn't believe he'd break my tooth. I figured whatever he needed, it wasn't me any more."

"And you left?"

"Yes."

"And you divorced him?"

"Well, actually, he divorced me. He had the lawyer."

He shook his head. "How old were you?"

"Nineteen."

"Just nineteen?"

She nodded.

"A long time ago, then."

She nodded again.

He finished his float.

"And you've been alone since?"

"Well, not really." For all her interest, she'd hardly touched her float. "I was married again."

"Not to a baseball player, I hope."

"No," she smiled, "not a baseball player. He was a business man. Very successful, really. Very clever. I had my own car, and a Weimaraner. They have blue eyes, you know. It's very unusual. And I took tennis lessons at Gladhill, and . . . "

"Well?"

"He had some trouble with the IRS. Actually, I guess it was a lot of trouble. And then we had trouble. And then one thing led to another, and . . . "

"Well, I hope this time you got a good settlement."

"The IRS got the settlement."

"Oh."

With her encouragement he gathered the cups. Her ice cream had melted, but floated nonetheless atop the milky root beer in a rigid, non-dairy froth. He watched it tilt and disappear into the plastic liner of the trash bin. In the car she was silent, and he was uncertain how to broach a conversation.

"Would you like to go somewhere?"

"I don't think so. It's late, and I have to work in the morning." She told him where she lived.

They were silent for a long time, but he was not ready for silence.

"So you've been divorced twice."

"Well," she said as if she'd only been waiting for the question, "the truth is, I've been divorced three times."

"Three?" He tried to disguise the astonishment in his voice, but he was not a natural soprano.

"Yes, my last husband was a lot like me. In fact, he'd led my exact life. His first wife beat him up, and his second one was a shoplifter. I thought we were made for each other."

"But you weren't, huh?" he asked when it was clear she had finished.

"Nope."

"Well, how come you're back again?"

"Back?"

"I mean at that special obsession thing or whatever they call it."

"Oh, that. I go because Carmen insists on it. She means well. She's actually a dear."

"You mean you're not looking for a husband?"

"Not really."

"You're not?" His astonishment was immense.

"I don't think I'm very good at it. Do you?"

He laughed. "You go because you're under the same inquisitional duress that I'm under."

"I don't know what that means."

"Yes, you do. You just don't know that you know."

He laughed, and she laughed, and the silence between them on the way home now seemed comfortable and salutary.

He was watching her, glancing in her direction more than the driving required or than, really, he wanted to. In the dark, in the settled moonlight, she seemed younger, with softness returned to her hair and her lips and erasing the self-inflicted line around her eyes. He imagined he saw her as he might have twenty years before, or twenty-five, or even thirty. Once, on the way home from his mission, he and an adventurous friend had gone to a nightclub in Berlin to see a young British singer whose chaste loveliness in the photograph on the marquee had seduced them utterly. Ravening inwardly like explorers on the brink of Eldorado, they'd waited through the long evening for her appearance, but when at last she came, emerging suddenly from the shadows into the smokey light, she was not at all the fabled golden temple they'd dreamed of, but, instead, its ruin, long raised and ravaged, and gaudily painted by the pitiful surviving natives in grotesque homage to an irretrievable past. The young adventurers had watched in riveted horror and then left in a deep archeological melancholy over so perfect a loveliness lost.

Now, decades later, driving in the moonlight on a pot-holed access road in the Midwest, he remembered. And he thought about the woman next to him in her amazing summer dress, about her many-husbanded childlessness, and about the goddess girl she must surely once have been. And he wondered bleakly whether, if he had known her then and known how to dance and to make small talk and if he had somehow, somewhere found the courage to ask, she would ever possibly, conceivably have gone out with him. At least, he wouldn't have hit her.

"I'm embarrassed to admit it," he said when he'd pulled up in front of the house she pointed out to him, "I've seen you at church, but I don't even know your name. Mine's Damon."

"I know," she said, "Damon Boulder. And my name is Thelma Rydell. Thelma Durzac Sealy Hunsaker Rydell, if you want them all." She grinned. And he grinned back.

"Well, it was nice meeting you, Thelma. I'm sorry if I was rude. I'm out of practice. I'm really not very good at these sorts of things. I guess that's obvious. Thank you for speaking to me, anyway, and for listening to me, and please tell Carmen Stavely that I behaved myself, or that I didn't, or whatever you think will encourage her least." He was looking straight ahead through the windshield, but could tell she wasn't moving toward the door, and he thought for a moment and with some misgiving that maybe she didn't really want to go in yet after all. But then why had she said she did? Probably, she just couldn't open the door. Japanese door handles were inscrutable. When he'd bought the car, he had himself spent several clumsy minutes seeking an escape. So in a flash of embarrassed realization, he reached across to help. "Look, you just grab that little gizmo right there . . . " but at that very moment, having suddenly and simultaneously realized that he was not going to get out and open the door for her, that he, in fact, expected her to let herself out, she also reached, with equal embarrassment and leaning forward to look for the handle, so that she obstructed his path, and so that his extended hand, though innocent of guile and of all dishonorable intention, plunged nonetheless directly through the wide opening in her summer dress and then onward and downward with irresistible inertia along and between and, finally, well up under her bosom.

There was a gasp. A duet of gasps, whistled through open throats. Then nothing. Neither breathed. Neither moved. Damon had no idea what had happened, but deep embarrassment burned the tips of his ears, and of his nose, and of his deeply embedded fingers.

"Oh!" he blurted in a drawn whisper. He tugged at his fingers, but they were securely lodged and cupped upwards under the far breast, so that he despaired at the violence it would require to remove them. Her eyes were as wide and round as flower pots, her body as rigid as a retaining wall.

"I am sorry." He pulled again. "I just . . . the door . . . " He was helpless.

Then, slowly, ever so slowly, he felt her soften and relax behind his fingers.

"It's all right," she said at last and calmly. Her voice in the pitched silence was like dark green glass. "It's my fault."

"No. No!"

"Really." She insisted and leaned forward again and turned a little toward him so that he was able gently to extricate his hand. She helped him.

"I'm so terribly sorry. I . . . I . . . "

"It's all right. Really, I moved in the way."

He didn't know what to do with the freed hand. He was afraid to look at it, and something autonomous, something heady and lost and adolescent in the palm was already palpably remembering. He made a fist before it could spread.

She was looking at him. "Really," she repeated. "It's okay." And there was an attentiveness in her eyes, a penetrating, generous, almost maternal attentiveness that held him like a comforted child. After a while she reached down and took his hand again, opened the reluctant fist and, smiling shyly, guided the upturned fingers alongside and gently under her covered breast. Then Thelma Durzac Sealy Hunsaker Rydell turned and kissed Damon Boulder as sweetly, oh, but far more knowingly and reassuringly, as any prom queen ever kissed any most preferred man.

When he got out to open her door, he went the long way round the back of the car, and breathed in the cool night air, and counted slowly backwards from one hundred, making a detour he had not made for a reason he had not had since his senior year in high school. The night sky was pristine and the stars in the perfect blackness overwhelmed the poor light leaching weakly up from the city. Damon Boulder knew that he knew what that song meant. And he knew he'd known it all along.

The Last Nephite

Harlow never really knew for sure. It might have been the corduroy jacket and L. L. Bean shirt, or maybe the wire-rimmed glasses and the mustache he'd started. The mustache was in that awkward beginning stage. All scruff and eyebrow pencil. Maybe it was that. Maybe not. Maybe it was none of the above. But whatever it was, out of the more than sixteen hundred assembled men, women, and children, stalwart youth and singing mothers, authorities, dignitaries, missionaries, members by blood and by adoption, friends, investigators, friends of investigators, visitors, and miscellaneous others . . . from all those milling hundreds, the stranger had selected him alone, Harlow Havens, doctoral candidate in sociology, author of certain controversial articles, night manager at Mountain Jack's, father of two, skeptic, thinker, and contributing rethinker of (and to) the one, restored, true and living gospel. He alone had been singled out to see and experience, not in dream or airy vision, but with his own eyes and protruding, earthly ears, a sign of the last days, a marvelous work, and, yes, a wonder.

During conference he had stood at a side door in the overflow area, assigned there by Arlon Crisp, his elders' quorum president, who'd called on Tuesday and explained with an economy of expression foreign to Arlon's normally trackless discourse that Harlow was being called to a special security group and would be personally responsible—in his assigned sector—for the welfare and safety of the visiting brethren.

Now, "security" is a calling not covered in the 107th Section, nor in the Handbook, nor even in the manuals, not yet anyway, but certain high and very general authorities from church headquarters were to attend the local stake conference to inaugurate a churchwide program. This much was known and widely published. The authorities' names, however, had not been disclosed. And this "security precaution" added measurably to the mystery and portent of the occasion. The faithful and even the not so faithful came out in droves to be surprised. They also came to be strengthened or validated, to have their hearts turned, their strides lengthened, and their lights nudged from under bushels. Some, of course, came merely from curiosity, and others for the martial spectacle of power. And yet others might in dark times have come for who knows what dark reasons. That was why Harlow and nineteen additional elders received special instruction from the special consultant sent in advance from Salt Lake City to secure and coordinate the event. The man was a professional.

Harlow's specific assignment was carefully to appraise all who entered through his exit. If anyone appeared unfamiliar or unusual, if anyone behaved strangely or acted nervous, if anyone carried an overly large bag or unusual package, he was to take note of where that person sat and signal the supervisor immediately.

He watched his sector diligently too, though, if the truth were known, with doubtful enthusiasm. He understood the letter of his new office, but had not entirely caught the spirit, and his diligence came at least in part as the search for some sinister and, therefore, reassuring sign that all of this was really necessary.

The Lord's mystery ambassadors, meanwhile, entered cautiously in among the Saints. When the congregation had finally been seated and the doors closed, each "usher" took up position in front of his assigned exit while a reserve crew swept the halls for strays and stragglers. After the all-clear had been signaled, a special van drew up to a side entrance. A special interdiction escort team from Salt Lake preceded the mystery authorities into the chapel, taking special seats reserved at strategic points around the perimeter of the stand. During the subsequent grand entrance, while the congregation, itching with suspense over who and what were coming, whispered news flashes in waves across the hall, these burly young men scanned the area with an edgily systematic thoroughness. The congregation sang the hymn of spontaneous welcome listed in the program. The announcements came and went. The most senior high councilman arose to pray.

During the long invocation, Harlow opened one curious eye, and then abruptly opened the other. Evidently, he had been slacking. The wide-eyed vigilantes on the stand, at any rate, continued their neck-craning surveillance uninhibited by prayer. Security in the last days, the consultant had said, would have to be as strong as the spirit, if not stronger. These were dangerous times.

And they were, of course, though not altogether in the sense the professional had intended, and it was not until after the conference, after the presentation of the new "Family Posterity Data Depository and Missionary Program," and, in fact, after the closing prayer, when the great men of the hour, their words ringing behind them, had safely disappeared and the doors could again be opened to release the pent and pepped-up faithful, that the very sign Harlow had been seeking nearly ran him down in the hall.

He had just stepped through the double fire doors, people streaming out behind him, and was headed off toward the foyer to find his family.

"Well, ah'll be!" a voice rang out. "I don't believe it!" The voice had a high, intermountain twang. "I haven't seen ya in years, y'old dog! How are ya anyway? Y'look great!"

A small, wiry-looking man moving hastily against the current in the corridor crooned all this at a pitch and volume that stunned the surging crowd into silence. Soon everyone was turning and straining to see who was being addressed and what exactly was going on. Harlow turned and looked as well, and while he looked, the same small man, whom Harlow had never seen before in his entire twenty-eight and a half years, grabbed him suddenly and solidly under the arm like some old arm-wrestling buddy. Harlow whirled and pulled away, but the stranger held him fast and hustled him with alarming strength roughly and irresistibly backwards through the throng. Down the hall they went. Around a corner. And straight into the men's room at the back of the building.

"Wait a minute!"

But protest was useless. Once inside the bathroom, the strange man quickly closed the door and then, turning back, forced his full weight against it, all the while holding tightly to Harlow's arm. No sooner had he set himself against the door than someone outside tried it, which, of course, was not surprising. What did surprise the already astonished Harlow was that almost immediately thereafter the door heaved in with tremendous force against his abductor's constraining weight, as if someone very large and very desperate to get inside were battering violently up against it. The door heaved inward once, then again and again, opening perhaps a quarter inch further each time, but, nevertheless, without success, for the stranger—as Harlow saw him now—diminutive in a rumpled western suit and glasses, and looking strangely like a cowboy cost accountant, managed each time to force the door resolutely back into the jamb—though more, it seemed to Harlow, through determination than any imaginable physical force.

While he held off the pile-driving blows from outside, the stranger reached inside his jacket with a free hand and produced a large brown envelope which he immediately forced into Harlow's own open jacket, high up under his left arm where it could be held easily with just a little downward pressure. Then, nimbly buttoning the jacket buttons with the same free hand, he looked him in the eye.

"What's yer name?" he whispered. Harlow was speechless and the stranger rejoined his own question. "Naw, never mind. I don't wanta know. You're a cynic, ain't ya?"

Harlow, to whom speech was gradually returning, stared stupidly at the little man. "I don't know what you mean."

"Yeh, yer one all right. Look," the stranger's voice dropped even lower, "yer name is Ralph. Understand? Ralph!"

The captive squinted. "Ralph?" he repeated, and suddenly, as if at that very signal, the man hurled himself from the door, dragging Harlow with him to the center of the washroom.

"Gee, Ralph," he announced loudly, stepping up to a wash basin and beginning to wash his hands, "I'd sure love ta. I'd really love ta come on over fer dinner, but . . . "

Instantly, the room was full of men. There were fellow security conscripts from the elders' quorum; there were the familiar hall and foyer haunters; there were teenagers, and children, and, right at the head of the phalanx, four more strangers. These new strangers were hale and burly and, to Harlow's rocketing astonishment, dressed uniformly in black suits, narrow ties, and synthetic white shirts that made them look like superannuated missionaries.

"Thing is, Ralph, I'm not travelin' alone. In fact," at the wash basin Harlow's abductor kept up both ends of their spirited conversation, " . . . in fact, these fellas here are ma travelin' companions. Hi, fellas," he nodded and spoke into the mirror. "I want ya to meet a young friend a mine. Name's Ralph. Small world, ain't it?"

Ignoring Harlow, the four glanced anxiously but systematically around the crowded washroom as if scanning pre-coordinated, interlocking sectors. Then, apparently satisfied, they all looked him over at once and with obvious suspicion. The envelope jammed under his arm suddenly felt heavy and precarious. As soon, however, as Harlow's bishop, looking alarmed and asking if there were anything wrong, joined the crowd in the washroom, the four seemed quite self-consciously to relax their manner and smiled blandly about them. And indeed, smiling, they looked for all the world like overgrown missionaries who had lost their way into early middle age. They even wore "LDS" name tags, which reassured Harlow considerably until he noticed that the space for the name on each tag was as blank as its owner's smile.

No one said much except his abductor, who never stopped speaking.

"Old Ralphie here's invited me to dinner, fellas. Told him I'd love to, yes sir, but we're on a tight schedule. Ain't that right?"

"That's right," repeated one of the traveling companions with his dairy smile, but without intonation.

"Well, that's what I told him. And I suppose we've got to be gettin' along. Say, Ralph, can I take me a rain check on that dinner?"

Harlow, who had been staring at the traveling companions, found his voice. "Sure, ah . . . any time."

The stranger shook Harlow's hand intensely like an old, old friend, and while the little man pumped his right arm, Harlow pushed the left harder against the envelope tucked way up in his armpit.

To his terror, the traveling companions shook his hand as well, each looking at him for an awkwardly long time and narrowing the space between his eyebrows in what seemed a kind of sinister warning. Then, quite as suddenly as the strangers had appeared, they were all gone again.

Leaving the bathroom, Harlow re-encountered the bishop, who was now standing at the back door watching the five men climb into a road-soiled silver and black van with dark-tinted windows. Two of the heavy-set men sat in the front while the bizarre and talkative stranger sat in the back, wedged precariously between the other two, even larger men, one of whom reached over with authority and slammed the side door shut. When the van had disappeared from view, the bishop looked back at Harlow.

"Ralph?" he asked, his forehead contorted with puzzlement.

Harlow shrugged. "I think he thought I was someone else." And then he shrugged again.

There was to this encounter a so wildly fantastical and hallucinatory quality that, if upon climbing into his Honda in the parking lot, Harlow had not found the envelope still lodged under his now cramped and sore left arm, he would surely have concluded that he had nodded off during conference and dreamed the entire thing. But the envelope, bent now and sweat-darkened, was still there, and Harlow held it gingerly by the ends, turning it over and over in the greenhouse heat of the Honda. He felt uneasy and, in fact, threatened. And when, suddenly, the door on the opposite side of the car opened, his alarm was so immediate and so convulsive that he bumped his lunging head against the thinly padded roof.

"Ouch!"

The envelope, meanwhile, floated an endless, airborne second or more in front of his ballooning eyes until he could grab it and force it swiftly, urgently down into the dark narrow space between the bucket seats.

The voice Harlow heard, when his body finally resumed its involuntary functions, belonged to Connie, his wife. She was complaining loudly that he hadn't told her he would wait for her in the car, hadn't thought at all to help her with the children. How was she to know where he was?

Listening to her assault, Harlow was overwhelmed with relief. He didn't respond, didn't defend himself. He merely slumped in his seat listening to his own pulse. Had Connie not been so angry and so preoccupied with the children, she would surely have noticed that there was something wrong. When she had finished wrestling the baby into submission and into her harness in the back, and when she had adjusted the other belts around her four-year-old son, she was herself flushed and distracted. Annoyed at Harlow's patriarchal indolence, she fell into a punitive silence, and it was not until sometime later, after leaving the church, when Harlow suddenly veered the Honda off of Cedar Road and onto the empty May Company parking lot, that she realized with a start that something more than oppressive August heat and the age-old oppression of women was in the air.

"What are you doing?" Her question reflected equal proportions of surprise and annoyance, but Harlow didn't answer. In silence he drove across the vast parking lot to a remote section far from the busy street. Then he turned the car and backed it into a protected corner from which he could readily oversee all possible routes of approach across the acres of steaming asphalt.

"Harlow," Connie bleated, and by now her annoyance had given way entirely to astonishment, "what are we doing?"

He looked at her intently, importantly, but remained silent. The motor was running, and he had put the car into neutral and let out the clutch. He carefully surveyed the parking lot and, reassured that all was quiet, reached down between the seats and drew out the brown envelope. He held it up between them.

"What is it?" she asked, looking back and forth from the envelope to her husband.

"Something happened today," he replied grimly. "I don't know what it was, but I think it may be dangerous."

"Dangerous?" Connie's eyes dilated.

"I don't know. There was a man at the church, I mean, I think he was a . . . " he looked at her wide eyes and, in fact, surprised himself with the word that came out of his mouth, " . . . a prisoner."

"Prisoner?" In the course of three syllables, Connie's tone fell perceptibly from alarm through incredulity in the direction once again of annoyance.

"Look," Harlow insisted, "he pushed me into the bathroom and then forced this envelope into my jacket. I mean, he didn't just hand it to me; he forced it into my jacket like . . . " he struggled for an analogy, "like a secret agent drop or something."

"Harlow, that sounds totally stupid. Is this a joke?" Connie's surmise that she was being made the butt of something distinctly male and nefarious did not register in Harlow's preoccupation. He had taken the letter into his lap and begun to open it. The heavy brown paper tore easily along the end where it had been softened by his sweat. And when he had torn it open, he blew the end gently into a trembling ellipse supported by pressure from his fingers. But as he gazed across the opening, his eyes widened.

"That's them!" he nearly shouted.

"What?" Connie, who had been engrossed in the envelope too, jumped with renewed alarm.

"That's them, Connie." He pointed directly across the parking lot at a silver and black van just pulling out of the take-out lane at the Burger King and onto Cedar Road.

"Who?" she pleaded, "What are you talking about?"

"The prisoner. He got into that van. I'm sure of it."

"Harlow, how can someone be a prisoner, if he's driving around in a van?"

"He's not driving!" Harlow looked at his wife as though she had said something infinitely stupid. "Prisoners don't just drive around in vans. He's in the back with guards. You should see these guys. There are four down linemen in there, and I mean monsters, in missionary suits. I'm not kidding. I shook their hands."

"You what?"

"I – shook – their – hands!" He pronounced the sentence emphatically word by insistent word as if it were his wife who made no sense, and then returned his attention immediately to the van. "I don't think they know we're here. I don't think they have any idea. They just stopped for something to eat. That's all."

He watched the van signal and pull into the left turn lane at Warrensville. Harlow slipped the car back into gear, and when the van turned left, he released the clutch slowly and began to creep toward the Warrensville exit of the May Company lot. As the van passed out of sight, he pounced on the gas and shifted.

"What are you doing, Harlow?"

He ignored her, waiting at the exit for traffic to clear and at the first slender opportunity speeding in front of two startled drivers into the far lane. The van was already nearly a block ahead of them.

"Are you trying to follow them?"

"I just want to get the license number."

"Harlow!"

"All I want is their license number."

"Harlow," she sounded deceptively calm, "I am hungry. Your children are hungry."

Harlow glanced back over his shoulder. "The kids are asleep."

"Yes, they're asleep, but they won't sleep long, and when they wake up they'll be starving. They've been in conference all morning; they haven't eaten since 7:30; I have a chicken in the oven, and you are racing all over the city in front of oncoming traffic because down-men or whatever you call them shook your hand. Is that right? Is that what you're telling me?"

Harlow didn't answer. While she'd been clarifying his activity, he'd been weaving back and forth between lanes of traffic. Now only two cars separated him from the van. But the light up ahead was already yellow. He decided to run it. Calculating like a professional, he checked left and right for cross traffic.

Then, the car in front of them stopped.

"Harlowwww!"

He nearly ran into it. He was furious. He had to watch the van slip a full block away again and into the left turn lane at the next intersection. When the light changed he took a calculated risk. There were two lefts up ahead. If the van turned half-left up Northfield and got into traffic, it would be a crapshoot. He might never find it again. But if it made the hard left up Chagrin toward the interstate, he could turn where he was, cut through the back streets and catch up to it before the next major intersection. He made the turn, sped past 25mph-limit signs and through a school zone at fifty or better, and when he thought he'd traveled far and fast enough, made a quick right, arriving at Chagrin Boulevard just in time to see the van glide by. "Damn!" he said triumphantly under his breath and pounded smartly on the steering wheel in front of him. He had to wait for traffic to clear again, but he knew that now, no matter what, he would catch up to the van on the interstate at the latest. And he would get the number.

Harlow sat back and glanced over at Connie. He would have liked to declare the victory and explain the victorious strategy, but his wife sat in travertine silence, arms folded over her smoldering fury, staring at nothing at all through the side window. He knew better. He held his peace.

As the interstate sign approached, Harlow had nearly caught up with the van again, but it surprised him by turning right, not onto the interstate, but beforehand on the commercial access road. He hit the brake and the turn signal and followed. After a few hundred feet it turned left again, abruptly this time and without signaling, into the parking lot at the Marriott.

Harlow stopped the Honda right in the middle of traffic. He didn't know what to do. Should he follow? Maybe they had spotted him. Maybe they were taking evasive action. Maybe they weren't sure and were just waiting to see if he would follow and, therefore, actually was following them. The cars behind him began to honk. Finally he slipped the clutch, lurching suddenly ahead and turning, not into the Marriott lot, but into a smaller parking lot on his right and across the street from the Marriott. He found a space and pulled in. When he looked up, he was at McDonald's.

"All right," Connie unfolded one arm, "what are we doing here?"

"I thought you said the kids were hungry."

"At McDonald's?"

"Yeh, McDonald's." He pointed.

"It's Sunday, Harlow. What about my chicken?"

"Look," he was already opening his door, "just get the kids something to eat. I'll be right back."

"Harlowww!"

Harlow Havens dropped into a crouch next to the Honda and scowled.

"Look," he said again. "Someone is in trouble over there, and I am going to get that number." There was patriarchy in his voice that would countenance no further bleating, glissando 'Harlowww!s' from his wife. "See that the kids get something to eat," he ordered, "I'll be back when I can."

Fuming, Connie glared her compliance through the far window while he stood again and struck off importantly through the heat.

The van was not on the street. They probably hadn't seen him after all, hadn't been waiting or testing to see if he was following. In any case, the access road was a dead end. If they tried to make a run for it, they'd have to go right past him. He'd get the number. Dodging heavy traffic, he danced across to the Marriott lot, then keeping the exits in sight worked carefully and systematically through the crowded rows toward the hotel. It was several minutes before he rounded the corner of the building and saw the silver and black Dodge van parked at the curb not fifty feet away. He leaped backward, then slowly peered around the corner again. There was no discernable movement, no activity. The van seemed empty, but because of the tinted windows, he couldn't be sure. If he approached directly, he would be seen and probably recognized. He withdrew around the corner of the building again and then backtracked a hundred feet or more. When he felt he'd gone far enough, he struck off to his left, crossing two double rows of parked cars, then turned left again, walking casually along parallel to the side of the hotel. When he was directly behind the van he stopped at the tailgate of a Buick station wagon and slid into a crouch. Leaning out slowly and peering between the parked cars, he could see the back of the van, but not the license plate. He waited, then crouching close to the ground moved slowly forward through the first double row of parked cars. He was sweating, and he felt the drops trickle icily down his steaming sides. When he crossed the intervening traffic lane to the next row, he moved slightly to the left in order to be directly behind a red Ford pickup and, thus, securely out of view. But from behind the truck he could still not see the license plate. He moved one more vehicle to the left and then another and edged part way forward so that raising his head just enough to look diagonally over the hood of the car next to which he crouched and across the trunk of the car standing kitty-corner to it, he could finally see the entire back of the van.

The plate was from Utah. Harlow fumbled in his pocket for a pencil and for something to write on. The only paper he could find was the conference program. He pressed it up against the fender. But when he began to write, he wasn't sure. Harlow was near-sighted. The plates were still some distance away, and from this angle the numbers didn't have edges. He squinted and adjusted his glasses, but still wasn't sure. When he'd written the number he thought he saw on the program, he resolved to take one last risk. He would return to the red pickup, stand, and walk around it between the remaining parked cars and out directly behind the van where he could see the plate clearly. Then he would turn and walk away. If there were any discrepancy between the number on the plate and the one in his pocket, he would note it down as soon as he rounded the corner of the hotel. If there were any trouble, he would run like hell. In any case Harlow, who abhorred slipshod research, was going to get it right.

When he emerged, standing, from between the parked cars, the sun was shining at an angle that allowed him to see through the tinted windows of the van. It was empty after all. In fact, there was not a soul anywhere in sight. The whole world, he thought, must be inside with air conditioning. Harlow stood for a moment sweating like Cannon on television, and then like Cannon stepped impetuously across the street to check out the getaway vehicle. He pulled the program from his pocket. The numbers were identical. He stepped to the rear window and peered into the luggage space. He saw luggage. The back seat was empty, as was the front. Harlow tried the door on the driver's side, then went around to the passenger side. The front was locked, but the sliding side door gave when he pushed the handle. Slowly, because the door was noisy, he inched it open.

"Somethin' in there ya want?"

Harlow whirled to find a scowling nose tackle, one of the huge down linemen he'd tried to describe to Connie, in a two-point stance on the curb, his hammer arms folded across the polyester lapels of his black suit. In almost the same motion Harlow whirled again to see two defensive ends in the same black uniforms take up the same menacing stance at the back of the van. He was trapped.

Harlow knew football, but he was no power runner. He wasn't athletic at all. In a dozen years he hadn't jogged a dozen yards. Nor was he a fool. There was not a soul within eye- or earshot to whom he could appeal. In seconds he found himself inside a climbing elevator surrounded by three glowering monoliths and the overwhelming smell of Mennen Regular; within minutes he was standing in front of a double-locked door on the chilly eighth floor of the Marriott.

The nose tackle knocked three definite, well-defined knocks. There was an answering knock, and the outside signal caller knocked again in different sequence. Then, after a moment, Harlow heard a key in the lock. The door opened, carefully at first, then swung wide, and there across the big room and the beige carpet and the two king-size beds with blue quilted bedspreads in a club chair under a swag lamp at an octagonal table with his glasses gleaming, a smile on his lips, and a Whopper with cheese in his hand, sat the captive stranger from the washroom.

"Ralphie!" He sang the name out calmly and without particular surprise, but there was genuine pleasure in his voice. "Now, there's a pal. Can't make it ta dinner at his place, so he comes over fer dinner at mine. Now, don't that just beat all, fellas. They's some things on this poor old turnip ya kin still depend on." He winked.

"Come on in here, son, and take a load off. I saved ya somethin' t'eat."

Harlow wandered numbly across the room. "What's going on here? Are you all right?"

"Hey, I'm livin' good. These fellas invited me . . . 'scuse me, invited 'us' ta dinner here't the hotel. It's ther treat, so eat up." Harlow looked back across the room. All four down linemen were there now in silent formation and with their arms folded. "I saved ya some a this." The western stranger pushed half a vanilla milkshake at Harlow and handed him a new straw. "The rest a this is in there." He waved the hamburger fragment in his hand and pointed to the styrofoam tray on the table. "It's a little raw fer my taste, but you eastern fellas like it recent." Harlow accepted the milkshake. He sat down nervously on the front edge of the other club chair, and, with one finger, opened the lid of the styrofoam tray. The meat under the glistening cheese was as grey as March. He wasn't hungry.

"Why are we here?"

"Well now, that's a good'n. Yes, sir. Fellas! Ma friend Ralph would like to know why it is that we're here. I mean other than this fine Sunday dinner, a course." He looked across the room with genuine curiosity. But no one answered. The four linemen stood silent as doom on the far wall. "Well now, I could a told 'm all that m'self." He shook his head, smiled wearily, and looked back at Harlow. "Drink yer milkshake, Ralphie. We may be here a spell."

But almost before he'd finished speaking, a door, not the door through which Harlow had just come, but the connecting double door to the next room, opened. The man who entered was in a hurry.

"All right, they're ready over . . . " He stopped in his tracks. "Who is that?" He was a florid man, flushed and red even in the air conditioning. He had a walky-talky attached to his belt issuing short, erratic bursts of static and unintelligible speech, and when he spoke, he spoke in terse explosions like his walky-talky. "Who is he?"

"He was outside nosing around the van." The sentinels broke silence to report.

"I caught him breaking in."

"Into the van?"

"Yes, sir."

The newcomer turned to Harlow glowing with perplexity. "Who are you? What do you want?"

"He was at the church this morning," one of the linemen continued. "The guy in the bathroom."

"He's the one?"

"Yeh."

"Yeh, that's him."

"The other one says it's his friend."

"Friend?" The newcomer's puzzlement rose another octave.

"Yeh. Name's Ralph."

"Ralph?"

"Yeh."

He turned toward Harlow again. "Your name is Ralph?"

Harlow shrugged and nodded uncomfortably and simultaneously, but he didn't really seem to be part of the conversation anyway.

"Well, what are we going to do with him?"

"I dunno." The linemen fell silent again while their interrogator paced nervously.

"I guess we'll just have to take him in there. I don't like it. I do not like it. But what else can we do?"

The four linemen shrugged synchronously.

"Well then, let's get on with it." He opened the connecting door again and disappeared.

The nose tackle stepped toward Harlow and the stranger and jerked his large head in the direction of the door. "Let's go."

"You want us to go in there?" The nose tackle grimaced condescendingly, but Harlow was actually stalling for time. He'd decided this had gone far enough. He didn't know who these people were. He didn't know what they wanted. He had no idea what was through that door, but the way things had been going, he didn't want to know. Maybe he should make a break for it now, or make a stand. Maybe he had nothing to lose.

"And if I refuse to go?" he announced defiantly.

The remaining linemen came immediately to attention.

"C'mon, kid," the stranger who was already on his feet pounded Harlow on the shoulder, "don't let 'em yank yer harness. This here is the good part. It's why ya come. Trust me, ya wouldn' wanna miss it." He winked broadly and headed for the open door.

Harlow stood deflated and perplexed for a moment, but then headed slowly for the door as well. He could have been at home now, eating chicken.

The room through the double door was a sitting room with sofas, a coffee table, easy chairs, and a fold-down desk along the wall. It was elegant, sort of. The furniture was light, and there was a huge, glass-covered seascape on the wall in distinctly non aquatic greys and greens and mauve. In the far corner by the window there were two octagonal game tables. On top of one sat a gleaming black vase with an arrangement of real flowers. The stranger was already seated on one of the white couches, leaning back comfortably with a scuffed yellow boot pulled up on one knee. He was smiling to himself, and when Harlow perched nervously on the same couch, he waved but didn't look up or speak.

The man with the walky-talky was on the phone. "Yes, sir. They're here now, sir . . . No, sir . . . I don't know, sir . . . Yes, sir . . . " Then there was silence with the florid sentinel standing over them, arms folded and at attention like a vice-principal in a study hall.

When he entered, Harlow recognized him immediately. From that morning, of course, when he had spoken briefly, but especially from his pictures. He was not tall, but he was commanding, lean and deliberate with eyes and hair as black as his suit. The suit was not polyester. The tie was as red and riveting as a cardinal's hat, and the shirt as white as forgiveness. Colors so stark they were almost allegorical. Standing in the doorway, he looked down at them with the canny cordiality of an inquisitor.

"Brethren," he said as he settled himself lightly on the couch directly across from them. "Thank you, for agreeing to meet with me."

Stunned, Harlow waited for some clarifying response from the talkative stranger at his side, but none came. The little man only sat in smiling silence.

"We didn't agree to any meeting," Harlow finally announced, "at least I certainly didn't. I was brought here against my will."

The authority cast an irritated glance at the florid sentinel with his walky-talky. "Of course, that is unfortunate, Brother . . . ? I don't believe I know your name."

Harlow didn't know what to answer. Should he tell the truth or was the truth precisely the wrong thing to tell? But while he struggled, the walky-talky man intervened.

"His name's Ralph."

"Brother Ralph?"

Relieved of the burden of decision, Harlow nodded.

"Well then, Brother Ralph, why *are* you here? Why did you come?"

"I . . . I came because . . . " he turned toward the smiling stranger on the couch next to him, "because my friend seemed to be in trouble."

"That's admirable, Brother Ralph. We should all have such loyal friends. But I fear you have it backwards." He fixed Harlow with his black eyes. "I am the one in trouble here. And you are in trouble. The good brethren who brought you here, they are in trouble. The church itself is in trouble. Oh," he waved his hand, "not terrible trouble, not catastrophic trouble, but serious and distressing enough that I must meet with your friend here, who is the cause of it, and who alone can resolve it." He turned from Harlow and narrowed his eyes at the slight, smiling figure on the other side of the sofa. "But your friend does not make it easy to meet with him. He's elusive. Uncooperative. Some even say he's a mischievous prankster. But I don't think that's true." He paused and relaxed his eyes and his manner. "I think what we have had here is a failure of communication. And sometimes, brother, and let me tell you this from long experience, sometimes in order to re-establish communication, we must resort to means which under ordinary circumstances we would ourselves deplore." He leaned back and returned his attention to Harlow. "Do you know who your friend is?"

Trapped, Harlow stared at the floor and smiled as mutely and as foolishly as the stranger at his side.

"Well, don't be embarrassed, Brother Ralph. Neither do we. Not for certain. Do you know who he thinks he is? No? Or where he's been? Or what he's been up to?"

Harlow fixed his attention tenaciously on the toe of his own penny loafer.

"Well, perhaps you'll forgive me if I say I'm not surprised. Perhaps you'll allow me to enlighten you. Brother Beazley . . . " He turned to the man still standing at attention at the telephone.

"Yes, sir?"

"May I have the file."

Brother Beazley went to the fold-down desk and retrieved a manila folder which he handed over.

"Thank you." He opened the file, leafed through for a moment, and ran his finger down a page. "Where do I begin? Perhaps with the visitations. We have received reports of his 'visitations' from California to Mexico to New Brunswick, New Jersey."

"Visitations?"

"Yes, visitations. Out of nowhere he appears at a member home, introduces himself as a traveling elder of the Church, and asks for a meal and a bed."

Harlow didn't say anything, but his eyes betrayed that he hardly saw anything sinister in that.

"Prays with the family, quotes the scriptures, retires early to his bed, and in the morning . . . in the morning when they go to wake him up for breakfast, the bed is empty and he has disappeared."

"Disappeared?"

"Without a trace. Along with a half gallon of milk, a loaf of bread, a dozen eggs, a pound of bacon, a bag of apples or oranges, a pie, a cake, a dozen donuts, or anything else that isn't strapped down to the refrigerator. Oh, but there is a note to the family, a reminder with scriptural citations that anything they may have done for the Lord's emissary will be repaid them an hundredfold in the life hereafter."

Harlow's pleasure at this report was irrepressible.

"Now, that may seem comical to you, brother, but it is not so comical when people who believe they've been singled out for a special test and blessing have, in fact, been made the means of avoiding the necessity of earning an honest living."

Harlow forced sobriety back into his face. "You mean, he's been posing . . ."

"I didn't necessarily say it was a pose."

"You mean he's really . . . "

The expression on the face of authority made it clear that that wasn't what he'd meant, either.

" . . . or you mean he really thinks he's . . . "

This time a slight nod and gently ascending eyebrows gave Harlow to know that finally he understood. He stole a glance at the innocent impostor next to him on the couch. The serene but silly smile hadn't fluctuated a degree.

"And if that were all, I'd hardly be sitting here speaking to either of you. But that is just the tip of the iceberg." He turned a page in the folder. "There are, for instance, the healings. In the last quarter alone he's been credited publicly with miraculous cures of," he read the list, "constipation, athlete's foot, bunions, hemorrhoids, plantar warts, heat rash, impotence, and nervous indigestion." He looked up from his reading this time directly at the beaming culprit. "Now, brother . . . dear brother . . . ? What *is* your name?"

The stranger was cheerfully attentive, but silent.

"No one, not your own friend here, not even Elder Beazley, who, I promise you, has left no stone unturned, seems able to provide your name of record. Won't you tell me?" Still no answer, and Harlow shrugged apologetically for his comrade's awkward recalcitrance. The questioner shrugged in return. "Well, whatever your real name, brother, I am here to assure you that we are happy to see our members relieved of any affliction, however minor, by whatever means, real or imagined. We are delighted, in fact. But we do not, nor does Brother Ralph here, nor would you, I should think, want to see the powers and ordinances of heaven associated with medical quackery . . . or," his voice hardened, "exchanged for money."

"You mean he was taking money?" Harlow was finally shocked.

" 'Accepted' is perhaps the better word, and not a lot of money. Not a great deal. Sometimes not even money. But it's the principle of the thing. Some of these incidents get into local newspapers."

Harlow nodded unamused agreement this time. The stranger, however, sat silent and motionless and beatific as ever.

"And then there are the warnings. Now, there is a tradition in the Church that the Lord from time to time sends certain messengers to warn threatened Saints of impending danger, but such dangers do not include," he paused, turned the page, and read again, "nutritional supplements, recreational vehicles, the law profession, schools of management, color analysis, inspirational cassette tapes, Tupperware, or voting Republican in Utah. When you make such statements," warning filled the lower register of his voice, "and when, as a consequence of your representations, some person or persons take those statements to be the official, ecclesiastical position of the Church, you make the Church liable not only to ridicule and defamation, but to possible legal action as well. And," he was speaking with momentum now and hardly took a breath before continuing, "when you go beyond this sort of prank and flirt with the very boundaries of legality in the name of heaven, then you have gone too far!"

"You mean," Harlow, now nervously enthralled, intruded, "he's actually broken the law?"

"Brother Ralph, there are a thousand and who knows how many souls out there who believe fervently on the basis of a vanished bunion or a regular stool or nothing more than a missing bag of grapefruits that this man is some special emissary of heaven. I have an archive full of letters and testimonies. Now," he scowled juridically, "don't you think it might trouble those trusting people to learn that this same man recently presented himself to an elderly sister, a defenseless widow and pensioner in Salt Lake City, as a qualified financial adviser? Do messengers from the Lord appear as confidence men? *Or*," he flipped the page, "do they volunteer to drive trucks loaded with apple cider from church farms to market and then deliver them up to thieves and looters not a hundred miles from here? *Or*," he was transparently angry now and didn't even refer to his folder, "do they break through security fences and lead illegal protesters and trespassers onto the private property of private foundations?"

"He did that?" Harlow was now wide-eyed with astonishment.

The last-named offense had been in the papers. The whole thing. Everyone knew about the private foundation, a complex on the hill above the city, and about the prominent church members involved, and everyone had read the charges that there was a buried waste dump on the land, a toxic dump. The owners, brethren of intensely rectilinear moral and political conviction, first denied the dump's existence, then all knowledge of the dump's existence, and finally any and all intent to cover up the dump's existence or any knowledge thereof. They were honorable men, but at the mercy of appearances. Documents had been inadvertently shredded. Certain crucial witnesses had imagined themselves encouraged to silence. Satan was afoot. Everyone knew.

And someone had alerted the Greenpeace people, and the Sierra Club, and the Consumers Environmental Alliance. Someone had shown protesters how to get through the fence and the security people and where on the grounds to look and whom to call and whom to malign. Someone had done it. An insider. It had to be, but no one knew who. And everyone not amused was furious. And Harlow, who had been amused, looked at his new friend now, silent and silly on the sofa beside him, with sudden respect. "He's the one?"

"Would you like to read the file?"

He held it out, but Harlow only shook his head and looked at the stranger. They both looked at him, though now with rather different eyes, as he sat in his western suit and string tie and incongruous glasses, smiling and wrestling his own thumbs playfully back and forth over the yellow boot on his knee and saying nothing at all.

The walky-talky on Brother Beazley's belt crackled, and he pushed a button shutting it off. He picked up the telephone.

"There's a call, sir."

"Now?"

"I'm afraid it's important."

"Can I take it here?"

Beazley looked uncomfortably at Harlow and at the man whose name of record he had been unable to discover.

"Very well, tell them to hold. I'll only be a moment. Brethren," he turned his attention back to the detainees on the sofa, "I'm afraid I'm out of time, and we need to come to some conclusion. I don't mind telling you we have considered legal action, even criminal charges. But who would gain by that? There are many who believe in this brother. We surely wouldn't want to make a martyr of him. Do you understand?" Harlow, at least, understood. "Faith is a fragile thing, Brother Ralph, a house plant. It does not easily survive the extremes of weather in a callous world. In the household of faith we operate a nursery. We manage and control the climate, artificially sometimes, but always to protect and nurture the flower of faith. In this case we will not bring charges unless he leaves us no other choice. And he alone, of course, has power over that. But surely he has no more desire to see his supporters troubled than do we. I have tracked him down and sought him out only to encourage him to do the right thing. And let me tell you something else. Your unforeseen intrusion into this matter has caused a great deal of inconvenience. It forced me to move this meeting here to the hotel. Forced me to delay my return. I've missed my plane on your account, brother, and I don't mind saying I viewed your interference as a meddlesome and unnecessary complication." Harlow winced internally, but held eye contact. "I am a busy man. But the Lord has his own timetable and his own ways, and I am wondering now if your appearance here wasn't the hand of providence after all. If truly you are a friend and brother to this obviously troubled man, then you'll help to see he settles down, finds honest employment, and, if and when he's ready, accepts some genuine, authorized responsibility in the Church. You may even want to see that he gets into treatment. I recommend it. Get in touch with the regional social services representative, and if there is any problem whatsoever, you have him call me directly. I'm going to give you a direct number." He took a card from his pocket and wrote on the back of it, then handed it to Harlow who sat up very straight and accepted the card and the commission.

"Yes, sir."

"Brother," now he turned his attention to the beatific delinquent himself, speaking loudly and very clearly as if to a child or a confused, elderly person, "Brother, I do not know your given name, but I know," his tone and his eyes became very kind, "who you are. And I have called you here today to thank you on behalf of the brethren for your long and faithful service, and to tell you that the programs and policies of the Church have changed. We are centralized now and correlated. The times are different and your talents are needed elsewhere. I am releasing you with our gratitude from all your past callings. All of them. Do you understand? No more burdensome traveling. We want you to settle down and take a well-deserved rest." He waited, but there was no answer. The stranger smiled his smile. "I want you to place your trust in Brother Ralph here. Listen to his counsel and follow his advice, and soon—when you are well and rested again—we'll have a new official responsibility for you . . . right here in your own ward. Now, how does that sound?" The silent smile persisted, but warmed suddenly and intensified. The bizarre little man was beaming, and his interrogator took heart. "Good, brother, you understand me then. I must go now, but remember, you've been released, and I want you to stay right here with Brother Ralph and take a long rest." He stood, and so did the stranger. He offered his hand in confirmation. "Agreed?" And the stranger accepted it, taking it enthusiastically in both hands and shaking it warmly while saying nothing. "Well, then, we are agreed," he looked hopefully in Harlow's direction, "aren't we?"

"Yes, sir."

"Yes." He shook Harlow's hand as well and turned to Brother Beazley. "Well, let's get on with it then."

"You can take it next door, sir. They're still on the line."

Harlow watched him withdraw across the carpet and disappear into the next room. When he stopped momentarily at the door and waved an amiable farewell, it was the wave of a chancellor from a balcony, or a president from the door of Air Force One.

Beazley, meanwhile, had stepped to the main door and, making a point of leaving it wide open, had disappeared down the hall. When his footsteps were no longer audible, Harlow stood and edged toward the opening. He checked the hallway. It was empty. The four apocalyptic linemen were nowhere in sight. He turned and addressed the stranger, who was sitting on the sofa again, grinning. "Why didn't you say anything?"

"Nice fella," he said.

"But why didn't you talk?"

"Whadya think I brung you here fer? Ya hire a man, ya let him do his work. That's the way I am."

"Hired me?"

"Done a pertty good job, too."

"But I didn't do anything!"

" 'Course not. Look," he squinted and for the first time all afternoon looked serious, "I learned a long time ago these fellas ain't listeners. They're talkers, Ralphie, paid talkers. Thet's ther job. An' yers was ta open yer mouth 'n talk 'n not say nothin' 'n stay outa the way. 'N ya done real good. Take any point on any subject and that fella's got a whole confernce address just burnin' to be turned loose. Me talkin' jus' irritates 'm. Fella like that alays figures I'm talkin' back. And that don't help him ner me either. Oh, it slows 'm down some, maybe, but it fires 'm up, too, and when yu've been through's many confernce addresses as me, y'aint anxious to prolong the affliction."

"But I thought you were desperate."

"I was. Big mouth like mine, I could a been here three days arguin'. Or he'd a got it in his head to haul me off fer some doctor ta feed on."

"He thinks you're crazy."

"Yep."

"He thinks that you think you're a . . . "

"Yep. That's what he thinks."

"Well?"

"Well what?"

"Well," Harlow grinned, "do you?"

"Do I what?"

With some discomfort Harlow recognized the probable delicacy of his question.

"I mean . . . ah . . . are you?"

"Well," this time the question seemed to have connected, "I sure don't need no job, if that's what yer askin'. I got all I kin handle right now, thank ya."

Harlow felt firmer but far more exotic ground under him. He had to make sure.

"Aren't there a . . . aren't there supposed to be three of you?"

"Now, that's true. We used ta do partners. Used ta have us a time." He smiled mysteriously, lost in a momentary reverie, and Harlow knew it was true. He was crazy. "But that's all histry."

"Why's that?" Harlow probed and humored him.

"Other two fellas give up. Reetired."

"Retired?"

"Well, one of 'm held out all the way ta 1964. But that was it. Correlation got him. Couldn't stand it no more. Went out ta Alaska a hunderd 'n fifty miles from nowhere and become a hermit. Won't see nobody. Won't talk ta nobody. Just summer 'n winter, winter 'n summer, 'n berries 'n roots 'n a little wild honey. That's it, waiting fer the end."

"And the other one?"

"He worries me some. Already give up in 1914 and went off ta become a heedonist."

"A what?"

"Heedonist. He's livin' serial polygamy in the Greek islands, only sometimes it ain't sa serial. Right now he's upset. Been livin' heedonism with a woman seventy-six years of age."

Harlow's jaw dropped.

"Yep. She's gettin' up there. And he claims when she goes, secrets'll die with that woman that'll be utterly lost to the world."

Harlow was unable to formulate a clinically appropriate response.

"Yep, jus' me now. The whole thing. And I'm danged if I'm gonna live off a Sego Lilies and mortification a the flesh. When ya get my age, a little comfort ain't no sin. It's a workin' necessity."

"And that's why you take the food?"

"I suppose, you go off fer a whole day's work without no lunch?" Despite his earlier silence, he was clearly irritated at what had been said and insinuated. Harlow answered what, in any case, would have been obvious.

"No, sir." He couldn't leave it at that, however. "But what about the healings?"

"What about 'em?"

"I mean . . . well . . . bunions and hemorrhoids? They don't seem very serious."

"Y'ever had a bunion?"

"No, sir."

"Didn't think so. You sure ain't never had no hemorrhoid."

"But isn't that . . . I mean . . . a . . . don't you save lives or . . . ?"

"We done some a that. Still give in ta it now and again, but it's a bad habit. Misleadin'. I'm tryin' ta forsake it. Folks alays dyin' ta live forever. Lemme tell ya somethin', Brother Ralph, longevity ain't what it's made out. Jus' one bunion 'n hemorrhoid after th'other."

"But the money?"

"How many doctors you know," there was more than just irritation in his voice now, "work for bus fare ta the next patient? How many doctors you know ever took a bus in ther whole life? Some a us'r tired a walkin'. And that woman," he wasn't through, "that woman in Salt Lake worked for the genealogy twenty-two years 'n retired on just about enough money ta pay tythin' and eat miracles. I give 'er a little help. That's all."

"Financial help?"

"A course."

"How did you help her?"

"I told her ta sell her house 'n take ever nickel she could lay hand on 'n invest it."

"Invest it?"

"Yep. Deseret Satellite Dish."

"And she lost it all." Harlow shook his head and anticipated the result.

"Lost it? She made a pot a money. Moved up ta Federal Heights." He shook his head, and gestured across the room. "Not five doors away from his holiness out there."

Harlow was baffled. "Then why is he upset?"

"She's the one's upset. Never fails." He looked at Harlow with a teacher's peevishness. "Don't ya ever read the Book a Marmon?"

Harlow shrugged. "Sometimes."

"Never fails. Help 'em out enough 'n ya make 'em mean, 'n nasty 'n thankless. She's drivin' him nuts."

"She is? But why?"

"Got the law on her."

"The law?"

"Think she's guilty a stock fraud. Called insider tradin'. Know what that is?"

Harlow knew.

"Right off she gets herself a ulcer 'n a whole outhouse full a lawyers. Then she runs down the street ta tattle ta the genral management." He hefted his thumb in the direction of the door again. "If the woman'd just use good sense 'n lay back 'n take a bubble bath or go shoppin' or watch some television or somethin', she'd be jus' fine."

"She would?"

"They'll never lay a finger on her."

"They won't?"

"Brother Ralph. Fer a intellec-chal, yer not too quick." He leaned forward and bobbed a finger against his own breast bone. "Her insider's me." He winked, and a clear western grin spread across his face. "Oh, 'n that cider. Nobody never stole that cider neither. I give ever last pint away m'self."

Harlow didn't ask. He was embarrassed. He knew he sounded like an echo. But the question was as clear in his eyes as it was heavy in the air.

"Why? Well, maybe, that'n was wrong. It was a kind a impulse. Got me an assignment down to the welfare farm, 'n that fella down there told us right out. Welfare ain't no charity. No sir. Not no more. That's policy, friend. Welfare's got to get itself off the dole and turn a profit jus' like anybody else. So he sends me down to the depot with that load a cider, 'n I'm on ma way through the city, 'n these kids is playing ball on the ugliest, scraggiest patch a dust y'ever seen. Made ya spit chalk jus' lookin'."

"So you gave it to the kids?"

"Yep. Impulse, like I said. And then ther brothers come along, 'n sisters 'n mothers 'n aunts 'n granpas 'n neighbors 'n friends 'n a whole passel a raggy strangers . . . Nice people," he said after a reflective pause, and then he paused and reflected again. "Thirsty."

"A course, still wan't right, in a way. Wan't authorized. Insider tradin', I guess. But I'll tell ya somethin'. I'm a little short on ree-morse. Now take that fella back there." He pointed at the door through which the authority general had just retreated. "Smart fella. Serious. Real hard workin'. But truth is a hell-bent responsible fella like that don't get three good clear impulses in a whole year. They jus' plain can't get at 'im. He's up over his ears in implication 'n ramification 'n a half dozen other poisonous varieties. It ain't healthy, that's all. It ain't even harmless.

"Now, he ain't a bad sort, no siree. Little govermental maybe, but bacon comes from hogs, don't it, 'n someone's gotta wear them suits 'n stay awake through confernce. Mostly they don't do much harm. Mostly. And mostly they earn ther keep. There's a lot a varmints out there, and a whole lot a crazies need lookin' out fer. Trouble is it sours a body. Truckin' with that lot turns a man artful 'n cynical."

A bell rang in Harlow's head. "Cynical?"

"Yep."

"You said I was a cynic?"

"Well then, let this be a lesson ta ya, Brother Ralph. It's the wages a worldly education ya seen here today." A wide grin returned to his face. "Maybe we oughta get on downstairs. I expect someone's waitin' on ya."

In the elevator Harlow stared at his unearthly companion and searched for the Solomonic question that would unravel his identity.

"How'd you know about the waste dump?"

He shrugged. "Someone in my line's jus' naturly specialized in treasures a th'earth. Ain't no big thing."

"Treasures?"

"Yep."

"But it's chemicals, isn't it? Toxic chemicals?"

"Yep, a whole mother lode of 'em."

"But . . . " Harlow stuttered and knotted his forehead in puzzlement, yet nothing in the stranger's eyes acknowleged paradox. Harlow tried another tack.

"Some of those men are ruined. Some may even go to jail."

"It's a darn shame."

"The foundation is out of business."

"Yep."

"Why'd you do it?"

The scrawny suburban cowboy thought a moment and scratched his chin, and then he came clean. "Cheemo-therapy, Brother Ralph, cheemo-therapy." He winked and cleared his throat and looked up at the ceiling, "Ya wouldn't have five dollars on ya, would ya?"

"Five dollars?"

"Fer the telephone?"

"The telephone?"

"Yeh, the telephone. Gotta call in 'n see what's cookin'. You didn' think that'd be a local call, now did ya?"

Harlow knew it was crazy, but he gave away his last five dollars.

"I'll put it on account at standard interest. It's a perty good deal."

"Sure." The door opened to the lobby, and Harlow put away his wallet and shook his head and looked up to find the stranger indicating discreetly over his shoulder.

"Harlowww!"

When he turned, Connie was barreling toward him through the crowded lobby with the baby, red and wet-eyed, thrown over her shoulder and his four-year-old son straining under tow. "Harlow!"

He turned again quickly, but the stranger was already gone, and before he could undertake anything to find him, Connie had him firmly by the arm. "They're awake now, and they're starving." She was sweating and angry. "I told you they'd be starving." She pushed the reluctant baby into his arms, and the baby promptly turned, arched her back, reached for her mother, who refused to take her, and began to wail.

"Why didn't you feed them?" He was trying to talk, hold the struggling baby, and look back over his shoulder all at once.

"I don't have a nickel, Harlow. How am I supposed to feed them without money?"

"Look, Connie," he tried to hand her the baby again, "I've got to find . . . "

"Harlowwww!"

She was near tears. He surrendered.

"All right, we'll just take them home then."

"What for," she shot back, "baked chicken ashes? Give me back the five dollars I gave you this morning."

Harlow groaned. He'd been taken, obviously, by a man he'd promised not twenty minutes before to take personal charge of. He'd let himself listen to him. Let himself fall under whatever spell he cast. Almost wanted to believe him. And he'd let the scoundrel escape with the very food out of his children's mouths. Harlow Havens felt naive and gullible and ridiculous.

"I haven't got it," he said weakly.

When they reached the Honda, both children were bawling, and Harlow wrestled them resignedly into their harnesses. When he turned around and slid, panting, back down into the driver's seat, he found himself staring at the brown envelope. It was lying on the dash. He picked it up.

"Harlow, take me home!"

"Here!" He handed it to her. "You tell me what's in it."

He started the engine, put the car into reverse, and then twisted himself around, placing his arm on the back of Connie's seat so that he could see clearly to back out of the parking space.

"Harlow."

"What?"

"It's . . . a certificate."

"A what?"

"It's a gift certificate."

He turned and read. "You," it announced in big red and yellow letters, "deserve a feast today . . . " It was a gift certificate, to the gaping eyes and mouths of both witnesses, a bona-fide FAMILY FUN FEAST certificate, signed, authorized, and certified in indelible facsimile by Ronald McDonald himself.

Harlow, meanwhile, had nearly backed the Honda into a rumbling, black Camaro. The teenage driver lay on the horn and shook his head in open disgust while Harlow pulled back into the parking space.

"It's still good, Harlow. It hasn't expired."

When Connie and the kids were out of the car again and headed up the walk, Harlow locked the door. He was still bewildered and distracted, and it took him a while, but he looked up in time to see an inter-suburban express bus go by. There, in the window just behind the driver, was the grinning stranger. He was waving.